Grace

Grace

Nancy Allen

M,

I hope you enjoy
my story,

Love,

Nancy

atmosphere press

In loving memory of my sister B

Prologue
July 2005

Catherine placed her laptop on the desk and pulled several books from her briefcase. She slid into the massive swivel chair and opened the cavernous bottom drawer, now empty. Secrets told. Conflicts resolved.

The Autobiographical Impulse in Literature, she typed into the syllabus. She'd have to explain the title in the first class. She smiled as she typed the tedious objectives for the course. All she really wanted was for the students to enjoy reading a few good stories, poems, and essays and, maybe, begin to believe that their own stories were worth telling.

The stories we tell, first to ourselves and then in a form that others can understand. Why do some writers feel comfortable—or is it compelled—to tell their stories as memoirs, anxious to get them down on paper before forgetfulness obscures the details? Others need the veil of fiction, constructing their reality so readers can see the character as a whole, not as a fragmented life in progress.

Catherine leafed through her notes on each text, thinking about the themes she would emphasize in class. Virginia Woolf, traumatized by the sexual assaults of her older half-brothers. James Baldwin, fighting against the impact of racism on his father's mental health. Sylvia Plath, slipping into madness at such a young age. Tim O'Brien, a self-proclaimed coward for going to Vietnam; then, writing his way to peace of mind. She pulled *Dreams from My Father* from her briefcase, a powerful memoir written by a little-known senator from Illinois. It might be good to include something so recent.

Would she ever have the courage to tell her own story of what happened at Franklin College last year? Would Chelsea or any of the students who had been impacted? A riveting novel or a tell-all memoir?

Would the nightmares end? She looked at her hands, at the nails that had scratched his face as she escaped his grip.

Catherine closed the laptop and walked the two blocks to the boardwalk. She watched the surf roll in, massive white caps dominating blue water. Grief over her father's death tugged at her heart as she watched an elderly man hobble to a bench and sit down. She hadn't buried the tangled story of her parents' loveless marriage with her father, but maybe that story wasn't hers to tell.

She ran the two-mile length of the boardwalk, letting the memories go and thinking instead about Woolf's "Sketch of the Past" and its fragmented structure.

Part I
Summer 2004

Chapter One

Catherine turned onto the campus and parked in front of Tyler Hall, perched at the top of the hill, an old stone building with a formal entrance. Multi-colored petunias filled the large clay pots along the twisting walkway and in the window boxes on the second floor of the building.

Balancing her briefcase and an over-sized cup of coffee, Catherine pushed open the outside door. Her red A-line skirt clung to her and several strands of hair fell over her eyes. I'll probably have to redo my make-up, she thought as she wiped perspiration from her face.

She placed her coffee cup and her briefcase on the floor, struggling with the lock on the outer office door. Her own office door opened more easily. Mahogany bookcases lined the wall behind the large desk. She imagined the empty shelves filled with her books. She'd come in on a Saturday and fill the shelves. Then, she'd feel at home.

Neatly stacked piles of mail had been placed on the left-hand side of the desk close to the computer. A desk nameplate, gold on dark wood, read, Catherine Finley,

Ph.D. Dean of Undergraduate Studies.

Catherine sat down in front of the computer and logged in. As she waited for the password prompt, she took in the beautiful arrangement of flowers that graced the coffee table in the area in front of the desk where two maroon chairs and matching loveseat seemed welcoming. A wall of windows looked out on the playing fields. No hint of the humid morning in the air-conditioned office. The day was clear and bright.

She poured coffee into a small, flowered mug that she pulled from her briefcase, spilling some. Coffee blotted one stack of mail. Damn. She soaked it up with a napkin.

Wiping perspiration from her face and neck, Catherine crossed the room and opened the card lying next to the vase of flowers. It read, "To my daughter, the Dean. I'm proud of you. Love, Dad."

"Those arrived Friday afternoon." Catherine turned and saw Bette, her administrative assistant, standing in the doorway.

Bette was in her mid-fifties. Tall, impeccably dressed in a black and white linen dress and jacket, she had been at the College for seven years and had been with the last Dean throughout his tenure.

"I'll walk you down to your ten o'clock meeting with Neil, so I can introduce you to his assistant Marie," Bette said. "She can always help you when I'm not available." Before Catherine had a chance to respond, Bette returned to her desk to pick-up the phone on the first ring.

Catherine poured more coffee into her mug and turned to the stacks of mail.

"Good morning, Dr. Finley."

Catherine looked up. Hal Doyle, Dean of Graduate

Studies, stood in the doorway. Catherine pushed back her chair and stretched out her hand.

"You can call me Catherine, Dr. Doyle."

"Well, that's a relief," he said with a grin. "Call me Hal." Catherine moved closer to him, looking at him intently. His blue eyes were warm and attentive. He ran his hand through his jet-black hair before he reached over and shook her hand.

"I won't keep you this morning, but I scheduled lunch on Thursday. I thought we could continue the conversation we started during the interviews," Hal said.

"Great. I'll look forward to it," Catherine said with a smile.

Hal smiled back and headed down the hall to his office. Catherine had made a connection with Hal during the interviews. A historian, he had been at the College for three years. Compared to the other senior administrators, Hal was young, probably about Catherine's age, and had been candid about the campus politics. "Take a few weeks, maybe a month to get to know people," he told her after she accepted the position. "Then, ask me anything you want about the cast of characters. I'm happy to share my view of campus politics."

A few minutes before ten, Bette knocked on the door. They walked down the hall to Neil's office. Bette introduced Catherine to Marie, and Marie, talkative and warm, dominated the conversation. The outer office where she sat was spacious, cluttered with stacks of paper and binders placed randomly on metal bookcases. The tiered computer arm of her desk showcased numerous pictures, probably her children and grandchildren.

As Marie showed her the mailings going out to new

students and explained her role in orientation, Catherine was distracted by Neil's angry voice coming from the closed door behind Marie's desk. Marie and Bette seemed not to notice.

Marie directed Catherine to a chair beside her desk, and Bette returned to her office after giving Marie some advice about the mailing to new students. Catherine shifted nervously, crossing and uncrossing her legs, wishing she knew what to do to deflect her anxiety.

"Sorry to keep you waiting, Catherine," Neil said as he emerged from his office. Despite the heat, Neil dressed in a gray pinstripe suit, crisp white shirt, and dark green tie. After a brief word with Marie, he motioned for Catherine to enter the office. She took a seat beside Neil's desk. Seated, his long torso and legs dwarfed his surroundings. He was brief as he talked about the projects he wanted Catherine to begin while he was on vacation.

"I leave Thursday, and I will be away for two weeks. I will check email occasionally, so if you need anything, you can reach me that way. Marie can also be a big help."

"Thanks."

"I had a good working relationship with your predecessor. Yes." He nodded his head and smiled as if something important just came into his mind. "We were a good team, and I expect the same to develop with you. Loyalty is important."

"Of course," Catherine said. "Loyalty," she repeated with some uncertainty. "I hope you have a good vacation."

"Unlikely. My wife's unhappy, and she'll be with me."

Catherine didn't know how to respond to this bombshell, so she excused herself and left quietly. Maybe Neil was just having a bad day, but the comment about loyalty seemed odd.

As she returned to her office, she thought about her first impressions of Neil. He had said little in the interviews. He seemed indifferent to the whole process, and she had been troubled about the way he looked at his cell phone and sent several messages while she was responding to questions.

"Catherine," Bette interrupted her thoughts. "President Ashcroft's assistant called. The President would like to meet with you at three, so she can welcome you to the College community."

"Wonderful," Catherine said. Putting aside her misgivings about Neil, she focused on working for a President who was known as a strong advocate for women in leadership positions. She hadn't known about Roslyn Ashcroft before her interviews at Franklin, but when she began telling colleagues about the offer when she was still considering it, several told her to take the position because of Ashcroft.

"She's an academic success story. A meteoric rise from the faculty to dean and then to president."

"She knows how hard it can be for other women, so she helps them in any way she can."

Catherine made her way uphill a few minutes before 3:00, hoping the stifling heat and humidity wouldn't reduce her to a sweaty puddle. She stopped in the portico of Franklin Hall and examined her reflection in a window. She took a small comb from her skirt pocket and ran it through her hair.

Franklin Hall, an old Victorian mansion, housed the President's Office, a few meeting rooms and the Admissions and Financial Aid Offices. This was the impressive first building that prospective students and their parents saw when they visited the campus. The main entrance was lined with live oaks, a reminder of the property's nineteenth-century ownership by a sugar magnate from South Carolina who wanted to recreate southern gentility on the outskirts of Philadelphia.

Cold air touched her face as she struggled with the heavy door to the main entrance. Inside, she took in the burgundy carpet, dark woodwork, and a central staircase leading to a mezzanine.

Startled by a voice coming from the large desk tucked under the window beside the main door, Catherine turned to see a woman seated behind a row of phones.

"You must be Dr. Finley."

"Catherine," she said, extending her hand to the attentive woman who stood to greet her.

"I'm Dolly. I run the switchboard. Every call, all the calls when people don't know where to direct, come to me," she said, a grin brightening her round face.

I bet Admissions loves that, Catherine thought, suppressing a smile. How many prospective parents and students have been lost to a "Please hold" from Dolly?

"Flower deliveries come here as well. Beautiful bouquet you got last week."

"Yes. They were from my father," Catherine said, somehow feeling satisfaction that she'd killed a story Dolly might want to pass along.

"Very nice to meet you, Dolly. I'm here for a meeting with President Ashcroft."

"Yes. I know," Dolly quipped, returning to her desk. "Go on in. Michelle will take care of you."

"Welcome aboard, Dr. Finley," Michelle said, reaching

out to give Catherine's hand a warm shake as she entered the office.

Michelle took Catherine into the conference room where tea service was laid out on the table.

"President Ashcroft will be with you shortly," Michelle said.

Catherine took a seat at the table. Windowless, each wall had several portraits of past presidents, their tenure reaching back to the College's 1810 founding. All men.

"Admiring my predecessors?" Roslyn asked, taking her place at the head of the table. Roslyn's flat-chested torso was covered with a red jacket over a white silk blouse, buttoned to her chin. A tapered black skirt drew attention to her slender, sculpted legs, but Catherine couldn't help but look at Roslyn's feet—heavy black orthopedic shoes that reminded her of the ones her grandmother used to wear with her house dresses.

"Not really," Catherine quipped, surprised at her own candor. "You're alone in this field of graybeards."

"Yes. Many were clergy who knew nothing about finances. That's one reason why President Corbett had so much to address when he took the helm in 1950."

Roslyn poured two cups of tea and offered Catherine cream and sugar.

"Just black," Catherine said, relaxing into her first sip. Roslyn shared some highlights of the College's history, ending with President Corbett's phenomenal fundraising and acquisition of land.

"He couldn't have done all of that by himself?" Catherine said, noticing how Roslyn's face lit up when she talked about Corbett.

"We have a good team here in Development. Corbett

didn't have that support. Even today, a lot depends on me. Trustees and business leaders want to hear what I have to say about the College. You will be important in our fundraising efforts, Catherine, because you'll have your finger on the academic pulse. Our alumnae, still predominantly women, want to hear your voice."

Catherine ticked through her academic mentors in graduate school and faculty positions. All men. To be mentored by a woman would be a welcome change.

"I've read your articles about your work in Jamaica, Columbia, and the Congo. Your stories are so engaging," Catherine said. She mentioned one book that outlined how four centuries of mercantile trade in the Congo shaped ideas about health, suffering, and healing. "You portrayed each historical figure as if she were a character in a novel."

"Well, that's high praise coming from you. Literary criticism can be so dull, but you write about poets and novelists as if you know them," Roslyn said, the gold buttons on her red jacket brushing against the table.

"I do," Catherine said, smiling broadly, "and I could tell you how they take their tea."

Roslyn leaned in to place her cup on its saucer, her laugh settling on the conversation.

"Was it difficult making the change from teaching and research when you became dean?" Catherine asked, feeling a connection with Roslyn and not wanting the moment to pass.

Roslyn sipped her tea before answering. "I was President Corbett's administrative assistant for a year before I was appointed dean. He included me in meetings with business leaders. I took minutes at Board of Trustee meetings. I learned by watching him in action, the way I imagine our students do today in internships. It was the best year of my life. I felt like I belonged. My first year as dean was difficult, but I met with Corbett on a regular basis. I never lost his support."

Catherine was drawn in by the story, wishing she could articulate how much she would welcome Roslyn's support, but she was afraid she might sound like a lovesick schoolgirl.

"We're all glad you're here, Catherine. I was crushed, simply crushed, when Nicole, our graduate dean, left for a more prestigious post at U. C. Davis. It's difficult for small liberal arts colleges to keep the brightest and the best, but I hope you'll stay a while and help us bring the College to the next level of excellence."

"I will," Catherine said. "I'm looking forward to working with you."

Tuesday melted into Wednesday, and Catherine met individually with members of her staff. Bill Stevens, who had been Acting Dean during the year that the committee searched for and hired Catherine, spent considerable time outlining the highlights of the past year.

"I made two staffing changes that I thought would make your first year more manageable," Bill said. Catherine listened carefully as he described the employee that he had reorganized out of a job. "He was a malcontent and demanded that his position be made full-time," Bill asserted without further explanation.

Hmm, Catherine thought. I am not sure I could have done that.

Tired from the long day of meetings, Catherine left the office at 7:00. She poured a glass of wine and popped a

Lean Cuisine in the microwave. When dinner was ready, she sat down at the dining room table and began reading the mail she had neglected all day. In bed by ten, she was too tired to return her father's call.

Catherine woke up early on Thursday thinking about her lunch appointment with Hal. After a shower, she took several different outfits out of the closet and laid them on the bed. The red sleeveless dress with the white trim and white buttons would look good with the new red shoes. The conservative blue suit would not do.

Standing in front of the full-length mirror, she examined her naked body. She pinched the flesh around her waist. Am I gaining weight? No. I just need to get some exercise and tone some muscle. She smiled and said out loud, "You're having lunch, silly. You're not getting laid."

The breakup with Peter still hurt. Sometimes, she wondered if she was even interested in a relationship anymore.

She chose the red dress and reluctantly put on stockings. She needed some more time at the beach so she could get some color.

The morning was productive, and Bette answered questions on several ongoing projects. Hal stopped by promptly at noon. He looked relaxed in a pair of khaki slacks and pale-yellow shirt. He walked Catherine to his car, a black Honda with immaculate white upholstery.

While Hal drove, Catherine took in her surroundings, houses on rolling hills with beautiful gardens draped either side of the wide boulevard. The houses reminded Catherine of her great Aunt Rita's house in Bryn Mawr with an English garden and a fountain with Athena gracing its center. She and her sister Caroline would visit every summer, and Aunt Rita would take them to a play in Philadelphia. She'd find a Saturday soon and explore the City and those childhood memories.

The restaurant was small, tucked under a bookstore that looked inviting. The dining room was crowded and noisy. Hal focused on work, explaining that he reported to the Vice President for Enrollment Management, Steve Dennison, who had been instrumental in getting the College back on its feet after some financial difficulties in the 1990s. "He was the driving force behind the development of all our graduate programs."

Hal ordered an enormous roast beef sandwich with french fries, and Catherine asked for a salad with chicken.

"I don't eat like this every day. Since Tina's death, I've gotten out of the habit of cooking. Most nights I work out after work and go to bed early."

"Tina?" Catherine asked, laying her fork down and sipping her water.

"My wife," Hal said, holding Catherine's gaze. "She had an aggressive cancer that took her quickly."

"I'm so sorry for your loss," Catherine said, feeling tears form in her eyes. She realized as she tried to keep her composure that she hadn't cried when her own mother died.

They ate in silence for a while, enjoying the energy of the busy dining room.

The conversation shifted to academic interests and courses they had taught recently. The tension in Hal's face disappeared. His hands moved in rhythm with his slightly raised voice as he described the oral histories he had written and published about the Civil Rights Movement.

"My academic interest comes from listening to my mother talk about her work. She was an attorney. Her parents had been poor when they started out together in the 1940s, but her father made quite a bit of money in real estate. They sent her to college, thinking this was a way to launch her into Philadelphia society."

"Instead, she decided to get an education?" Catherine asked sarcastically, thinking about her own mother who saw a college education as a way to snag a man.

"Exactly. She studied English Literature and then decided to go to law school. She clerked for a judge and worked with the judge's son, also an attorney, who got her interested in the Civil Rights Movement. She tried some landmark Civil Rights cases and practiced law in Boston until she died in 1987."

Hal took the last bite of his sandwich and leaned back in his chair. "What about your mother, Catherine?"

Catherine hesitated, wondering where to begin.

"My mother went to Bryn Mawr," Catherine said derisively. "She would have made your grandparents happy. She got the degree and then the coveted MRS. She snagged my father at a mixer, and they were married the summer after graduation. She never worked a day in her life and resented women like your mother for wanting a career. She never seemed happy, so I'm not sure what she wanted out of life."

"I don't think it was easy for women of our mothers' generation," Hal said thoughtfully. "Women who wanted a conventional marriage felt threatened by women who wanted a career and more equality in marriage."

"You're right," Catherine conceded. She was forming another question about his mother's work when Hal looked at his watch and motioned for the check. He didn't want to be late for a two o'clock appointment.

Tyler Hall was quiet when Hal and Catherine got back to campus.

"Let's have lunch again soon," Catherine said. "I would love to hear more about your research." Catherine liked Hal's deep, gentle voice, his confidence about his work. In a few weeks, she'd ask him about the cast of characters. She smiled, remembering the mischievous way he'd said those words.

Chapter Two

When Catherine arrived at the house in Spring Lake, her father was sitting on the porch, several books lying open on the small glass-topped café table. He got up slowly, measuring each step as he walked toward her. He stopped at the top of the stairs, holding tightly to the railing.

Catherine put down her bags and gave him a hurried hug, feeling his bony frame. He's lost so much weight, she thought. He placed a kiss on her cheek and took her hand. She squeezed his fingers, crooked from arthritis.

"The drive took longer than I expected," she said. "Traffic was heavy."

"Of course," he replied with a smile. "It's supposed to be a beautiful weekend, so everyone is headed this direction."

"How was your first week as dean?" he asked.

"Great. I already have stories to tell you. Thanks for the beautiful flowers. What a lovely surprise on my first day."

Catherine took in the wrap-around porch of the nineteenth-century Victorian. The white wicker rocking chair was still nestled in the corner. *For a moment, she saw her grandmother sitting in it. Flowered dress, a book in her lap, knitting basket at her feet. Eyes closed, snoring.*

Catherine smiled at the memory and pulled the rocking chair up to the table.

"I've chilled some white wine. Let's have a glass before we think about dinner," Douglas said, walking back and sitting across from her.

"Dinner's easy. I brought a casserole," Catherine said, getting up and going into the kitchen to get the wine. She carried the bottle from the refrigerator and poured two glasses. As she placed the bottle back on the bottom shelf, she noticed its only companions were half a melon and a bottle of orange juice. It was a good thing she'd picked up a few things on the way down.

Returning to the porch, she handed her father a glass and sat down in the rocking chair. The chilly ocean breeze was refreshing after the hot, tiring drive.

The gentle tinkling of the wind chimes called to mind another memory.

She's in a yellow sundress, reaching up as her grandmother lifts her into the rocking chair. Her grandmother brushes the sand off her cheeks and chubby arms. Catherine looks up into her face, running her index finger over a wrinkled cheek.

"Did you let Daddy sit on your lap when he was a little boy?" Catherine asks, wiggling further into her grandmother's lap as she waited for an answer.

"I did until he got too grown-up," her grandmother

says, running her fingers through Catherine's tangled chestnut curls.

"You're thinking about Nana," Douglas said, taking a sip of wine and bringing Catherine back to the present.

"This porch is incomplete without her," Catherine said, nodding.

Letting the memory go, Catherine looked at her father. He smiled, his wrinkled face relaxed and glowing in the late afternoon sun.

"So how about some of those stories about Franklin you promised?" Douglas asked, returning his gaze to Catherine.

"Neil, my boss, may have some anger management issues," she said lightly, describing the volatile phone conversation she overheard. "But Roslyn Ashcroft, the president, she's amazing." She told her father about their meeting on her first day and her hopes that Roslyn might be a mentor.

That evening, as they sat down to dinner, Douglas bowed his head to say grace. Catherine scanned her father's face as he said each word.

"Dad, have you been eating?" she asked as he took his first bite of the casserole. Douglas looked at Catherine sheepishly, and then, returned his attention to his food.

"I didn't think so," she said. "I'm going to make some dinners for you this weekend that will last you all week. All you'll have to do is heat them up."

They spent most of the meal in silence until Douglas said, "This was delicious, Catherine." He lay his fork across his plate. "Your visits since your mother's death have meant so much to me." Catherine put her arm around her father and squeezed his shoulder before she started to clear the table.

Guilt tugged at her, remembering the months before her mother's death in January when she hadn't come to visit. She couldn't face her mother's comments about breaking up with Peter.

"What's wrong with you? He comes from a good family... has money," her mother said. She remembered her mother's contorted face, the anger slicing through her slurred speech.

As if money and good breeding made your marriage to Daddy a success, she thought, rage building inside her.

"I'm sorry I didn't visit during those last few months," she said.

Looking into the distance, he said softly, "It's all right, Catherine."

But it wasn't all right. She had run away like a child, and her father didn't stand up for her. He never tried to stop her mother's attacks. And now, she couldn't say what she was thinking. He was too frail. She'd upset him.

Douglas wasn't up for the short walk to the ocean, so Catherine went alone. The surgeon wanted him to walk every day, but he often had no will to do so.

The lights on the boardwalk provided enough light to see the distant white caps. Catherine walked the two-mile length of the worn planks, stopping frequently to watch the waves pound the shore as the tide came in. Memories of childhood swirled in her mind as she descended the steps onto the beach... her parents' fights... that terrible night of the sirens when her mother slit her wrists...

She thought about her sister Caroline. Beautiful Caroline, insisting on marrying David before she finished college... Daddy wanting her to wait. Was it better for him now that Caroline didn't visit? It always seemed like it was Caroline and mother in one corner and she and Daddy in the other.

Thoughts about Peter rushed in with the first refreshing wave.

Catherine picked up a piece of driftwood and tossed it into the foaming surf.

She had met Peter at a friend's party. Dark curly hair. Brown eyes. Swimmer's body.

He was deep in conversation with another man about President Clinton and health care. His gaze fell on her, and she was embarrassed to be caught eavesdropping. He steered the other man her way so he could introduce himself. She gave him her name and mentioned that she was starting at Somerset College.

"I'm in the Finance Department there. This is my little brother Bobby," he said, turning and giving the other man an affectionate slap on the back. "He's studying law in New York but is home for the summer, enjoying the family lake house."

"Nice to meet both of you," Catherine said, smiling at Peter. "It's good to hear people haven't forgotten about the need for equal access to health care."

"Most have. But 'how can I, that girl standing there/My attention fix/ On ...politics'".

"Yeats," Bobby said, rolling his eyes.

"I know," Catherine said, sipping her drink. "Now I'm really impressed."

Bobby drifted off to another conversation, and Peter told Catherine about his hiking trips to Ireland.

"I was there in '98 on an NEH Summer Fellowship, studying Yeats in Sligo," Catherine said. They compared experiences, climbing Ben Bulben and hiking in County Claire.

The next day, Peter took her water skiing on Lake Sunapee. During the five years they were together, they spent many long weekends at his family house, sometimes with Peter's parents. Water skiing on the lake in summer and skating on the frozen lake in winter.

One winter trip when they were at the house alone, they left after dinner to take a walk to the lake. Starting out in darkness, they were startled by bright green light. Catherine turned to Peter, catching his smile.

"I knew it was possible tonight," he said, "but I wanted to surprise you." Catherine listened as he explained how the Northern Lights were created... something about fast-moving electrons and oxygen in the earth's magnetic field.

They walked on the frozen lake, the light still brilliant.

"We shouldn't go too far," Catherine said breathlessly, ice forming on her eyelashes.

"You're crying," Peter said, brushing her cheek with his gloved hand.

"It's so beautiful," Catherine said.

They made love that night and sat by the fire eating eggs and toast at 3:00 a.m. And just before dawn, Peter proposed and said they'd be soulmates forever. They talked about having children. He wanted three, maybe more. She insisted on two, one boy and one girl.

"Stop thinking about Peter," Catherine said out loud.

Be honest, she told herself. How much did you really want him when you were together? There were the magical times like the night he proposed, but what about his reckless behavior... the drinking and the drugs?

Catherine took a deep breath of the salt air. Turning away from the ocean, she walked down her father's quiet, mostly dark street. Lights upstairs in several homes probably meant unpacking and putting young children to bed.

When Catherine returned, Douglas was reading in the sunroom. She poured a glass of port for him, his nightly ritual, and sat down on the couch next to his recliner. He seemed tired and distant, so she picked up *The New Yorker* from the coffee table and looked through it. A review of a new biography of Dylan Thomas. Welsh Poet. American Legend. Maybe a little Dylan Thomas the next time she taught her autobiography course. Students would like his rock-star quality and his unorthodox behavior.

Douglas placed his book on the arm of the recliner. Catherine looked up, and her father was staring straight ahead. Her eyes followed his gaze to the wedding picture sitting on top of the television.

"It's six months today since your mother's gone."

"I know," Catherine said.

"I pray she's at peace. She had so little peace, so little joy in this life."

"I know," Catherine said again, reaching over to place her hand over his. She squeezed the bony fingers. She felt no grief for her mother, only sadness that her father felt such pain. Is this her father the priest, hoping she's at peace? Is it really anyone else's fault that her mother had no peace in her life?

"I'm going to turn in early, Dad," Catherine said, leaning over and kissing him good night. Upstairs, she opened the bedroom door and took in the room she had called home as a teenager. Light from the Tiffany lamp fell on the music box on the dresser. She opened it, and a few notes played from a melody she didn't recognize. A breeze stirred the satin window panel, and the gentle roar of the surf was reassuring.

Catherine undressed and pulled a nightshirt over her head. Climbing into bed, the sea air filled her lungs. She pulled the comforter over her and fell into a deep sleep. She dreamed about her grandmother, reading to her in the rocking chair on the porch.

Chapter Three

The clock registered 6:00 a.m. Douglas turned away from its light and reached his arm around a large pillow.

"Grace," he said softly as he closed his eyes and pulled the pillow closer to his chest. Eyes wide open, he saw long black hair falling against slender shoulders.

White buttocks, round as peaches, stood firm over long, slender, athletic legs. Douglas reached for her as she disappeared in the darkened bedroom.

"I wish Catherine had been your daughter," Douglas said aloud as if she was there with him, not a fleeting memory passing him by as he returned to sleep.

Pouring the coffee, Grace looked at him with sparkling eyes. He sat at the kitchen table and sipped the scalding liquid, taking in the early morning breeze on roses, the tap, tap, tap of a bird on the back fence. The New York Times *lay on the chair beside him in pieces, folded badly.*

"President Kennedy decided to withhold American aid

to South Vietnam's President unless they implement political reforms," Grace said, opening the newspaper to the article reporting this.

"It's a start, but not enough. Unless American advisors help with a plan, things won't change," he said, stroking her hand. Red blushing cheeks and green eyes, brightness that mirrored the morning sun and stillness of the warm October day.

Coffee finished, they walked in Valley Green, a park near Grace's apartment, walked in silence, soft tread on muddy pathways. Sun shimmering on the waterfall. His hand slid across her back, reaching for her right hand. He kissed her gently on the lips.

He stopped to show a little girl how to skim stones. She gazed up at him, with large, expressive eyes. Then, she looked at her mother to make sure it was all right to respond. The mother offered a shy smile, kneeling close to the edge of the water.

Douglas opened his eyes and pushed himself up slowly. Struggling to sit up, he reached for his glasses next to the clock radio. Sliding feet into slippers gingerly, he padded to the bathroom.

Hand to razor, razor to face, he looked at the elderly man looking back at him. Eyes bright in wrinkled lids and face.

He thought about mornings waking early, Elizabeth asleep beside him. Her back to him, she would sleep soundly, or so he thought. He made coffee before he showered and dressed, sipping the first cup before returning to the kitchen to make breakfast for the girls.

Most mornings, Flora would arrive while he was in mid-course. She'd shoo him away cheerfully and finish breakfast as the girls got ready for school.

By the time Caroline was four, she was dressing herself. Drunk or not, at least Elizabeth would have laid out Caroline's clothes the night before, but never Catherine's. When Caroline appeared at the breakfast table, Douglas would kiss her and head upstairs for his other daughter.

"Daddy," she'd giggle, reaching for him.

"Catherine," he'd reply, smile returning.

Catherine had pulled on brown corduroy overalls and had buttoned one shoulder. White socks and mary janes. No shirt.

"Honey, I'm no Pierre Cardin, but these shoes don't go with the overalls."

"Who's Pierre?" Catherine said with a frown.

"Never mind," Douglas said as he looked in her closet to find something more suitable.

"How about the yellow dress that mommy just bought? Caroline has on the matching green one."

Catherine nodded enthusiastically, starting to unbutton the overalls.

After the last stroke of the razor, Douglas wiped his face with a warm washcloth. Pulling a tartan plaid bathrobe over his pajamas, he headed for the kitchen. Tightening the belt, he took one step at a time, breathing deeply, salt air filling his lungs.

Douglas made coffee and cut a piece of crumb cake. Crumbs, buttery dough, stickiness. He rinsed his fingers.

"Daddy, Daddy," Catherine squealed as Douglas peeked around the corner. "Nana let us bake cookies."

Douglas launched Catherine from the booster seat, stopping short of his mother and a tray of cookies hot from the oven.

"Do I get to sample one?" he asked, warm cinnamon making his mouth water.

"Only if Santa says you've been a good boy this year," his mother said, taking the tray out of his reach and placing it on the counter to cool. Caroline looked up and nodded her approval. Then, she turned her attention to the cookies she was sprinkling with red and green sugar.

"Daddy's been very good, Nana. He's read to us every night since Mommy's been gone. He does all the voices in the stories," Catherine said.

Douglas placed Catherine back in the booster seat. She watched Caroline decorate the cookies. Taking great care to do it exactly as Caroline did, red sugar for the stars, green for the Christmas trees. Raisins for the snowmen's eyes and buttons. They worked quietly. Comfortable silence... unbearable pain.

For a moment, Douglas's attention returned to the beautiful summer morning. A squirrel skittered across the window ledge, seeming to stop and look at him as he sipped his coffee. Catherine had asked him many times that Christmas when her mother would come back. He told her he didn't know.

Decorated cookies were placed in the oven. Douglas carried a sleepy but happy Catherine upstairs, stopping in the bathroom to wash her sticky hands before tucking her in.

"I'm sleepy. No story tonight," Catherine said.

"Okay. I'll start a new one tomorrow night."

Still holding his hand, Catherine fell asleep immediately. Not wanting the moment to pass, Douglas held tight to her chubby fingers, remembering another hand in his on a warm October day. Lavender perfume mixed with the fresh air as they walked in Valley Green. "I wish you had known Grace," he said as he placed a tiny bear in Catherine's hand. Hugging the soft fur, Catherine rolled on her side, a smile faint on her lips.

"I hope you remember this, Doll," he said out loud.

Chapter Four

Catherine breathed in the smell of rich coffee. 9:37 a.m. *Hmm. Daddy's up early.* Slipping into sandals, she went downstairs and found her father in the sunroom. A book was open on the table in front of him, and his eyes were opening and closing as he repeated the words on the page.

> I yearn to belong to something...
> I yearn to be held
> in the great hands of your heart—

"Good morning, Catherine," he said, tilting his head up so she could kiss him on the cheek. "Ruth brought two crumb buns for me yesterday, so I would have something nutritious to give you this weekend."

Douglas looked up at Catherine impishly, and she laughed as she walked to the kitchen and located the crumb bun on the kitchen counter and spread a generous serving of butter on a piece. She poured coffee and returned to the sunroom, touching her father's hand gently as she sat down close to him.

Ruth and Al had been members of Douglas's parish and had become good friends. Since her mother's death, Ruth called or looked in on Douglas every day. Catherine called her if she was worried about her father. Ruth always seemed to know what to say.

"Douglas recovered physically from the bypass surgery," Ruth told her in a phone conversation two months after her mother's death, "but he's depressed. His friend Ray calls him every day. Their talks always lighten his mood."

Catherine finished the coffee cake and sipped her coffee.

"It's good to be here with you, Dad," she said, once again squeezing his hand. Reaching for Douglas's book, she turned it toward her and read aloud:

> I want to mirror your immensity.
> I want never to be too weak or too old
> To bear the heavy, lurching image of you.

Catherine looked at her father as his trembling hand carried his coffee cup to his lips. He drank slowly and then placed the cup in the saucer. Morning quiet, a bird chirping softly near the window, settled over the rattling cup as he placed it on the table.

"I first read Rilke's poetry when I was young," he said. "It awakened in me a sense of connection with the creation in the same way that Hopkins's poetry did, an awareness of the sacredness of every living thing."

Catherine listened to her father, imagining him as a

professor, teaching these texts that he loved so much. Making a difference in the world had drawn him to ministry, but the church had disappointed him. The war on poverty failed. The church never integrated. Hearts weren't changed. At least as a professor, he could have inspired a few to love the things he loved.

"When I was a young man in 1968, a difficult year for me," he continued, looking at Catherine intently, "I went to Maine. We spent a day hiking in Acadia National Park. I've never felt so overwhelmed by physical beauty. Tranquil lakes... we canoed on Long Pond." He stopped for a moment, his gaze far away. Then, smiling wanly, he continued, "A rainstorm came up when we were on the pond. At first, I was frightened because two bolts of lightning lit up the sky, but once the drenching rain stopped, the air was still and full of possibility."

"Dad," Catherine asked, "Do you remember the time you took me to Maine?"

"Yes. I took you a few years later because I wanted you to feel that sense of God's immensity too, even as a little girl."

Catherine sat quietly for a few moments, drinking her coffee. Silences were easy with her father. She had so many adventures with him as a little girl. Even something as mundane as going to the grocery store was an adventure... a time to wander down an aisle, looking for the right box of cookies or a new flavor of ice cream.

After a few minutes of this reverie, she stood up and went to the kitchen to clean up the breakfast dishes.

"Dad, I'm going to the beach for a while," she said as she watched him shuffle back to his recliner. "I'll be back in time to make you some lunch. I called Ruth on the way down yesterday and invited her and Al over for coffee afterward."

Catherine headed for the beach, a new novel in her bag. She left Douglas in his chair, reading, but she knew he would soon be asleep. This had become part of his daily routine since his surgery.

Catherine placed her chair in the hard sand, a few feet from the water's edge. The morning was still, and the sun was climbing slowly over the ocean. A few surfers walked past her and waved, the only others on the beach. She pulled *The Hours* from her bag, running her fingers over its shiny cover.

She didn't open the book. Her thoughts wandered to her time at Acadia on Jordan Pond with her father.

The day had been clear and cool. With a knapsack and hiking boots just like her father's, she felt very grown-up. They walked the path briskly until they reached rocks submerged in water. Her father lifted her into the air and placed her on top of a large, dry boulder. She turned and watched him struggle over the wet ground, slipping once but catching himself. Going forward, he stayed a few steps ahead of her to make sure there were no loose rocks or slippery spots. They walked at a good pace until they came to a small wooden bridge, which traversed a shallow stream.

Her father stopped and settled himself on a flat boulder. He pulled two apples from his knapsack and handed one to Catherine. The apple, shiny and deep red, tasted sweet.

Catherine rubbed sunblock on her face and shoulders.

Why was that memory of her father so vivid? He had seemed so alive, unlike the tense, shy man navigating her mother's anger.

Catherine opened her novel and lost herself in the story. Virginia Woolf wading into the river and drowning herself. Laura Brown, a depressed housewife reading *Mrs. Dalloway* in sterile 1949 Los Angeles, struggling to live amid thoughts about death. Clarissa Vaughan, a modern-day Mrs. Dalloway wading into memory as she tries to make sense of her life at the end of the twentieth century. Had her mother's story been like this? Had she struggled to find those moments of happiness when all Catherine saw was her mother's suicide attempts?

After reading a few more pages, Catherine realized the beach was filling up around her. She saw people she knew who lived in Spring Lake year-round, and then there were the tourists struggling with umbrellas, coolers, and buckets and shovels. They looked like characters in a cartoon trying to look relaxed in a foreign country.

Catherine put the novel in her bag and decided to head back to the house. Cunningham understood the power of stories. Woolf's exquisite "moments of being" making stories out of the "cotton wool" of life. Writing those stories kept Woolf alive. Reading *Mrs. Dalloway* helped Mrs. Brown choose life, a life she couldn't continue without stories.

When she got back to the house, her father was asleep in the recliner, Rilke face down on his stomach. Without disturbing him, Catherine went into the kitchen and opened a can of soup. She took ham, cheese, and wheat bread out of the refrigerator, putting two slices of bread in the toaster.

While she was doing this, her father shuffled into the dining room and sat down at the head of the table. Rain started, tapping on the roof, then pounding with authority.

"Just half a sandwich, dear," Douglas said. "Some of this medicine I'm taking has killed my appetite."

"I know," Catherine said, glancing at her father with a worried look. "You have to try, though. Maybe you can eat more frequently... just little meals or snacks."

Douglas smiled as he took a bite of the sandwich and said, "When I was in business with Ray, we could really put it away. Cheesesteaks... pasta at the little restaurant on Nassau Street."

"I loved that restaurant," Catherine said. "Uncle Ray always convinced us to try something new. Lasagna, fettuccine alfredo, but I couldn't say *fettuccine*."

Catherine caught a troubled look on her father's face. Were those tears? she thought, placing a plate of chocolate chip cookies on the table.

"Are you okay, Daddy?"

"Yes, dear. You are so kind to make me lunch... Your mother..." His voice trailed off. Catherine squeezed his shoulder and moved toward the living room as the doorbell rang.

Ruth stood in the doorway with the rain coming down hard. She stepped across the threshold, and Catherine hugged her tightly.

"Al sends his love to both of you," she said, following Catherine into the sunroom. Douglas followed and settled himself in his recliner. Ruth reached down and kissed Douglas on the cheek. "He's worn out. We did some yard work together this morning."

"You shouldn't be working in that hot sun," Catherine

scolded, placing cups of coffee in front of Ruth and her father.

"We worked in the shade mostly, but you're right, dear. It may have been too much for both of us."

Douglas offered Ruth the plate of cookies. Rain beat a staccato backdrop to the conversation.

"I was just saying to Catherine that it's so kind... her visits, making me lunch, dinner," Douglas said.

"That's a lovely way to put it," Ruth said, nibbling on a cookie. "I've been making dinner for Al for fifty years. That's what everyone does. At least they did in my generation."

"Well, not everyone," Catherine said, looking only at Ruth. "My mother never cooked. I remember awful TV dinners when I was a teenager. Mother was usually hammered by the time she put them in the oven. I'm not sure I ever saw her eat. She'd keep drinking while we ate the wretched things."

Her father's coffee cup slipped from his grasp. Catherine turned toward him. His shaking hand fell to his side.

"Douglas, are you all right?" Ruth asked, reaching for his arm.

"The Episcopal priest with a drunk for a wife," he said in a whisper. "I didn't know how to help her... to keep you and your sister from the pain."

Catherine picked up the cup and went to the kitchen for a dishtowel. Tears came silently, anger and sorrow all at once. Fingers gripping the counter, she looked at the tiny kitchen table.

Drunk the day of her First Communion. Drunk at nine

o'clock on a Sunday morning. Did Mother do it to spite her father because she hated his job so much? Or had all her mother's rage been focused on Catherine?

She thought about how her mother would scoop up her sister every time she cried, wipe her tears and pat her head. But she never held Catherine. If Catherine cried, she smacked her hard.

It had only happened once in front of her father. Her mother's diamond turned around on her finger, scratched Catherine's face. At fourteen, the acne was bad enough, but the scratch took weeks to heal. She told people the cat did it. They didn't have a cat.

Her father had taken her into the kitchen and wet his handkerchief. He sat down next to her at the kitchen table and gently mopped up the blood.

"Why does she hate me?" Catherine asked. Silence filled the space between them. "Say something," she screamed. "Say something!"

"I don't know what to say," he said, pulling her close to him and placing the handkerchief on the kitchen table.

"But you know why she hates me," Catherine said, her tears stopping. She realized he wasn't denying it. He was incapable of lying to her.

She heard her mother's glass rattle in the living room. She set the bottle down hard.

"Tell her, Douglas," her mother said. "Tell her it's your fault. You decided her fate before she was born."

Her father looked stricken. Catherine didn't want him to cry. She didn't think he knew what her mother was talking about.

Catherine never asked her mother what she meant

that night. What was her father's fault? Was there a story she needed to know, one shaping what her mother had become?

She reached for a tissue and wiped away some tears, touching the cheek where the scratch had been, remembering her mother's slap, the diamond tearing her cheek.

When Catherine returned to the sunroom, Ruth was seated close to Douglas, patting his arm. Catherine mopped up the coffee with the towel, then left the towel to cover the stain.

"I'll put some stain remover on it later. It will be fine."

"Catherine, I'm sorry," Douglas said.

Catherine sat down on the couch across from her father, tears still creeping down her cheeks.

"People said such awful things about Elizabeth's drinking," Ruth offered, "but most of us just wanted to support you, Douglas, and the girls." She leaned back in her chair.

"Catherine, I'm sorry," Douglas said again, his hand rubbing his twitching eyebrow.

A simple *I'm sorry* wouldn't wash away years of silence. He was so good at carrying everyone else's pain. What about hers?

Brushing tears away she said, "You don't need to apologize. I have good memories too. When I was little, you'd get me up in the morning, pick out my clothes. Caroline was always a little jealous since Mother laid out her clothes the night before."

"Good for you, Douglas," Ruth said. "Al never helped much with the children. Some mornings, he was on the road before they got up. When I help my daughter with her babies now, I wonder how I did it."

"Catherine, your mother never had a good model to learn how to be a mother," Douglas said, shifting in his chair and turning towards her.

"Most of us didn't," Ruth added. "We just made it up as we went along."

Ruth finished her coffee and said she was heading home for a nap.

"That sounds good," Catherine said, walking her to the door.

"He's so glad you're here," Ruth said kissing Catherine on the cheek. "You should try to talk with him about how you feel, but remember, he carries a lot of pain and guilt."

Catherine nodded, squeezing Ruth's hand. She leaned against the door as she closed it, wishing she hadn't talked so openly about her mother. There were stories she should keep to herself.

Chapter Five

Hal walked briskly uphill, not wanting to be late for his meeting with Steve. He passed the library, built in 2001, the year he'd started at Franklin. After accepting the position, he and Tina had come down and spent a long weekend exploring, deciding where they wanted to live.

They'd come on the campus that Sunday afternoon, walking through each building to get a feel for the College.

"A library without card catalogs," Hal had said, shaking his head as he stood in the first-floor lobby, seeing only computers.

"It's the twenty-first century, Dr. Dinosaur," Tina said, laughing.

Hal laughed too, taking her hand as they moved on to the next building.

Tina was right. Things moved too fast for him. He'd master the applications on his phone, and it would be time to upgrade. He missed wandering through the stacks in a library, plucking a book from the shelf and perusing the table of contents.

"This is beautiful," Tina exclaimed, as they entered the Hemingway Reading Room, a dark-paneled room furnished with round cherry tables and chairs nestled in alcoves with large windows. A Tiffany lamp graced the center of each table. Bookcases filled with classic literature lined the interior walls of the alcoves.

"Mary Hemingway," Hal said to Tina, as he removed a leather-bound copy of The Tempest from a top shelf. "She left money to the College for an endowed chair in Comparative Literature. Her children donated her library, over 7,000 books, a few years ago."

"I wonder if she read them all," Tina demurred, reaching under Hal's hand to touch the soft leather cover.

"I never met her," Hal said, moving closer to Tina, "but colleagues who knew her found her memory amazing. She memorized more poetry than most of us have read."

Chest tightening, Hal stopped for a moment on his walk to his meeting, taking in the petunias outside the bay window in front of the Hemingway Reading Room, the circular rose garden on the commons, adjacent to Smith Science Center. He had looked at all of this with Tina. Everything looked more beautiful when he could see it with her eyes.

They met in college during his senior year. She was a sophomore. She sat next to him in an eight o'clock Abnormal Psychology course that he'd selected as an elective. At the end of the first class, she'd asked him a question, something about the first essay for the course. It took him three weeks to ask her to have coffee with him after class. They sat in the cafeteria and talked until lunch service started at 11:30. Her family didn't have a lot of money, she told him, and she got to college on a full scholarship.

"Why am I only meeting you now if you've been here almost two years?" he asked.

"I don't go to fraternity parties. Hmm. Now that I say that, I guess I don't go out much at all. My first year, I was worried I wasn't smart enough to be here, but I got a 4.0 and started to relax," she said.

Hal enjoyed listening to her talk about herself. He'd dated lots of women in his four years at Amherst. He'd spent most of his junior year with Shirley Watson, only to find out she was also sleeping with a fraternity brother. Even now, he flinched at his own naivete.

He'd slept with Tina for the first time the week before finals. It was after they'd walked one night to the observatory and lay in the grass, watching the stars in a clear sky. She'd nestled in close to him and began kissing him. He marveled at her fearlessness. She had no concern at all about the other students walking past.

She left the day after finals for her family home, a small town outside of Philadelphia, and he didn't see her again until she returned from a semester abroad in Italy in December. He'd written to her every week that summer and fall. It was easier for him to tell her about himself in letters. He told her about his mother's cancer and his trips home to Boston on weekends to care for her.

She wrote back occasionally, telling him about

Florence and Rome and the little towns in Tuscany she was visiting. In one letter in October, she asked if she could fly to Boston and spend some time with him at Christmas. He wrote back immediately, "Stay as long as you like. My mother wants to meet you."

She stayed the entire Christmas break, and he drove her back to Amherst in the new year.

"I'm glad I met your mother," she told him later that spring when she came to Boston for his mother's funeral. "If I ever have children, I want to be a mother like yours."

"You will be," Hal had said, wanting her close, wishing she didn't have another year of school away from him.

"Hi, Dr. Doyle," a petite brunette in Franklin shorts and t-shirt said, approaching him as he got back on the path that led to Franklin Hall. He'd helped the Dean of Students interview orientation leaders, and Katie had been one of the students selected.

"I'm back for orientation," she said, stopping to face him on the path. "I heard we've hired a new dean."

"Yes," Hal said. He encouraged her to stop and introduce herself to Catherine.

As he approached the entrance to Franklin Hall, Steve emerged with three students.

"This is Dr. Doyle, our Graduate Dean," Steve said to the three students. "Paul, Hassan, and Mike are giving some last-minute tours to prospective transfer students."

Steve and Hal moved through the spacious foyer and climbed the wide, central stairway to the second floor. Steve's office, once the dressing room for the plantation owner's estranged wife, was tucked back in the front corner of the second floor. The masculine furniture—

mahogany desk, computer table, and conference table—created a stark contrast to the feminine tapestries draped on several walls.

"Numbers for fall look good," Steve said, passing a report to Hal as they sat down at the small conference table. "Transfer numbers are up, and the number of transfers living on campus has increased by thirty percent.

"We have some soft numbers with our graduate enrollments, which I'm not happy about. Most programs are new, and we haven't done the needed marketing to get the word out. Neil's no help here. He's encouraging faculty to speak out against the new programs. We need to be strategic in how we move ahead."

The spin, Hal thought, still nodding in agreement but wishing the politics were less contentious.

Hal headed downhill, planning to go home and do some reading for class. He thought about the meeting with Neil and several faculty members when he was three months into his position. They were more interested in talking about his predecessor than the topic at hand.

"She came in here like a bat out of hell, pushing through a program we didn't need," a Psychology professor said, who'd published his only article in 1982.

"A program the College can't sustain financially," Neil added, sitting back in his chair and grinning at his colleagues. None of it true, but Hal sat speechless.

Hal described the encounter with Tina at dinner that evening.

"Men have such a hard time with bright, accomplished women," Tina said simply, "especially the ones who don't seek their approval."

It might not be that simple, Hal thought. Or maybe it was.

His mother had been like Nicole. Strong. Focused on getting the job done and guiding the client through to the end.

Huddled in bed one night when he was nine, he overheard a conversation between his mother and Uncle Vince, her good friend and law firm colleague. Vince was reassuring her that everything was going to work out. "The vote went our way," he said more than once.

"Don't they know she's sick?" Hal asked Vince when he came in to say good night. She was just home from the hospital after the breast cancer surgery. Hal remembered the fear. Fear she wouldn't survive the pain and nausea. Fear she would leave him like Gramps and the father he had never known.

Vince shook his head. "She didn't want them to know. It would make her too vulnerable."

"What's vulnerable?" Hal asked.

Uncle Vince was blunt. Some of the men in the firm didn't believe women should be allowed to practice law. They should stay home and care for their children.

"But my mother takes care of me," Hal said, his tiny fists pummeling his Winnie the Pooh.

Vince nodded. "Some men have a hard time believing women are just as smart as they are. Your mother knows that, so she doesn't let them see any weakness, any vulnerability, like being sick."

Hal wasn't his mother. He wasn't a fighter.

Chapter Six

Catherine walked past the lanky student in a tailored navy-blue suit and high heels talking with Hal. Returning Hal's smile, she walked into his office and stood in front of the bookcases lining the walls. She scanned the titles until her eyes fell on Bobby Kennedy's *Thirteen Days: A Memoir of the Cuban Missile Crisis* and *Robert Kennedy: In His Own Words*. She pulled a slim black volume from the shelf. *Strength to Love* by Martin Luther King Jr. She wondered if her father had read this.

Putting the book back, she turned to several pictures on the middle shelf. A woman in an emerald green bikini, dark hair falling over her slim shoulders, held a baby in navy blue bathing trunks. One small hand lay against the woman's cheek while the woman playfully kissed the fingers on his other hand. Hal and his mother.

The second frame held a collage of photographs—Hal in a cap and gown, doctoral hood displayed proudly by a petite blond. A wedding picture, the blond bride wearing an off-white dress with pearls trimming the neckline and bodice. The groom, hair as dark as hers was light, smiled contentedly as he looked at his bride. Catherine lingered on the picture, imaging herself in white satin with a veil made of Italian lace. The third picture was that blonde bride, a few years older but much thinner. Still beautiful, her smile seemed disingenuous, perhaps suggesting pain of some kind, or, maybe, she simply didn't want her picture taken.

As Hal came in and stood beside her, Catherine turned to him and sighed. "Hal, your mother and your wife were so beautiful."

"I think so too," he said with a smile. "I have so few pictures of either of them. For some reason, neither one of them liked having their picture taken."

Hal directed Catherine to a small table and pulled out a chair for her. He took a piece of paper out of a leather binder and handed it to her, then slid into a chair.

"Roslyn expects fundraising ideas to support academic programs to come from us," Hal explained. "We have a strong alumnae base, providing much of the support."

Catherine nodded, remembering her conversation with Roslyn. She scanned the list of potential donors.

"Use first meetings to get to know them. Relax like you're at a cocktail party."

"That's right," Catherine said, her frame convulsed with laughter. "You don't know me yet. I'm the shrinking violet in the corner at the cocktail party, gulping wine to fuel my courage."

"Not recommended," Hal shot back lightly. "Don't like cocktail parties? Okay. Picture a Board meeting, and you're on the agenda. I'm happy to talk you through some scenarios."

"I welcome your help, coach," she said.

"Steve will be part of the team as well," Hal said, jotting a note on his agenda.

"And Neil?" Catherine asked, watching Hal's relaxed posture stiffen.

"Steve has tried to include Neil in meetings and events, but he's shown little interest. Steve's take is Neil is still angry with Roslyn because I report to Steve, not to him. I try to stay out of it."

Another bombshell. Which landmine will find me first? Catherine mused.

Hal stopped by Catherine's office ten minutes before the meeting with Roslyn. He looked tired, and his tie hung crooked against his white wrinkled shirt. She tried not to notice and began chatting about one of the issues on their agenda.

As they walked brusquely uphill in the stifling heat, little boys on campus for soccer ran past them like miniature soldiers, quiet and orderly.

Catherine smiled. "Poor little guys. They must be melting."

They entered Franklin Hall and said a hurried hello to Dolly before moving into the President's Office. Roslyn's door was open. She ended a phone conversation and waited for Michelle to announce them.

The office was spacious. A formidable mahogany desk faced out from an alcove filled with large windows. Wrought-iron trim and latches on the windows appeared to be the original windows when the house was built in

1893. Roslyn got up from her desk and walked around to greet them. She led them to the other side of the office where a high-backed love seat and two Queen Anne chairs surrounded a coffee table.

"Let's be comfortable," Roslyn said as she sat down in one of the chairs. "If we need to move into the conference room, we can do so later." Catherine settled into a corner of the love seat and listened attentively as Hal moved from one item on his agenda to the next. She nodded in agreement, intimidated by how easily Hal conversed with this formidable figure.

Roslyn must have sensed Catherine's uncertainty. As Hal talked about some of the alumnae he had courted for the capital campaign, Roslyn turned to her.

"Catherine, did you have any fundraising experience when you were Acting Dean at Somerset College?"

"No. I was aware of the academic vice president's strategy for outreach, but I never did any of the fundraising."

"I have no doubt you'll be successful. I was impressed in the interview with your idea for a Professional Development Program for our students. You can introduce the idea as you begin conversations."

"But don't I need to get buy-in from the faculty and staff first?" Catherine asked, leaning in.

"Nonsense. You have the staff to start the program, and the faculty will get on board when they see how successful it is."

Catherine felt like she was being washed out to sea by a large wave. Fighting the anxiety, she heard Hal's reassuring voice.

"Anything I can do to help, just say the word,

Catherine," he said.

Roslyn produced a schedule for a three-day trip to Boston beginning Wednesday of the following week. A dinner meeting with two alumnae would be followed by a reception hosted by the Boston Alumni Association where Catherine would be introduced and asked to speak. Individual appointments with three alumnae were scheduled for Thursday, and a luncheon meeting with two trustees was slotted for Friday.

As Catherine and Hal walked downhill, Hal stopped, faced Catherine, and gave her a reassuring smile.

"Roslyn gives new meaning to 'hit the ground running'."

"I'll say."

"You need to learn how to pace yourself," he said thoughtfully. "Roslyn is a workhorse. As far as we know, she has no other life than this, and she assumes the same for us."

"Thanks for the advice, Hal," she said with a wan smile. They walked the rest of the way to Tyler Hall in silence, tired from the long day and oppressive heat. Catherine wondered if she was like Roslyn. Without Peter, without her father, she would be working all the time, filling all the empty spaces.

Bette was putting a few things in her briefcase as Catherine entered the office.

"I was just writing you a note. Chelsea Williams from the Music Department stopped by earlier. She seemed upset. I offered to schedule an appointment, but she said no. She asked if you would call her."

"I'd be happy to," Catherine said, taking the note from Bette with Chelsea's home number. "Have a good evening."

Catherine checked her emails and responded to several before she returned Chelsea's call. Chelsea picked up on the second ring and was immediately apologetic for bothering Catherine. Catherine assured her it wasn't a problem, but Chelsea seemed hesitant to go on. Finally, she said, "I need some advice about how to handle a situation with Neil Rhodes. Could we schedule a time to have coffee off-campus?" They agreed to meet the following morning at Catherine's home.

Catherine arrived home that night to two hungry cats, Molly and Maggie, and an almost empty refrigerator. She opened a small container of yogurt and called her father to let him know she would be in Spring Lake by dinner on Friday.

Finishing the yogurt and pouring a large glass of water, she phoned her friend Judy in Vermont.

A vivacious voice asked, "How is the Dean doing?"

"I'm doing very well, my friend, and I have some good news and bad news."

"Does the good news include me?"

Catherine chuckled softly at her friend's narcissism.

"The bad news is I have to go to Boston next Wednesday for three days of fundraising, and the good news is I could stay for the weekend if you could come down for a visit."

"Catherine, that would be perfect. Email me where you are staying, and I will see you next Friday."

Catherine turned off her cell phone and walked upstairs to run a hot bath. As she lowered herself into the soapy water, she smiled as she thought about the first time she and Judy met in graduate school almost two decades ago.

Judy had begun the program a year before she had, and at the beginning of the fall semester, Catherine had to attend a meeting of all the teaching assistants. As the group made introductions, Catherine began to feel uncomfortable. Most of them were men and very sure of themselves, bragging about the essays they had published and courses they were designing for the undergraduate program. Catherine was younger than all the other students, having graduated from college in three years and gone directly to graduate school.

When Judy introduced herself, she did not go on about her publications. Instead, she apologized for being out of sorts. "I was up reading when I realized at about three o'clock that there was a bat in my apartment. I chased the bat until I was able to subdue him with the broom." After the session, Catherine asked Judy if she wanted to get some coffee. She got more details about the bat story and started a conversation which turned into a deep friendship that had sustained her through many difficult times. "You're always looking for the right man," Judy told her after one painful breakup, "but you will never find a man who can listen to you and talk with you like I can."

Maybe Judy's right about me, she thought. Perhaps having a man in her life did mean too much to her, but Judy's cynicism could be overwhelming at times.

But I do wish I had more of Judy's confidence, Catherine thought, reaching for a towel. *She could still hear her mother's voice when she broke up with Peter. "Stupid, stupid girl. You're just like your father. No sense of reality. Do you think reality is those stories you read?"*

Catherine shuddered and wrapped the powder-blue robe around her. She crawled into bed and was asleep before she could think about anything else.

Chapter Seven

The narrator claims she's an authority on all the characters. Hmm. Not convincing. Knowing them is possible only when they're ready to reveal themselves. She admits it at the end, admits her arrogance.

"...thinking my space, my view was the only one that was or that mattered..." and "It never occurred to me that they were thinking other thoughts, feeling other feelings, putting their lives together in ways I never dreamed of."

Running her fingers over the tattered cover and tucking a loose page into the book, Catherine thought about how many times she'd read Morrison's *Jazz*, how many times she'd taught the novel. Always something new. In Morrison's worlds, time and experience are circular; imagination ignited, ready to change the outcome. Community, an ensemble. Catherine placed *Jazz* back on the bookcase, craning her neck to see if Chelsea had pulled into the driveway.

Lost in thought, the gentle knock sounded a second

time before Catherine answered the door.

White capris covered Chelsea's slender hips and long legs; a salmon-colored camisole fit snugly against her tanned arms and chest. Catherine envied the tan and the faculty dress code, casual like the students.

Chelsea apologized for taking her time as Catherine poured coffee and invited Chelsea to join her on the patio. The still morning was already hot and humid.

Chelsea started right in. "My third-year review is coming up in the fall. In late April, Marie called to set up a meeting with Dr. Rhodes. He wanted to talk with me about the new jazz curriculum and my third-year review. After asking me a few questions about the curriculum, he told me how beautiful my eyes were and how much he enjoyed watching me at faculty meetings. I tried to change the subject, but he started making comments about my breasts, the curve of my..." Her eyes filled with tears.

"How did the meeting end?" Catherine asked as she nervously picked up her coffee mug and put it down again without drinking.

"He said he would speak on my behalf in my third-year review if I would sleep with him. I told him no. I told him I'm in a committed relationship, and before I could finish, he just started laughing at me."

Catherine picked up her mug again and this time took a sip. She looked at Chelsea, slowly shaking her head.

"Why did you decide to tell me about this?" Catherine asked, feeling tightness in her throat. Wrong thing to ask, she realized almost before the question was out of her mouth.

"I didn't know who I could talk to. Barry has been a good colleague, but I wasn't comfortable telling him."

Chelsea seemed to relax as they continued talking, and she gave Catherine some background on her interest in teaching and the politics involved in getting the music program approved.

Barry Champlain, the chairman of the Music Department, had worked for several years to develop the curriculum for the jazz program. Neil opposed the program because it was expensive. With President Ashcroft's support, the program was approved more than two years ago.

"Chelsea, you need to find some ways to protect yourself and your bid for tenure. Talk with Barry and to Bill Stephens as President of the Faculty Senate. I'd talk with Barry first."

"Catherine, there's something else." Chelsea hesitated, drinking more coffee, then shifting in her chair and looking at her feet. "I was an undergraduate at Middlebury, and I did a lot of drinking then."

"Neil was a professor at Middlebury," Catherine blurted without thinking.

"Yes, and one night, some of my friends and I went skinny dipping in the fountain on the academic quad. Neil and another professor from the Psychology Department had followed us there from the pub where we'd been drinking." Chelsea's eyes filled with tears. She couldn't catch her breath. Catherine moved close to her and rubbed her back gently.

"Take your time," Catherine said.

Chelsea took a deep breath and got up, clasping her hands as she walked away from Catherine. Turning and facing Catherine, she said, "Neil followed me to my room. When my roommate saw him, she left. It's a blur. I woke up the next morning, sore, bruised."

How does a woman carry this searing, painful memory? First kisses, the first boyfriend, and sex the first time were all good memories for Catherine. What if all that was erased by this violence, this loss of control over her own body?

"I wished I'd nailed him then, but I was drunk. I didn't have a good case."

Catherine was at a loss to say anything helpful. She paced the length of the patio, clutching her coffee mug. Still standing, she faced Chelsea and said, "Chelsea, you need to protect yourself. Talk with Barry about what Neil's done now. What happened in the past at Middlebury is more egregious... a professor assaulting a student... but I'd only reveal it if you need more ammunition for shutting Neil down. No one deserves an assault or rape just because she's had too much to drink."

Catherine walked along the edge of the patio, looking at the roses in bloom, wishing she wasn't having this conversation. Chelsea started to cry, softly at first, and then sobs shook her frame. Catherine stood beside her and put a hand on her shoulder.

After several minutes, Chelsea regained her composure. "Catherine, I appreciate your listening. I will talk with Barry."

"Let's talk again soon," Catherine said.

Chelsea picked up her coffee mug and carried it to the kitchen. Catherine gave Chelsea a quick hug before closing the door behind her. Nothing ran through Catherine's mind at first. Then, she began to think. *Why did I take this job? I was uneasy about Neil during the interview. Should I have asked more questions? I'm questioning Chelsea's* motives for coming to me. Why? I should be willing to help, willing to help any woman in this situation.

Turning off the coffee pot and placing the mugs in the sink, she picked up her purse and her briefcase and headed out for the College. She ran through the conversation with Chelsea.

He will speak on her behalf if she'd sleep with him... He's unhappy in his marriage, so he's preying on other women. He thinks he can do it because she's loose. Loose? Where did that come from? My mother, of course.

He assaults her at Middlebury... Was it rape? Was it consensual sex and Chelsea doesn't remember?

...a prank, skinny dipping in the fountain, and she's attacked. "I wish I'd nailed him then, but I was drunk. I didn't have a good case." Chelsea's words played over and over in Catherine's mind.

Keeping the peace, protecting the College, was the issue. She remembered a graduate student, Kristin, who'd been harassed by an obese Linguistics professor when she was studying for her Ph.D. Catherine encouraged Kristin— yes, Kristin was her name—to talk with the department chair about what happened. How naïve Catherine was, believing the world would right itself for Kristin. The chair was sympathetic to her but disclosed that this had happened before.

Keeping the peace... protecting the College's secrets. "Institutions have no heart," she remembered her mentor and department chair in graduate school saying when a beloved dean had been fired by a cost-cutting vice president. Within months of the dean's dismissal, the vice president was accused of embezzlement and left quietly with a generous severance package. Money and sex...

secrets protected.

The office was quiet when Catherine got to work. Hal stopped by, and they talked about Catherine's trip to Boston. Hal had a deep, soothing voice that always drew her in, but she realized she was scanning his face, looking for something. What was it? Her gaze turned to his large hands, wrapped around the oversized coffee mug. Long tapered fingers with fat knuckles. Daddy held a coffee cup that way, pausing to think or make a point, the cup a prop in the immediate drama.

"Catherine, is something wrong?" Hal asked, shifting his weight against the door jam.

"No. I'm sorry, Hal. For some reason, a thought about my father just ran through my mind, and I lost track of what you're saying."

"No harm done. I should let you get back to work. I'll be taking vacation days at the beginning of next week, so I just wanted to wish you a good trip. I know it'll go well.

"It's all in the relationships. Mistakenly, many people believe it's the extroverts who make great fundraisers. Not necessarily. Find what the alumni is passionate about, and you'll find your way in from there."

Catherine thought about Hal's comments as she reviewed the biographies of the alumnae she'd have dinner with before the program.

Lisa Ferguson, Class of 1960.
>   Phi Beta Kappa
>   Economics major
>   Varsity Basketball
>   Stockbroker
>   Mother of Margaret, Emily, and James

Annette Lombard, Class of 1980.
>   Political Science major
>   Villanova Law School
>   Clerk, Pennsylvania Superior Court

She'd see how well the profile fit the person when she got to Boston.

Chapter Eight

Catherine used her key to let herself in when she got to Spring Lake, thinking her father might be sleeping. After changing into a bathing suit, she wrote a note and placed it on the dining room table: "Went for a swim... be back in an hour. – C (4:00 p.m.)"

A strong wind blew off the ocean. Dropping her towel and t-shirt on the hot sand, she raced into the water, diving under a large wave. She smiled, remembering this was always what she did as a kid as soon as she got to the beach.

The warm water, cluttered with jellyfish, floated around her. She dove deep and surfaced several yards further from the shore. A conscientious lifeguard blew her in, and she obeyed. Leaving the water, she spread her towel out and sat on the edge of it. Her mind wandered to days as a teenager when she spent long mornings on the beach, out of the way of her parents' angry silences and fights. After a morning of reading on the beach, she would return home, shower, and dress for her job as a waitress in a local restaurant. Avoiding dinner with her parents and sister meant less worry about what would happen to their family.

Her thoughts turned to Hal, his warmth and professionalism. She often found him in his office, still working, when she was on her way home in the evening. That didn't happen when Tina was with him, she was sure. Work filled the emptiness like it did for Catherine.

Douglas was shuffling around the kitchen when Catherine returned from the beach. A jar of cashews sat beside the corkscrew on the kitchen counter. Douglas reached for a bottle of red wine on the rack.

"I wanted to have happy hour ready for us by the time you got back," he said, kissing her gently on the cheek.

"Give me a few minutes. I want to rinse off all this sand and saltwater."

Catherine showered quickly and slipped into a tank top and a baggy pair of denim shorts. She carried the opened red wine to the porch and poured two glasses. She talked at length about her upcoming trip to Boston and her plans to get together with Judy.

"You'll be a natural at fundraising. It's all in building relationships," Douglas said.

"That's what my colleague Hal said. He's the Graduate Dean and has been such a help to me since I started this job."

"Not a love interest?" her father asked, mischievously.

"No," she shot back.

Douglas sipped his wine and looked toward the ocean. The pounding surf filled the still afternoon. He seemed far away.

"Catherine, I have so many regrets about my life with your mother," Douglas said slowly. "In the few months before her death, I tried to talk with her, to ask for her forgiveness, but she refused to talk with me. She told me it was too late. I'd done too much harm." Catherine looked at her father, not sure she wanted him to continue.

"I married, knowing little about what is involved. I was a terrible husband. I didn't know how to love your mother the way I should."

"Is that what you are thinking about when you look so far away?" she asked, moving her chair closer to his. "All mother's years of drinking. It hurt all of us. It was never your fault. You need to believe that." Catherine searched her father's face, looking for a sign that he heard what she said.

Douglas continued to look toward the ocean. "Your mother and I never spent much time alone during our courtship. Once we married, she seemed uninterested in anything but our social life. I didn't know how to ask for what was missing. When Caroline was born, I thought your mother was happy, but it didn't last."

Catherine shifted in her chair, toes pirouetting against the wooden slats, and then flattening. *Does he know he's talking to me? Is this something you tell your daughter?*

Douglas sipped the wine, placing the glass on the café table. "You never knew your grandmother, your mother's mother. She committed suicide when your mother was thirteen. Your mother and your grandfather had gone to the movies one Saturday in October. They returned to find your grandmother in a bathtub filled with blood. Your mother never told me about this, but your grandfather did right before your mother and I were married."

Catherine's heart felt heavy. Was this why her mother tried to kill herself? Is this why she drank? Drinking to forget her mother's suicide? Why is Daddy thinking about this now?

Douglas picked up his wine glass with both hands, a few drops splashing on the table as he raised the glass to his lips. "Your grandfather was a cold, cold bastard. When I tried to talk with him about your mother getting some help to deal with her mother's suicide, he dismissed me. He said it was your grandmother, not your mother, who was sick, but I don't think she ever worked through this tragedy. She carried it deep inside of her."

"Daddy, I'm so sorry."

Catherine poured her father another small glass of wine and went to the kitchen to get dinner from the oven. I don't want to hear this, she thought, as she placed the chicken on a small platter.

They ate in silence. Catherine had questions she wanted to ask her father, but she hesitated. Was there some story she didn't know behind her mother's drinking, her meanness? She never made peace with her mother while her mother was alive. Was it pointless to dredge things up now?

Douglas was up for the short walk to the ocean after dinner and took a seat on a bench while Catherine walked the boardwalk. She didn't understand her father's guilt, his regrets. Her mother was a drunk. He'd done nothing wrong.

Her mother was drunk the day Catherine had her first date with Billy Johnson in the eighth grade.

"I don't want him coming to the house and see what

she is," Catherine declared to her father. Douglas picked up the phone and called Billy's father. He said he had a call to make in their neighborhood and could he drop Catherine off?

Another memory followed the first.

Dressed and ready for the junior prom, Catherine heard a loud crash in the dining room. The table had been set for the after breakfast... fine china from Catherine's grandmother... a yellow rose in a glass vase at each place.

When Catherine got to the dining room, her mother was on the floor, holding one end of the white lace tablecloth. Broken glass and china, yellow roses in puddles of water littered around her.

Her mother looked at Catherine with glazed eyes.

"She doesn't even know what she did," Catherine whispered to her father as she crouched down and began picking up pieces of the china. "If she did, she wouldn't care." Her mother continued to lay on the floor.

Catherine picked up two pieces of a shattered teacup, remembering the tea party her mother had for Caroline's seventh birthday. Cucumber sandwiches, scones, and apple juice in the tiny cups instead of tea. Her mother's elegance, then, in camel-colored chinos with black buttons and a black silk blouse. As she reached over to cut the birthday cake, Caroline touched her mother's arm and said, "No. It's beautiful. Don't disturb Alice."

Her mother smiled and stepped back. Caroline's friend Missy said, "Alice and Mad Hatter don't mind. I had a cake like this for my birthday with Cinderella and a big glass slipper. She plays with my Kiddles now."

Catherine placed the broken cup on the table and looked at her father in his crisp Oxford shirt and jeans, permanent sadness mirrored in his blue eyes and the curl of his lips.

"Catherine, I'm sorry," Douglas said. "I don't want you to cut yourself on any of this glass or ruin your dress. I'll get your mother to bed, and I'll clean up the mess before anyone gets here. After we take the pictures, I'll reset the table and have it ready for breakfast."

Catherine looked at her father in disbelief and headed upstairs to wash her tear-stained face.

When Catherine returned from her walk, she sat down close to her father and linked her arm in his.

"It's a beautiful night. Surf's really up." She held his bony hand in hers.

Dusk had turned to dark. Douglas lifted his head to look at Catherine, tears moistening his cheeks.

"You, Catherine, are the best thing that came of my years with your mother. I love you, Doll." Douglas got up from the bench slowly, and they headed back to the house.

Another early night, Catherine thought, as she watched fearfully as her father climbed the steps. She picked up her copy of *The Hours* and went into the sunroom. Curled up on the couch, she finished the novel. The modern-day Mrs. Dalloway looking for the moment of happiness. That moment at nineteen... kissing Richard after the drunken night... was that the moment of happiness?

What was that moment for her father? Did he want to tell her? Did she want to know? The trip to Ireland with Peter, so many moments, then, filled with laughter, conversation. Was that her moment of happiness, one she couldn't sustain?

Why is it so hard to find what makes us happy? Her mother always insisted that it was about finding the right man. Was this because she never did herself? Was she happy when she first married Catherine's father? He was making a lot of money, but did she feel left behind when her father decided to go to seminary and become an Episcopal priest? The arguments. Her mother ridiculing her father's passion for protesting the war, helping blacks get registered to vote. Why was he unable to explain to her mother why this was so important to him?

Laying the book aside, Catherine curled up on the sofa and fell asleep, smelling the salt air and hearing the gentle surf just blocks away.

Chapter Nine

The grandfather clock in the foyer struck eight. Time started up again as if it never stopped when I spent those few days with you, Grace, Douglas thought. Brother Andrew writes about practicing the presence of God. "Was I practicing the presence of God with Grace then?" he asked himself.

Douglas reached for the collection of Rilke, worn from years of use. The book fell open to a page he had read often.

I am praying again, Awesome One.

You hear me again, as words
from the depth of me
rush toward you in the wind.

Grace always mocked him for what he believed, but there were moments when he caught her passion for a case she was trying—the black woman in Memphis, raped by white teenage boys—and then he wondered if she wasn't also practicing the presence of God.

"Whatever you do for the least of these, you do for me," Douglas muttered as he walked across the living room, tan slippers shuffling beneath baggy khakis.

Douglas gazed out the window toward the ocean...

Grace in the kitchen of her tiny apartment, chopping lettuce and cucumbers in rhythm to "Blowin' in the Wind."

He opened the window so he could feel the gentle breeze...

Tell me, how many ears must one man have
Before he can hear people cry.
How many deaths will it take till he knows
Too many people have died.

"*The war needs to end. Things need to change,*" she said, popping a cherry tomato in his mouth.

He heard Elizabeth's voice. "*You want so much, don't you Douglas?*" she said, anger flashing across her porcelain cheeks and strawberry lips. "*You want life to make sense, but it doesn't.*"

She said this to him before the first breakdown, the first suicide attempt. He tried to hold her, make sense of what she said about her mother. She was right. None of it made sense. He went to see her every day the first week. She was talkative, asking about the girls. She said she'd go to D.C., but he didn't trust her sincerity. Then, more silence.

Douglas did want life to make sense. He had wanted his girls to have parents who loved each other as much as he loved them, he thought, breathing in the salt air. Every time he thought about his daughter Caroline, he was reminded of his failure.

"Where are you now, Grace?" Douglas asked, hands clutching the open book.

She always said, "Your God, Douglas" and then there would be a question... "Why does your God make black people wait for social justice?" she asked as they talked about opposition to Johnson's Civil Rights agenda.

Forgive me, God, for my questions. Forgive me for being old and broken.

He picked up Rilke and continued reading.

> It's here in all the pieces of my shame
> that now I find myself again.
> I yearn to belong to something, to be contained
> in an all-embracing mind that sees me
> as a single thing.
> I yearn to be held
> in the great hands of your heart—
> oh, let them take me now.
> Into them, I place these fragments, my life,
> and you, God, spend them however you want.

Lord, hear my prayer.

Chapter Ten
June 1968

Douglas rolled out of bed and went to the kitchen to make coffee. Catherine was already up, reading to her dolls in her father's study. She was turning the pages of a book, showing them the pictures as she repeated the words on the pages that she was too young to decipher. When she heard his footsteps, she threw her arms around his legs for a big daddy hug. He lifted her up. She smelled like sleep and baby powder.

"We have a special day planned," he said. "Once Flora has Caroline off to school, we're going to see Uncle Ray and have lunch with him." Catherine nodded her head and smiled as she climbed onto the chair to eat her cereal.

"Good morning, Mr. Finley," Flora said as she entered the kitchen. "It's a beautiful day." She laid her bag and umbrella on the chair in the corner.

"Yes, it is," he said softly as he sat with Catherine as she finished her breakfast and thought about what he needed to do today. Classes had ended at the seminary. He'd stop at the seminary and pick-up his gown and chords. He hoped to see two professors to say goodbye while he was on campus.

Douglas didn't have a job yet, but he was sure that the work he'd done in D.C. would yield a position there. He'd built a multiracial youth program in a predominantly white church. Weekly discussions at the church spilled over into History classes at two local high schools, struggling to make integration work. Unofficially, he'd been asked to stay on as a youth minister. Elizabeth had already told him she'd never go to Washington with him. "I'm not going to indulge your need to save the world," she had said maliciously. "You can do that on your own."

She had said this to him only two days before she broke down. The explosive anger, then silence. He tried to talk with her, asking her what he could do differently to make their marriage work. What are the words to say what happened? She tried to kill herself again... slit her wrists in the bathtub... Was she trying to relive what her mother had done when Elizabeth was a teenager? He didn't know.

He sat on the small love seat in his study reading when Flora came in with a letter in her hand. Catherine was on the floor, reading to her dolls.

"I'm sorry to interrupt, Mr. Finley, but one of Mr. Fulton's secretaries just dropped this off." Douglas took the letter from her and noticed the Boston postmark. He began to read, and a frown creased his brow. Catherine saw the dark expression on her father's face and crawled into his lap.

"What is it, Daddy?" she asked.

"A friend wrote to me, honey, someone who is very sad because a great man was killed last week."

Catherine hugged him as he read the letter.

Dear Douglas:

I hope this letter finds you well. I've been busy with several cases. Work seems endless sometimes, but I'm often preoccupied with the news, the violence. How can we bring children into a world like this—a world filled with hate where white men can bomb a church and kill little girls, girls like your daughters, who should have the same freedoms?

I was in Memphis the week Dr. King was killed. The case was a 24-year-old black woman living at home with her parents. She was repeatedly raped by a group of teenage white boys. Her father was broken because he was unable to defend his little girl.

I left Memphis the day of the assassination, and I didn't get the news until I was home in Boston. Memphis was exploding with violence, and I worried about the people, the neighborhood in Memphis, impacted by Loretta's assault and rape. It wasn't until the next morning, when I picked up The New York Times, that I read Bobby Kennedy's calming, comforting words. Did you hear the speech he gave in Indianapolis? He quoted Aeschylus, saying, "'Even in our sleep, pain which cannot forget falls drop by drop upon the heart, until, in our own despair, against our will, comes wisdom through the awful grace of God.'" He said that he believed that the vast number of people in this country want to live together and work to improve the quality of life for everyone. Do you believe this is true, Douglas?

Did Bobby Kennedy die because he believed this and so many others do not? So much hope shot down

with one bullet. Hope of ending the war in Vietnam...
hope of stopping the divisions between rich and poor...
black and white.

Where is your God in all this, Douglas? Are we
still waiting for him to show his face? When will he
hold us in the 'great hands of his heart'? Do you still
believe he's here for us?

Grace

Speechless, he held Catherine close and stroked her
hair.

"I want a better world for you, Catherine, and for
Caroline... better than the one we have now."

He placed Catherine on the floor and went into the
kitchen. He spoke with Flora about staying with the girls
so he could get away for a few days. She said she was
willing. He went back to the study and dialed information
for Boston, asking for the number for Grace's firm. He
called and left a message for her. He asked that she call
him in the evening.

Douglas and Catherine met Ray at the Italian
restaurant on Nassau Street, the best and cheapest food in
Princeton. They made small talk and described different
dishes on the menu that Catherine might like.

"Spa getti," she giggled, taking a big bite of her
buttered roll.

"Daddy wants you to try something new," said Ray,
suggesting the lasagna.

"Okay," she said. "I'm so hungry, I could eat a bear."

"Little girls don't eat bears," Ray said laughing and
tucking a napkin under her chin.

"Yes, we do. Bears without fur like Fuzzy Wuzzy," she
chortled. Ray shook his head and laughed.

While they waited for their food, Ray asked how Elizabeth was doing.

"I don't think the doctors know yet," Douglas said softly so Catherine wouldn't hear.

"Mommy went away to rest," Catherine said to Ray.

"That's right, honey. Your mommy needs to rest." Turning to Douglas, Ray asked, "Why did Grace write? It's been a long time."

"Four years," Douglas said. "She's upset about Bobby Kennedy's death. It's a beautiful letter. She's questioning everything. I can only read between the lines, but I think she is starting to doubt that any of us can make a difference."

"Maybe that's good, Doug," Ray said thoughtfully. "Life would be better for both of you if you stop fighting everything and accept things as they are. You'll make a great priest, but you'll feel defeated all the time if you keep fighting the status quo."

The steaming hot food arrived, and Ray reached over and cut Catherine's lasagna. "Let it cool a minute, honey. It's too hot right now." Once Catherine started to eat, Douglas turned to Ray and said, "I called Grace today and left a message for her to call me this evening. I want to go to Boston to see her."

"Why? And stir up old feelings?"

"Yes. I'm going to ask her to marry me. Once Elizabeth is well enough, I'm going to ask for a divorce. None of us can keep living like this," Douglas whispered, his brow furrowed.

"You've lost your mind," Ray said in a hushed tone.

"No. I've come to my senses finally. I've asked Flora to stay with the girls while I'm away." Douglas looked at his food, refusing to meet Ray's gaze.

Ray changed the subject and began talking about a new client. Catherine listened quietly, eating her lasagna. Douglas took her hand lovingly, enjoying the moment free of worries about Elizabeth.

By the time Ray dropped them off, Caroline was home from school. Catherine told her about her lasagna, and the two played quietly until Flora made both a light supper.

Douglas put the girls to bed and waited for Grace's call. The phone rang at nine o'clock. His hands shaking, he picked up on the second ring. Her voice was warm and soft. After a few minutes, she said, "I'm sorry if my letter sounded so negative. I've been feeling extremely low since Dr. King was killed."

"The letter didn't sound negative to me," Douglas said. "It often feels hopeless, though, but Dr. King or Bobby Kennedy wouldn't want us to give up. We fight because it's the right thing to do, not because we expect to win. Change never comes easily; it comes, usually, with a lot of pain."

"I miss you, Douglas," she said. Douglas was overwhelmed with emotion to hear her say this.

"I want to come to Boston to see you. I've asked our nanny to watch the girls while I'm away." Grace asked where Elizabeth was, and Douglas explained she was hospitalized after she tried to commit suicide again.

The next two weeks were busy. Graduation. Two interviews with a search committee for a parish position in D.C. Ray and Rosemary had a party at their home, one both the children and the grown-ups enjoyed. Many of their mutual friends didn't know that Elizabeth had been hospitalized. Douglas said little, never mentioning the suicide attempt but telling them that Elizabeth needed some time away to rest.

Elizabeth's father and Suzanne came to the party but kept their distance from Douglas. They blame me, he thought. I've let her down by going to seminary and changing the course of her life.

Several of the women helped Rosemary clean up as the party came to an end. Rosemary put all three girls down for a nap and headed out to run some errands, while Ray and Douglas nursed beers in the backyard.

Douglas told Ray he was leaving the next day to go to Boston to see Grace.

"I want you to be happy, Doug, but I think you're doing the wrong thing. What about Caroline and Catherine?" he asked, sipping his beer.

"I don't have any answers right now, but given all that's happened, I can't imagine that Elizabeth will be considered a fit mother," Douglas said, looking at Ray closely.

"You'd take her children away from her?" Ray looked stricken as if Douglas had just confessed to murdering Elizabeth.

"Never, but this isn't a marriage. I need to find an attorney who will see that and help me get joint custody of my children."

Ray shook his head and finished his beer.

Sleepy from their naps, Caroline and Catherine said goodbye. Holding Catherine, Douglas took Caroline's hand, and they walked the three blocks home.

"Daddy," Caroline asked, "When is Mommy coming home? Susie's mother asked me today, and I didn't know what to say." Douglas saw anger flash across her face. Was she angry at him? At her mother?

Gossip, Douglas thought to himself, but to Caroline, he said, "I don't know. The doctor says she needs rest. He'll let me know in a few days how she's doing. When I talk with him, I'll ask him when we can go and visit."

"I don't want to visit," Caroline said defiantly, stamping her foot, her green gingham dress swaying with the movement of her foot. "I want her home."

Douglas squeezed Caroline's hand and said nothing.

The girls played quietly as he packed a small bag. A little after eight, Douglas said goodnight to the girls and tucked them in. Caroline said little, but when he was leaving Catherine's room, she stood up on her bed. "Daddy," she said softly. He went over to her, and she put her arms around his neck and whispered in his ear, "I love you, Daddy. Tell me a story about Mommy, a happy story."

Douglas sat down on the bed as Catherine crawled under the covers.

"Once upon a time, when your Uncle Ray and I were in college, we met two princesses named Rosemary and Elizabeth."

Catherine smiled and nodded. "Two princesses. One for you and one for Uncle Ray."

"Exactly."

"Was it a ball? What was Mommy wearing?"

Douglas tapped Catherine on the nose. "Don't rush the storyteller, but if you must know, it was a party with yummy food and champagne. Princess Rosemary wore something red, a dress your Uncle Ray still talks about. Princess Elizabeth wore a powder blue dress with sapphire earrings and a locket with a sapphire stone. Her eyes sparkled, and her smile melted my heart. I introduced myself, and we danced and talked all night."

Douglas looked at the photograph on Catherine's bedside table of Elizabeth holding Catherine. Her smile, the same smile he remembered from the night he met her.

As he thought about where this story would go next, Catherine rolled on her side, sound asleep. He kissed her on the forehead and said, "I love you, Doll."

Chapter Eleven

At her hotel in Boston, Catherine reviewed her notes and the list of alums in attendance before she showered and dressed. The dress for the evening was upscale business attire, so Catherine put on a sleek black suit with a dark green blouse. A small green and black silk scarf she had purchased in Ireland added just the right touch to the dark colors.

Catherine walked the three blocks to the restaurant, passing the Faneuil Hall "Cheers." Judy and I should go there Friday night for dinner, she thought. She can eat a "Norm Burger" and have a beer or two. Judy could eat like that every day and never gain an ounce.

Catherine reached the restaurant early, so she checked her phone for messages. A few minutes later, an attractive woman, petite with snow-white hair, touched her elbow.

"Are you Catherine Finley?"

"Yes," Catherine said, her throat catching. She

realized how nervous she was. Can I do this, she thought?

From her research, she recognized Lisa Ferguson, a retired stockbroker who had been generous to Franklin since graduating, Class of 1960. Lisa asked the waiter to seat them while they waited for Annette Lombard, Class of 1980.

"Annette and I are good friends," Lisa said. "We got to know each other well when we were working on the last capital campaign. She's running about thirty minutes late. That's Annette for you."

Lisa ordered a bottle of wine and asked Catherine a lot of questions about her work at the College.

"We were all so pleased that you took the position, Catherine. The other finalist was a man, and, frankly, we think there are too many men in the administration as it is. Although Franklin isn't a women's college anymore, many of us old-timers wish it were."

"I understand, Lisa. As you know, I was an undergraduate at Smith," Catherine said, sipping the cold Chardonnay.

Both finished a glass of wine before Annette arrived, chatting about the fundraising needed to complete the library renovation. Annette apologized for being late. A meeting with a client had run over. They ordered, and Catherine steered the conversation to the new program to help students connect their academic interests to career paths. "I want students to hear your stories, how you made decisions about jobs and how you balanced this with decisions about your personal life."

"Catherine, the program's a great idea," Lisa said, "but we didn't have the choices students have today. My father, an attorney, was scrutinized by McCarthy. I grew up living those divisive politics and wanted to run for office, make things different, but that wasn't possible for a woman in 1960." She described a dead-end corporate position she endured until she met her husband in 1963.

"I graduated from college with no money to go to law school, so I worked as a secretary and went to law school part-time. I felt the pressure to marry because everyone else was, but it didn't last long," Annette said, a note of resignation in her voice.

"I was more fortunate than Annette," Lisa said, sending a warm smile across the table to her friend. "My husband was the love of my life, still is, and it was his position at the state department that opened my eyes to what could be possible for women."

"Young women now feel the pressure to have a career but still take on all the responsibilities of a home and children," Catherine said. "That's why your stories are so important. Life isn't as linear as many of our students think."

"You're right," Lisa said, motioning for the waiter to bring her the check. "My oldest granddaughter has traveled and done exceptional work as a photojournalist, but the other two have fallen into early marriages."

Lisa picked up the check before Catherine could, and they left for the reception in the ballroom upstairs. The room was crowded, and Catherine could feel her anxiety returning.

"We'll introduce you to as many alums as we can," Annette said warmly. "If we miss a beat, it's because we're blanking on a name."

Catherine noticed Steve Dennison across the room, so she moved in his direction until Mary Houston, one of the

Board members, waved her down. She greeted Catherine and ran through the agenda for the evening, including her introduction of Catherine.

"I'll go into some detail about your position since we know it's been expanded, but I'll also mention your scholarly work on autobiography," Mary Houston said.

Catherine was about to ask a question when a man in a black suit and bow tie approached Mary.

"Philip, how good to see you." Mary reached out and gave him a kiss on the cheek before introducing him to Catherine.

"Catherine, this is Philip Reynolds," Mary said. Philip extended his hand and gave her a warm welcome.

"It's a pleasure. I've heard good things about you from the other Board members," he said. She looked at him closely.

"Have we met?" she asked, smiling broadly.

"No. No. My term on the Board ended in June. I live in Philadelphia, but I have an office in Boston, so I thought I would stop in tonight and wish you a warm welcome."

"Well, thank you."

Someone touched Catherine's shoulder, and she was drawn into another conversation. Mary started the program promptly at eight o'clock. Catherine enjoyed Mary's gracious introduction about her work on autobiography, describing her as an expert on storytellers. Catherine spoke enthusiastically about what she had experienced thus far at Franklin. She fielded several questions about the new program for students and talked with several alums afterward who volunteered to be part of the program.

Catherine moved through the room, saying goodbye

to several people she had just met, working hard to remember names.

Only a few people were still chatting, so she decided to go back to her hotel room. Relieved and happy with how things went, she moved toward the ballroom door. As she approached the elevators, she heard someone calling her name.

"Catherine."

"Philip."

"May I buy you a night cap?"

"No, thank you. It's been a long day."

"Breakfast, then?" he persisted.

"Yes, I can do that. My first appointment is at ten o'clock, and it is only a couple of blocks away."

"Good. Then I will meet you in the restaurant on the mezzanine at 8:30," he said, smiling warmly.

"That sounds fine," Catherine said softly as she reached for the elevator button.

"Good night," Philip said.

Catherine got to her room and ran a hot bath. As she eased herself into the tub, she dialed Judy's number.

"Hello."

"Did I wake you up?"

A sleepy voice responded slowly, saying she had fallen asleep on the couch reading student essays.

Yawning, Judy insisted that she stay on the line.

"No. I just called to say I love you and can't wait to tell you about my new job."

Adding hot water and more bath oils, Catherine started thinking about Philip. His dark brown eyes seemed kind. The black tailored suit seemed to hide a rather lean body and a slight pouch around the middle. Mary had mentioned he had two children, a son, and a daughter. She would find out more tomorrow.

She arrived at the restaurant before Philip, so she ordered a cup of coffee and began reading the newspaper. Up at 6, Catherine logged five miles on the elliptical in the hotel's fitness room. Last night's program had been a success. She had enjoyed meeting the alumnae, one face of the College. Annette had promised to call her to have lunch sometime soon. She wanted to talk with Annette about what had happened to Chelsea.

"Good morning, Catherine." Catherine turned and saw Philip dressed in khaki trousers and a long-sleeved sports shirt.

"Good morning, Philip. You look rested and relaxed."

"I am. When you own the company, you can dress down when you feel like it." Catherine scanned his face, looking for the arrogance she heard in his voice. All she saw was a boyish grin.

"So, what's on your agenda today?" she asked, leaning in to pour coffee from the pot on the table.

"I'm meeting with the woman who manages my Boston office, and depending on how that goes, I will be heading back to Philadelphia this afternoon."

"Mary mentioned last night that you have a son and daughter who went to Franklin."

Yes. Stephen graduated five years ago and runs my office in New York. Megan graduated last year and is working for *Vogue* in London."

"Two success stories. That's what I like to hear about our graduates."

The waiter came and both ordered Eggs Benedict.

"I took you for a black coffee and bowl of fruit kind of woman," Philip said with a twinkle in his eye.

"I did five miles this morning, so I can justify it."

"So, you said no to the nightcap because you had to get up early?"

"Life is all about choices," she said, sipping her coffee. She was enjoying this. He was already pouting because she chose something over him.

"Tell me more about your business," Catherine said.

"I used to teach at Babson. My background's in Philosophy, and I taught Business Ethics and Social Policy. Then, about ten years ago, my father had a heart attack and wanted me to join him in his export business. I did, and within a year of that, he died."

"Do you like the business world better than teaching?" Catherine felt like she was interviewing someone for a job, but if she kept the focus on him, she felt more comfortable.

"I have enjoyed aspects of both. I got tenure two years before I left Babson. I enjoyed the students and the writing I was doing, but I hated the politics."

Catherine laughed. "Politics in a college? Really?"

Philip laughed and took a bite of his breakfast. "I'm sure you could write a book."

"Not yet," she said, thinking about Chelsea and the stories she couldn't tell.

"So, what do you do for fun?"

Catherine told Philip how much she enjoyed the City but hadn't had time to do much yet with a new job and her father's poor health. "He lives in New Jersey, and I spend a lot of weekends with him. "

"My mother lives in Miami, and I see her fairly often because I have an office there."

"An office in every port, but not a woman in every port?" Catherine asked.

Philip laughed. "I thought you'd never ask. No. I haven't dated much since my wife died five years ago. She was driving from Philadelphia to Baltimore on a rainy Friday night. We were planning a weekend together, attending a friend's wedding. She was hit head-on by a drunk driver. Many days, I still wake-up believing she's alive."

"I'm so sorry," Catherine said.

"In many ways, I think it has been harder on my children. Anne chose to be a stay-at-home mom, and this was particularly important to the children when I was building the business. I was away more than I was home."

Catherine sipped her coffee and studied Philip's face. His lower lip trembled when he talked about Anne, his voice softened and slowed.

"Catherine, are you involved with anyone right now?"

"No. With a new job and caring for my father, I haven't had time." She had a fleeting thought about how different this trip would be if Peter were here. His humor would make her forget how nervous she had been last night.

"Would it be all right if I called you when we get back to Philadelphia? I would like to take you to dinner."

"That would be fine. But can we keep the shop talk to a bare minimum?"

"I can do that," he said.

Catherine looked at her watch and said, "I better wrap this up." She waved the waiter down and handed him the check with a credit card. "I'll look forward to hearing from you."

Catherine breezed through her appointments on Thursday and Friday. Philip was on her mind. How old was he? Maybe a little too old, but she had dated several older men when she was in her twenties. Men her own age, then, seemed immature. Older men knew how to treat a woman.

After a short run along the Charles River, Catherine showered and changed into jeans and a cotton sweater. She headed for the lobby bar to wait for Judy.

"I'll have a pinot grigio and a glass of water, please," she told the bartender.

"Why is a beautiful woman like you drinking alone?" he asked, winking at her. He was balding and rotund, probably sixty.

"It's only temporary," she said. "I'm waiting for a friend."

"Good," he said, placing the wine and the water on the bar in front of her. Catherine sensed someone approaching behind her before Judy placed her hands over her eyes.

"Guess who?" a female voice asked, tapping her slender fingers on Catherine's forehead.

"The love of my life!" Catherine said playfully.

"You finally got it right," Judy said, giving Catherine a big hug. She settled in on a barstool and ordered a beer.

"How was your drive?" Catherine asked.

"Uneventful. I really didn't hit any traffic until I got into Boston. But enough about me," Judy said enthusiastically. "Tell me how the new job is going."

Catherine talked about the alums she met and the new program for students. "You know what a wallflower I am, but I really enjoyed this."

"You're not a wallflower," Judy said, laughing. "You're a good listener. I bet every one of those women want to be your new best friend. Plus, you're asking them to be part of a program where they are invited to come and talk about themselves. It's a win-win."

They finished their drinks and headed back to the room. While Judy showered, Catherine started *Dreams from My Father*. So young to be writing an autobiography, she thought. In the preface to the new edition, he reflects back on the last ten years. During this time, Obama loses his mother to cancer. If he had known his mother would die, he wonders if he would have written a different book, one focused on his mother rather than on his absent father. His mother had been the constant in his life. Hmm. Was Catherine making the same mistake? Her absent mother, distant because of alcohol and valium. Why chase that ghost when her father has been her constant and still is today?

A few minutes later, Judy appeared wrapped in a large white towel. "I just finished *The Hours* by Michael Cunningham. Have you read it?" Catherine asked, putting the book down and going to the bathroom to brush her teeth.

"Not yet. It's on my nightstand with three or four other books I want to read now that my summer term is over. How have you found any time to read?"

"Weekends," Catherine said through a mouthful of toothpaste. She described her visits with her father in Spring Lake. "I spend some time on the beach, and he's usually in bed by nine o'clock."

"How's he doing?" Judy asked, poised in front of the

mirror with a mascara brush in her hand.

"He's frail, but something else is going on inside his head."

"Dementia? Not your father?" Judy asked.

"No, but let me explain when we get to the restaurant. I'm starving too, and I had lunch."

"Are we really going to 'Cheers'?" Judy asked, chuckling

"Yes, and I'm going to have one of those killer burgers myself," Catherine said. "My appetite has been crazy since I started this job."

They strolled to the restaurant. The night was muggy.

They settled into a booth at "Cheers" and ordered immediately.

"Now tell me what's going on with your father," Judy said. Catherine began slowly, taking small bites of her burger as she talked. She described how far away her father seemed at times as though he was living in the past. "Then, last weekend, he told me that there was always a lot of distance in his marriage. He said I was the best thing that came of all his years with my mother."

"Wow. That must be hard to hear!" Judy said sympathetically.

"It is and it isn't. I grew up with my parents fighting and living through their long silences. I have too many memories of my mother saying threatening things to my father."

"You never told me any of this before," Judy said, sipping her second beer.

"I've only talked to a therapist about it after my break-up with Peter," Catherine said, thinking it was time to change the subject.

The conversation turned to Catherine's new job. She told Judy about her meeting with Roslyn. "She's an anthropologist and did some groundbreaking work in the field. I wonder why she'd leave that work to become a college administrator."

"Power," Judy said thoughtfully. "Or, maybe she got to the point where she didn't have anything more to say or any more worlds to explore."

"All possible," Catherine replied.

"No knight in shining armor, yet, at Franklin?" Judy asked as she started a hot fudge sundae with two gooey brownies underneath several scoops of ice cream.

She told Judy about Philip. "He runs an export business, based in Philadelphia, but he also has several other offices in port cities from Boston to Miami."

"Sounds intriguing."

"It might be," Catherine said.

"Always a knight on the horizon for my friend, Catherine," Judy said, slipping a generous tip under her water glass.

Catherine let the comment roll over her.

They walked for miles after dinner, enjoying the bustle of the city streets. Shopkeepers were in no hurry to be rid of customers who lingered at closing time, so they browsed in several bookstores.

As they stopped to watch boats on the harbor, Catherine asked Judy if she ever had a student confide in her about sexual harassment. Judy thought for a moment and shook her head. Catherine was formulating her thoughts about Chelsea when Judy shifted the conversation to stories about graduate school.

"Remember the asshole who taught linguistics?" Judy

asked derisively. "He had red boxing gloves in his office."

"Two pairs," Catherine interjected.

"Yes," Judy countered.

Catherine felt her stomach lurch as she remembered the obese professor whose odor overpowered her if he passed her in the hall or in the tiny walkway to the English Department where the secretary sat and tiny mailboxes lined the wall for the professors and graduate assistants. When a female student would meet with him about a paper, he'd close the door and ask her if she'd be willing to box him topless.

"Did it happen to you?" Catherine asked Judy, looking at her with wide eyes.

Judy nodded her head. "Yes, it happened to me, and I told that bastard I wouldn't box with him. I would attend every class, and if he tried to screw me with a bad grade, I'd take it to the president."

"Do you remember Kristin?" Catherine said, her gaze on the harbor. "It happened to her. I went with her to the chairman. It was only later in a private conversation with the chairman that he told me he was already aware of the situation," Catherine said slowly, the memory crystallizing in her mind. She had tried to help.

Judy nodded her head. "Don't you love how these bastards say, 'I was aware of the situation' as if the situation was running out of milk for coffee?"

"Ah, yes, he was aware of the situation because when the chairman married his third wife, Dr. Linguistics gave him boxing gloves for a wedding present."

Judy leaned back on the bench, pushing her sunglasses down on her nose and wagging a professorial finger. "Ah, yes, he was on wife number four when we knew him."

"After that," Judy said, "I stopped taking it all so seriously. I wanted to study. I wanted to teach, but I wasn't willing to play the crazy game."

"But we stayed in the game," Catherine said, thinking about Chelsea's situation.

"We've stayed in the game differently," Judy said, taking a deep breath. "You're so much more tolerant than me. I keep my distance from the crazies."

Catherine started to say something about Chelsea and then thought better of it.

Judy was already on to another topic... an associate dean who wears baggy trousers like men wore in the 1940s. "He wears a toupee that lies on his scalp like a squirrel wrapping itself around a tree branch."

Catherine let go of the tension in her stomach and laughed. "It can't be that bad."

"It is," Judy said, imitating his walk and his negative demeanor. "We don't know what he really does, but he has a lot of power."

Catherine shook her head and said, "Someday you'll be telling stories about me, that is if I survive the politics." Catherine got up from the bench, and they headed back to the hotel, ready for sleep. Graduate school was a lifetime ago. She had tried to help Kristin, but she had no power. Now, she had a responsibility to help Chelsea.

Chapter Twelve

Philip and Catherine met for dinner on Friday night at an Italian restaurant in a leafy Philadelphia neighborhood. Catherine relaxed immediately, telling Philip about her fundraising experience in Boston. He knew some of the alums she had met because of his experience as a board member. After a second glass of wine, Catherine suggested that they order. The scallops were large and tender, and Catherine found herself absorbed by her food.

"Philip, I have to admit. This job is already having a strange effect on me," she said.

"How do you mean?"

"Some days, I run on nothing more than coffee and yogurt. Then there are days like today when I'm eating like a horse. I had a huge hoagie for lunch, and now I'm ravenous again."

He laughed. "Don't worry. New jobs are always stressful. When I first went into business with my father, I was petrified. My father was a great guy, easy-going, but

I was so used to being judged by academic standards, so I wasn't sure I could succeed in business. I gained thirty pounds the first year."

"Now, you're scaring me. I'm not having dessert," she said, putting another large piece of scallop in her mouth.

Phillip asked Catherine about her decision to teach and become a dean. She tried to describe her experience, how she never really saw it as a decision.

"I never felt the pressure a lot of students feel, especially today, to get a job and make a lot of money. My father had been successful in business back in the sixties, but when I was a baby, he changed career paths and went to seminary. He was an Episcopal priest when I was growing up. He worked in a large parish in D.C., building a multiracial youth program and helping to integrate the church. He was opposed to the Vietnam War and worked with other clergy to try to bring an end to it."

Philip listened and told Catherine how different his experience had been. "I was a young man in the late 60s and early 70s trying to stay out of Vietnam. I suppose that is one of the reasons I went on and did the Ph.D., but not the only one."

She smiled at Philip, and her thoughts turned to those three years in D.C. where she started school.

She and Caroline would bring books home from the school library and show them to their grandmother. Her Nana would pull Catherine into her lap and read to her. Caroline, older by almost two years, would pull a chair close to Nana and listen. Sometimes, Nana would hand the book to Caroline and ask her to read. Caroline's blue eyes would sparkle as she leaned over the book and pronounced each word carefully with Nana nodding her approval.

Her father would be up early on Saturdays in those years, packing a lunch for a trip to a museum or a national monument.

"Is Mommy coming too?" Catherine inevitably asked as her father placed orange juice and a soft-boiled egg and toast in front of the sisters.

His blue-gray eyes would cloud over as he sat down next to Caroline and cracked her egg. "Not today. She's not feeling well." Nana would glance at their father, her face inscrutable.

The routine was shattered one morning when Catherine was six. "She's not sick. She's hungover," Caroline said, hands on her hips, lips pursed.

Catherine envied her sister's anger. Her tummy doesn't hurt like mine, she thought, putting her fork back on her plate. Caroline sensed Catherine's fear of the ongoing conflict. Letting go of her anger toward her father, she'd say, "Don't worry, Catherine. We're going to have a blast, and Nana will buy us treats. Right, Nana?"

"Yes, dear," Nana would say with a smile, and Daddy would reach down and give Caroline a kiss.

Catherine went to peace marches with her father, watching him talk with young people who wore dye-died shirts and carried colorful signs. Lying in bed one night, she heard her parents fighting.

"She's a little girl," her mother said. "I don't want her going to marches. She could get hurt. Or worse, she could become a low life like those nuts who want to change the world." The next morning on the way to school, Catherine asked Caroline what a low life was.

"It's complicated," Caroline said, shifting her bookbag

from one shoulder to the other. "People mother doesn't like who lack social graces. Or worse, they're black."

"Daddy and I were close," Catherine said, spearing the last piece of scallop on her plate, "but it wasn't until I was much older that I understood the connection between protesting the war and social injustice and his job as a priest. He believed the Gospel message was revolutionary, and we could eliminate the walls between rich and poor, black and white."

"Admirable idealism," Philip said as he motioned for the waiter to bring more wine. Tables filled up around them.

A polite answer, Catherine thought. Vietnam, part of our history, was part of her father's story. He had a heart for the men who fought and for the many who came home broken.

"Perhaps," Catherine said. "Ultimately, the church failed to be part of the progress my father wanted, but he continued to believe change came through fighting in the courts."

She searched Philip's face, and her gaze fell to the dark hair on his chest under a light blue shirt, unbuttoned at the neck. He had rolled up his sleeves before dinner, and she was drawn to his muscular arms. Philip handed his credit card to the waiter and suggested they have a nightcap at the bar.

"Philip, I couldn't drink anything more, and you said you need to be up early to pick-up your daughter at the airport."

"You're right, Catherine. I just don't want the evening to end. May I see you again?"

Flushed from the wine, she said nothing, but when he drove her back to the College, they sat for a moment in his car. She reached over and kissed him lightly on the cheek. Her hand glided across his body, stopping once to touch the exposed area around his throat and a second time to spread her fingers across his chest. His lips met hers, and he kissed her deeply.

"Please call me sometime soon," she said, letting him go. "Have a good weekend with your daughter."

He waited as she got in her car. She drove the short distance home and undressed slowly in front of the mirror. This feels good, she thought, pulling a nightshirt over her head. Does it just feel good because it's been so long?

Sleep didn't come easily. "Admirable idealism" kept running through Catherine's head. A polite response to something Philip doesn't understand or mocks?

She was seven when they moved to Spring Lake. Mother stopped drinking. She was buying new furniture, having work done on the house. She'd take the train into New York to have lunch with friends, go to the Met. Her father just looked sad. Young people from the D.C. church stayed in touch with him, asked his advice about college and careers.

Idealism perhaps, but he made a difference in people's lives.

Catherine drifted into sleep, thinking about Philip. Just another man who wants to get laid or something more?

Chapter Thirteen
June 1968

Douglas woke before the alarm. It was only four o'clock, but he could leave now and miss all the traffic in North Jersey and New York. He left Flora a note, thanking her again for taking care of the girls. He left the number at the Charles Street Inn and told her he would call her if he needed to give her another number.

It was dark, the traffic was light, and Douglas was over the Tappan Zee Bridge before the road became congested. It had been almost four years. Douglas remembered every detail of their meetings in her apartment in Chestnut Hill, a wealthy neighborhood in Philadelphia with large stone homes built in the early part of the twentieth century. Coffee in the backyard. Lovemaking. Simple but elegant dinners she cooked for him. Douglas always bought her flowers. Even a single rose gave her such pleasure.

"Yellow roses are my favorite," she told him once.

Was she telling him the truth? He'd found out since then that yellow means friendship. Did she fear that the passion wouldn't last?

His heart pounding, he'd never felt such yearning. Grace's touch was electricity, moving through his body. She never resisted his tongue, gently probing her mouth. After making love, once, she stroked his chest gently and asked, "What does it feel like to be inside of me?" He didn't know how to answer, but she insisted on an answer.

"I don't know, Grace," Douglas said, pulling her head to his chest, caressing the curve of her hip. "Like I'm drowning but don't want to surface. Like I will always feel loved, complete." She said nothing, kneading his forearm with her long, tapered fingers.

Douglas stopped at a diner on the outskirts of Hartford for some breakfast. He ordered and began reading *The New York Times*. "Kerner Commission concludes that the United States was becoming 'two societies, one black, one white—separate and unequal.'" The country was exploding with anger, and it would only get worse as the Democratic National Convention in Chicago approached. None of the candidates looked appealing to Douglas. Grace is right... Bobby Kennedy's death. So much hope shot down with one bullet.

He got back in the car and continued the long drive, sipping hot coffee. Radio stations faded in and out, so finally, he settled for a Boston station with mostly contemporary music. He was humming along to Simon and Garfunkel's "The Sound of Silence" when he realized how much the words meant now, this year of assassinations.

Douglas was in Boston before noon. He parked his car

and stopped at the hotel's front desk.

"You can check in at two o'clock, Mr. Finley," the attractive woman at the desk informed him. "Will anyone be joining you?" she asked.

"No," Douglas said, but his thoughts were already focused on Grace wanting him as much as he wanted her. Could passion still be there after all this time?

He walked along the Charles River. The day was warm and muggy. He returned to the hotel and fell fast asleep for several hours. After a hot shower, he ventured down to the restaurant in the lobby. He ordered a glass of wine at the bar and waited. A few minutes before seven, he looked up, and there she was.

Her black hair was pulled back, piled on the back of her head, clasped with a large gold barrette. She wore a yellow chiffon blouse, sheer enough that he could see the lacy bra beneath it. An A-line black skirt and black pumps made her look taller and thinner than he had remembered.

Douglas felt awkward. He wanted to hold her in his arms, but it had been so long. Spontaneously, she gave him a kiss on the cheek. He studied her face, remembering the softness in her eyes when she touched him.

He ordered a glass of wine for her. "I don't know how much time you have," Douglas stammered, "but I'm sure you're hungry."

"I'm in no rush," she said. They talked for hours, first about her work with the law firm and some cases she had tried with William Thompson.

"You remember William and Rebecca?" Grace asked.

"Of course. We met the night before the March on Washington." Douglas's mind flashed to his meeting her in the bar and how easily he fell into conversation with

William and Rebecca at dinner that night. If things had been different, they would have become friends.

"Sometimes William reminds me of you," she said.

"How so?" he asked.

"He believes in Dr. King's philosophy," she said. "He believes we can make a difference."

"William's right," Douglas assured her. "We *can* make a difference." He described the work he hoped to do in D.C. "Young people are leading this movement. They're open to breaking down color barriers," he said confidently.

"So much has changed since I saw you last," he said cautiously, "but one thing hasn't changed. I'm still in love with you."

"And Elizabeth?" she asked, motioning for the waiter to bring her another glass of wine.

"Soon after Catherine was born, she became very depressed. After several weeks, she didn't seem any better. She was drinking. One day, I came home to find both girls crying, and Elizabeth was "asleep"—that's what the girls said—on the living room floor.

"A combination of valium and alcohol nearly killed her. We got her the best care, and three months later, she was home. I thought she was okay until several weeks ago she tried to kill herself again."

"Douglas, I'm so sorry. How are your girls doing?"

"Caroline is very distant from me. I think she blames me for what is happening to her mother. Elizabeth wants nothing to do with Catherine."

Grace looked at Douglas intently. What was she thinking?

"Grace, I will never know if I'm the cause of all Elizabeth's pain. Her father says I am. He says I haven't cared for her as I should. I seem to have no answers for him because I'm not convinced she ever loved me. Perhaps if I had been someone else..."

"You can't be someone else, Douglas. You were true to her when you found out she was pregnant. You stayed with her." Grace took several bites of her salad.

"Yes. Now I can only tell you that I did so to save the life of my child. We have no marriage and lead totally separate lives. When I got your letter this month, I thought that perhaps, I hadn't lost you. I felt your passion and your pain, and I missed you more than I have any day since I was with you." Douglas stopped, fearful about what might come next.

"I miss you every day, Douglas," Grace said softly. "I don't know what happened when I met you, but something changed in me... changed dramatically." She leaned in, her voice softer, her eyes searching his face.

"I had been with many men before I met you, perhaps proving to myself that my mother was wrong. I didn't need a husband, but with you it was different."

He didn't like hearing she had been with other men. He wanted her to love him, no one else.

"Grace, I want to start over with you." Yes, these were the same words he said to Elizabeth the night he meant to leave her and found out she was pregnant with Catherine.

"But no judge will give you custody," Grace said, sipping her wine. "With your father-in-law's money and your infidelity, it's impossible."

Douglas reached across the table and took Grace's hand. She didn't resist.

"Let me try again because I'm not saying what's really important. I love you, Grace. I want to marry you. That sense of how I feel about you has nothing to do with Elizabeth or anyone or anything else."

Grace caressed his hand and muttered, "It's not possible, Douglas. So much has happened. How do we sort things out?" She moved closer to him and gently touched his lips with her fingers. She took in the rhythm of his words as he spoke.

"Is there someone else? I'll understand if there is," Douglas said.

She shook her head.

"Will you stay with me tonight, even if it's just tonight?" Douglas asked. She nodded and sat back, placing her hands in her lap as she waited for him to pay the bill. They took the elevator to his room, and he led her to the bed. He undressed her slowly, touching every crease and curve in her body. Grace moaned with pleasure and responded to every advance. They fell asleep in each other's arms.

Douglas awakened early and propped himself up on one elbow. Grace slept soundly beside him, breathing shallowly, her naked body stretched out without covers. He began to gently stroke her buttocks, fingers delicately caressing her tiny waist. She turned to face him, dark hair cascading over her left breast. He moved toward her as she wrapped her long, milky white legs around him.

"Is this my wake-up call?" she purred softly.

"No, my love. We're not getting up for a long time."

Before falling asleep, they had talked about driving to Maine for a few days. He wanted to take her to Bar Harbor and places in Acadia National Park that he remembered from childhood, the last vacation with his parents before his father died.

They checked out close to noon, stopping at Grace's house so she could pack a bag. He waited in the foyer, noticing the books and legal pads on the floor by the couch in the living room.

Douglas decided to make a stop for dinner in Camden, a small town in Maine that he had visited as a child on a family vacation. The day was brilliant—Siberian iris in bloom, hanging balls of petunias, and the warm sun penetrating the windows of the restaurant as sounds from the bay played in the background. Large cumulus clouds splashed against a deep blue sky, which faded to pale blue as it reached down toward the water.

Grace nibbled on calamari, playfully placing one on a cocktail fork and reaching over to place it in Douglas's mouth. The silence between them was pregnant with meaning. Douglas was overcome with how easy it was to be with Grace, still after all this time. No pressure to talk, but when they did, he hung on her every word and never wanted to stop talking to her. He was talking to someone who saw into his heart and soul and truly knew him. He looked out at the harbor as they left the restaurant and took a deep breath of the fresh, cool air.

When they got to Bar Harbor, it was almost dark. Before checking in, they found a bench in the small park facing the harbor. The grassy knoll was alive with small children, running up and down. Others sat with their parents, enjoying an ice cream cone on the warm, clear night. Douglas put his arm around Grace, breathing in the smell of her along with the night air.

"Wake up, Douglas," he heard her say. He had been dreaming about her. The scent of her lavender perfume lay over him like a soft blanket. He didn't want to wake up or she might be gone.

"Douglas." He felt her warm breath on his back.

"Wake up. We're going to watch the sunrise."

It wasn't a dream. She stood above him, already dressed in Levi's and a heavy navy-blue sweater.

"Come on, Rip van Winkle. Dress warmly. You told me it's cold on the top."

His lips brushed the hair falling over her forehead as he reached for his boxer shorts.

"We need to get you some jeans," she said playfully as he pulled on brown, corduroy trousers. She tugged a chocolate brown sweater over his head. Her fingers fondled the Princeton insignia on the breast.

The air was frigid as they drove toward the park. Her warm hand lay on top of his, only letting go to allow him to shift. Douglas thought about their lovemaking. Long kisses, his hands on her breasts, her hands or tongue caressing him. After they came, often together, they cuddled and talked about anything on their minds.

"I'm afraid of heights," she said fearfully, bringing his focus back to the winding climb to the top. He couldn't see her face. He'd never seen her fear.

"But you want to see the sunrise?"

"Yes."

"Don't worry, love," he said reassuringly. "There's lots of space at the top."

Black and still, the only sound was the car's steady motor, momentarily hesitating now and again on the steep climb. The taillights of a car ahead of them shed some light on the rock face but still no light from the sky.

Douglas parked the car, anxious to find a spot with a

good view. Grace exhaled and smiled at him as he took her hand and helped her out of the car. As promised, there was a lot of space and a cold wind swirled around them.

"My parents brought me to Bar Harbor when I was a little boy... 1936," Douglas said. "I'll always remember the morning we drove up here to watch the sunrise. Mother had left my pajamas on, layering over them a pair of pants and a sweater. I slept in the backseat as my father drove up the mountain. I woke up and heard my father tell Mother he would always love her. My father died the next summer." Douglas looked toward the horizon. "There was more light that morning, at least that's what I remember."

"Look, there's some light. Let's walk closer," Grace said, squeezing his hand and picking up the pace.

The cold wind cut through them. Strands of gold emerged from the blackness, a sliver of orange appearing stage center. Gray to black clouds filled the sky around the tiny puddle of light.

"I wish we had a clear day," Douglas said. "That day in '36 was magnificent. The sky was azure blue. My mother picked me up and placed me on a rock, so I was as tall as she was. I watched the sun, like a cannonball, burst onto the horizon. Everyone cheered. My father kissed my mother and held her close. I felt safe, loved."

Grace said nothing, but Douglas saw tears in her eyes. She pulled him close to her. "You're loved, Douglas, but I don't know if either one of us will ever feel safe."

"I feel safe with you," Douglas whispered in her ear.

The sun appeared and disappeared among the clouds as it rose, and they stood for a long time, watching light hidden, then revealed, in the cloudy sky. They walked around the top of the mountain in silence.

Safe. He wanted to be safe with Grace, but he was sure she had already given her answer.

They drove down the mountain, her right hand held tightly to the door handle. Her left hand had fallen from his and clutched her left thigh.

"We'll be down soon," he said, catching a glimpse of her grimace as he rounded a curve. Her face relaxed as they reached the bottom and wound their way out of the park.

"One more trip down memory lane," he said, turning onto Cottage Street.

"What's that?" she asked, squeezing his hand again.

"The best blueberry pancakes in Maine," Douglas said. The Jordan Pond Restaurant was a gray, square building with a line of people waiting at its front door. They took their place behind the others, content to wait for the first cup of coffee of the morning.

"Hot coffee and two stacks of blueberry pancakes with sausage," Douglas said, without waiting to ask Grace what she wanted. The redheaded, freckled waitress in a gold uniform smiled and nodded as she wrote down their order. Long legs reached down to white sneakers and socks. She moved easily among crowded tables and other waitresses carrying armloads of plates with steaming eggs and pancakes.

"I've read your letter over and over again," he said after his first bite of pancake. "I wish I could have been with you in Memphis. Tell me about the case."

"Do you remember James Porter?" she asked.

"Of course. I introduced you to him at the March on Washington." Douglas had met Rev. Porter in '62 at a conference in Atlanta.

"Yes. We saw him again in Selma. He spoke so eloquently about marching with Dr. King and how the March was a turning point for him in making a commitment to the Movement," Grace said.

"We shared a pint of whiskey and talked Theology, while you were busy working the crowd, if I recall correctly. He thought you were my wife, and I did nothing to cause him to think differently," Douglas said, remembering the brief time they shared on the last night in Selma.

Grace sipped her coffee and smiled. "When the ACLU asked me to be co-counsel for his daughter's case, we met, and he remembered you as my husband. I didn't correct him, either. He was so distraught over what had happened to his daughter, and he had made a real connection with you... one I could not provide."

"How do you mean?" Douglas asked, already sure he knew the answer.

"As I worked with his daughter, Rev. Porter helped me realize that the religious and the political message are one and the same. There's no focus on heaven like the church taught when I was growing up. The New Jerusalem is built here, something Rev. Porter called the Beloved Community."

"Where's his daughter's case now?" Douglas asked.

"William and I were in Memphis in April for the trial. We got convictions for assault and rape for all three boys, but the sentencing was lenient," she said, blowing on a freshly poured cup of coffee.

They left the restaurant and planned to head out for Long Pond. During their drive to Bar Harbor, Grace had insisted they go canoeing. He protested, but she wouldn't listen.

"You did crew at Princeton," she said. "How hard can this be?"

"That was a long time ago. I'm out of shape," Douglas protested.

"I don't believe it," she said.

He turned onto Kebo Street and stopped in front of a gray clapboard house with shutters in need of paint.

"Where're we going?" she asked as he opened the car door for her.

"If we're going canoeing, we need a canoe," he said smiling. "Wait here. I'll just be a few minutes."

Grace watched as Douglas made his way up the path, decorated with small terra cotta pots filled with petunias. He rang the bell twice before a small man, wearing dark trousers and a plaid jacket, came to the door. Douglas disappeared inside and a few minutes later, reemerged.

"Who was that, Douglas?" she asked as he got in the car and laid a set of keys on the dashboard.

"Mr. Kent. It's a long story."

"And I want to hear it," Grace said, laughing.

"Well, my great grandfather had a summer cottage here," Douglas began.

"One of the blue bloods?" she asked, teasingly.

"He was a professor at Princeton and spent his summers here. He was a poet, an author, someone I'm rather proud of. He was also an expert on birds. In 1919 he was appointed—don't laugh—chief ornithologist at what was then Lafayette National Park, now Acadia. My family and the Kent family have been friends for generations."

Grace hummed the Birdman theme song. "Did the Maine Birdman have an eagle sidekick named Avenger?"

"I thought only little boys liked Birdman until I heard Caroline humming that tune," Douglas said. "The Maine Birdman passed his hobby along to his son and to my father. I might have learned from my father if he had lived longer."

The dock was busy when they arrived on Long Pond. Several canoes were already on the water. Douglas found Mr. Kent's locker and pulled the canoe out onto the water. They rowed easily to an island on the lake. Dark clouds rolled in quickly and obliterated any blue in the sky.

"We need to head back, Grace," Douglas said. She didn't say a word as he skillfully turned the canoe around. He rowed hard against the wind. She followed his lead, and they almost reached shore before the heavens opened. Lightning, like elongated spears, pierced the black sky.

"I'm sorry, Douglas," she said, wringing water out of her windbreaker.

"Don't be," he said. "It would have been a wonderful adventure if it hadn't rained."

Douglas stopped at a coffee shop on the way back and filled his thermos. When they got back to the inn, he poured a cup and lifted it to Grace's mouth.

"Have a few sips. Then, let's get out of these wet clothes."

He ran a hot shower, and she was in it before he had a chance to undress. Still warming up, they crawled under the covers.

"So, you came from money, Douglas?" she asked, snuggling close to him when she had finished the coffee.

"Yes and no," Douglas answered. "My great grandfather was an academic whose family had come to this country in the seventeenth century. His connections in Princeton made it possible for him to marry money, but from what my mother told me about him, the wealth never tainted his interest in a simple lifestyle.

"Your family, Grace? I remember that first day I met you, you said your family had been poor."

"Irish potato famine," she said. "My great grandfather settled in Philadelphia when he came from Ireland. He was a roofer and worked hard to provide for a large family. My parents were poor when they first married, but by the time I was about fifteen, my father was making a lot of money in construction. Money made my mother happy, so he kept making it, but he was home less and less.

"As I walked home from school one day, I could hear my parents arguing. I stood outside and listened. Mother was accusing him of seeing another woman. He didn't deny it. I never heard them fight again after that day."

He absorbed her words and thought about his little girls. They were already experiencing this kind of pain, knowing or at least sensing that their parents didn't love each other. He wanted it to be different for them, but he couldn't make it different with Elizabeth. He kissed Grace on the bridge of her nose and suggested one more adventure.

"Let's take a walk around Jordan Pond," he said, another place in the park that he remembered from childhood. Although the morning was chilly, he put the top down on the Pontiac Lemans. Grace's dark hair was covered by a Kelly-green scarf. The sun was warm, the air cool and filled with the smell of pine and lilacs. The stillness filled Douglas with wonder. Dark gray shadows on soft blue; brown and beige pushing through the shiny surface. Rocks emerging from the water like tiny mountains in the distance.

A black hawk moved majestically above the trees, black against white clouds, black against powder blue until he disappeared behind the trees. Grace ran ahead on the rocky path, laughing and imitating the birds who seemed to talk only to her.

They drove back to Boston that afternoon. Before she got out of the car, she took his hand and placed it on her chest, so he could feel her heartbeat. She reached over and kissed him on the cheek.

Douglas drove home through heavy traffic, a thunderstorm, a chilly New Jersey summer evening. Her words ran through his mind repeatedly: "'You are loved, Douglas, but I don't know if either one of us will ever feel safe.'"

He never did, but he had to do what he could to make sure his little girls did.

Part II

Autumn 2004

Chapter Fourteen

August and September were a blur of activity: the beginning of the semester, the tedious weekly and monthly meetings with academic departments, other administrators, and navigating the constant tension between divisions, all part of the College landscape. Hal hated most of it and knew it would be less tedious if Tina were still here with him.

He pulled the rocking chair up to the living room window and sat in the dark, sipping a glass of wine. His thoughts turned to one summer afternoon last year when Tina came home from work early. The memories of Tina's last days ran through his mind like a movie he had seen many times.

"Is everything okay?" he asked as she wrapped her arms around him from behind, kissing the top of his head.

"Yes," she said, but he didn't believe her. He could feel the tension in her body, rigidity grafted onto softness.

"I want to walk in Valley Green."

"Let's go, then," Hal said as Tina went upstairs to change her clothes. It had been four months since the diagnosis, and Hal rarely saw Tina's fear or panic, a state he was in, it seemed, constantly.

Since their move to Philadelphia in 2001, they had taken many walks in Valley Green. In summer, it was a place to escape the heat, old trees shading the path winding around the stream, waterfall, and covered bridge. In fall, it was the place to watch yellow, orange, and red disappear as November's gray touched barren trees and the darkness of short December days became a reality.

After their walk, Tina had prepared a simple dinner— lamb chops, asparagus with hollandaise sauce, and a tossed salad. They ate in silence, Hal pushing his fear of losing her to the back of his mind.

"Penny for your thoughts," Hal said, running his fingers across the open palm of her hand lying on the table.

"You hate being a dean, don't you?" she asked, more a challenge than a question. "You only took the job because I wanted to move to Philadelphia."

"I do miss teaching and research," he said cautiously.

Tears welled up in Tina's eyes. She took a small bite of the lamb and sipped her wine.

"You could get your old job back," she said. "I'm sure they'd be glad to have you."

Hal moved his chair next to hers and pulled her into his arms. He said nothing, and silent tears rolled down his cheeks.

"You've lived for me, Hal," she said in a whisper.

"We've lived for each other." His response was hushed.

"When I'm gone, you need to live for yourself."

Icy fingers lingering in his hand until they warmed to his touch. Icy feet running up and down his leg until warm and ready for sleep. She fell asleep easily, tired from the long walk in Valley Green. How much more time does she have? Hal thought as he lay still, listening to the steady rhythm of her breathing.

Streaks of light, pink, then orange, fell across the tangerine slippers on Tina's side of the bed. Hal reached over and looked at the clock. 7:00 a.m.

She let me oversleep, he thought, pulling on sweatpants and heading for the smell of coffee.

"Why didn't you wake me up?" he asked sternly.

"Happy birthday, Hal," she said, wrapping her slender arms around his bare chest. "Go put a sweatshirt on, and I'll give you some eggs and sausage before you have to go to work." She smiled, loving the surprise and refusing to be scolded.

Hal headed upstairs for his sweatshirt. He stopped in his tracks when he heard a crash... glass breaking and the bounce of a bowl on the linoleum. He grabbed his sweatshirt and his cell phone and headed for the kitchen.

Tina slumped against the refrigerator, egg yolks stuck to denim, eggshells on the floor and coating the dark wood of the bowl. He dialed 911 and gave his address. With every muscle straining, he lifted Tina and carried her to the den. She was breathing shallowly, face pale, eyes closed.

"I'm sorry about the eggs," she said as he lifted cold water to dry lips.

"I'm sorry about your birthday," she said, licking her chapped lips.

Hal's hand went to Tina's heart. No breath. He took

her hand, tracing lines, circling her wedding ring with his left thumb, pressing his index finger to the tiny diamond on her engagement ring.

A cool breeze cut through the foyer as the paramedics followed him to the den. No life. No breath. The paramedics left silently, heads bowed.

Hal sat on the ottoman, looking at Tina across the room. Moving to the couch, he kneeled and took her right hand. Warmth of warmth. Warm holding a cold and soon, icy hand.

He stroked her slender arms, angry at the killer cells that destroyed the good, the good that was Tina.

Hal was relieved that he had made the decision one evening last January to get a course on the fall schedule. That night, Hal had come in from a long walk in the neighborhood. Snow had begun to fall, and it was snowing steadily by 9:00.

Hot chocolate would taste good if Tina were here, he thought. She loved the tiny marshmallows, bobbing like tiny buoys in the steaming liquid. As he watched it snow that January night, he knew he couldn't handle looking for a new job or moving back to Boston, but he could teach a course at Franklin. He needed to fill the empty spaces with things he loved.

The next day, he talked with the History Chairperson about a course for the fall semester. He designed a new course called Reflections on the Civil Rights Movement.

Hal placed the folder with copies of his syllabus on his worktable along with a copy of his textbook and his collection of oral histories. Rolling up the sleeves of his blue Oxford shirt, he took a deep breath. The class list included fifteen students, most History majors. He picked up his materials and headed for the classroom on the third floor. He passed Catherine in the hall.

"Have a good class," she said with a smile.

"I will," he said, noticing the black silk blouse and Kelly-green skirt she was wearing.

Two students were seated in the back of the class, eating hoagies and talking softly. The first looked at Hal with some interest and said hello. Her friend, in an over-sized t-shirt and sweatpants, looked down at her sandwich. As the rest of the class shuffled in, Hal handed out the syllabus along with a small card.

"Please put your name on the card and two bits of information: why you took this course and one book or article you have read about the Civil Rights Movement. Give me a one or two-sentence critique of the work you read."

"What if we haven't read anything?" asked a young man with wet hair, wearing shorts, a t-shirt, and flip-flops.

Without answering the student's question, Hal went on, "The syllabus I handed you only includes the readings for the first four weeks of class. I hope to add readings from the selections you give me today."

Hal collected the cards and asked what the class knew about the Civil Rights Movement.

Meghan raised her hand politely and said, "President Kennedy responded to the strife in the country by proposing legislation to provide equal rights for African-Americans. The legislation wasn't passed, though, until after President Kennedy was assassinated. President Johnson was the one who got it passed in 1965."

"That's right," Hal said, smiling broadly at her response.

"The March on Washington in 1963 was important too," said a thin boy with dark square hair and glasses. "Blacks and whites marched together, and politicians could no longer close their eyes to the movement or claim it was just about blacks." He lowered his eyes to the syllabus on his desk, nervously doodling on the margins.

"We'll talk at length about the March and the legislation. In fact, one of the oral histories in my book is told by a white woman who was at the March. 1963 is an important year for the Movement, but I would like to mention another date—1958—which is important. Does anyone know why?"

"Eisenhower was President, and *Leave It to Beaver* was on TV," said the other student in the back of the room.

"That's true," Hal said, laughing softly. He looked at the class list. "You're Suzanne?"

"Yes, Professor," she said, looking at him for the first time.

"The 1950s are often idealized as years of prosperity in the post–World War II America, but 1958 is important because millions of Americans were living in poverty, about 17 percent of the population. The first marches were about poverty. Let's start there."

"Dr. Doyle, why did you get interested in this part of American History?" a woman with almond skin and turquoise jewelry asked.

Hal smiled and perched on the edge of the large desk where he had placed his books and syllabi. He held the class list in his hands.

"Are you Mikayla?" he asked. He was looking at the

pictures on the class list and noticed that she was the only African-American student.

"Yes," she beamed. "My grandfather marched with Dr. King. When I was little, he told me lots of stories about what it was like growing up in the segregated South."

Hal nodded. "Your grandfather has an important story to tell."

"He died when I was thirteen," she continued, not allowing Hal to finish his thought. "I miss him. I loved his stories."

"Write the stories down while they are still in your mind. Write them down as you heard them, in his voice. That's what an oral history is."

"Read the first three chapters in the text for Thursday. We'll start there when we meet next time."

The students filed out quietly, and two students who arrived late apologized and took a syllabus from Hal's desk. Mikayla waited for all the other students to leave before approaching Hal.

"Dr. Doyle, I keep a journal. I've kept a journal since I was ten, and I've already written down many of my grandfather's stories."

"Great."

She held a notebook and her textbook tightly and looked up at Hal. "Will you teach me how to write an oral history?"

"I'd love to. Start reading the oral histories in my book. Then, we can talk about strategies I use when I'm writing someone's stories."

"Thanks, Professor. See you on Thursday."

Hal headed down the steps and stopped to fill his water bottle in the lounge. His office was quiet, and he easily tackled paperwork and responded to several emails.

Lost in thought, he did not hear footsteps approaching.

"Hal," Catherine said softly, standing in the doorway of his office. "It's 6:30. Time to go home."

He looked at his watch, which was lying beside the computer. "I lost track of time," he said as he logged off. "I'll walk out with you."

"I had a great class today," he said.

"I knew you would," she said. "I'll get back to teaching next year when I feel like I know my job better."

Hal didn't respond to Catherine's comment. He said good night and got in his car. The class had made him realize how much he missed teaching, missed the life he had as a professor. No one scheduling his day.

Hal had enjoyed the last few months since Catherine had started at Franklin. He'd had little rapport with her predecessor who was tangled in Neil's political web. No independent thinking. Just second-guessing what Neil wanted.

Catherine was empathetic when he told her about Tina, but she didn't suffocate him. Her independence was refreshing.

Chapter Fifteen

Hal rolled out of bed before the clock radio came on. Placing his feet on the floor, he felt shaky. He had been dreaming about Tina.

He placed his journal and pen on the bedside table and moved slowly toward the bathroom. He showered and shaved mechanically, smiling at the memory. Clutching a towel around his waist, Hal sat on the edge of the bed and continued to jot down details from the dream.

Hal drove to work, unaware of anything around him. As he got out of the car, Catherine pulled in next to him.

"Good morning, Catherine. How was your weekend?"

"It was difficult. My father called to say his friend Ray died last week."

"I'm sorry," Hal said, his thoughts still on the dream.

They lapsed into silence as they walked into the building. Hal waved a "good morning" to Bette and continued down the hall to his office.

"Good morning, Tom," Hal said to the student worker

in his front office. A young woman sat in the chair by the door, her head down, a large backpack at her feet.

"Good morning, Dr. Doyle," Tom replied. Tom was slumped over the desk, staring at the computer screen, a Phillies baseball cap perched backward on his head. He sat up as Hal moved through the office. "I put a letter on your desk that came FedEx this morning."

Hal logged in and looked at the phone messages on his desk. He ran his finger over the Eliot, Winthrop, and McKenzie insignia on the envelope and started to remove the letter when Tom came into his office and closed the door.

"Dr. Doyle, the student waiting for you said she had a really bad run-in with Professor Bennet. She met with Rhodes, and he blew her off."

"Give me five minutes. I need to return two phone calls, and then I will see her. What's her name?"

"Sarah Walsh."

"Please tell Sarah I will be right with her."

Hal made a quick call to Steve to let him know he would take the interview with the local newspaper about the new transfer student program, but he wanted someone from the Enrollment Management staff to be present. He called the faculty chairman of the MBA review committee with two questions he wanted covered at the faculty meeting.

"Sarah, please come in. I'm sorry to keep you waiting," Hal said, smiling warmly as he closed the door behind her.

Sarah perched on the loveseat, eyes downcast. Her navy-blue backpack bulged with heavy textbooks. She dropped the backpack on the floor, never raising her head.

"Tell me what happened," Hal said.

Silence.

"Is it harder to tell me than it was to tell Dr. Rhodes?"

"No. Yes, because he didn't believe me."

"Well, I am going to believe you. Please go ahead," Hal said, steel-blue eyes taking in Sarah's brown eyes and troubled expression. Her bottom lip quivered as she tried to speak.

"Last Tuesday, I went to see Professor Bennet about my mid-term. I got a 47, and I was really upset. I asked him if he would go over the essays where I had lost points. He sat down next to me, and he reeked of alcohol. He tried to speak, and his words were slurred. I told him I could come back another time. As I got up to leave, he grabbed my arm. He didn't say anything. He just started kissing me and grabbing at my breast." Sarah started to cry softly.

"What did Dr. Rhodes say about this?" Hal asked, leaning in closer to Sarah.

Sarah rubbed the palms of her hands on her thighs. "He told me that I exaggerated. He said that I was already on academic probation, and I should concentrate on my work. I went to Professor Bennet for help. I *was* focused on my work!" Anger flashed across Sarah's face, and Hal was quick to acknowledge that she had done the right thing.

"I never would have gone to Professor Bennet if I knew this could happen. I want to withdraw from the course, but I can't right now. Keeping my current job depends on my making adequate progress on my master's degree."

"Sarah, I don't want you to withdraw. I will see about placing you in another section. Let me talk with the other professor, and I will get back to you later this week before the next class."

"I'd really appreciate it if you can get me into the other section."

"Sarah, do you have friends you can be with tonight? I don't want you to be alone when you're this upset."

"Yes. I can hang out with my boyfriend."

"Good."

A faint smile crossed Sarah's face. "Thanks for your help," she said, reaching out to shake Hal's hand before she left the office.

After Sarah left, Hal walked over to Neil's office. Neil was standing next to Marie's desk, reading a memo.

"Good morning."

"Good morning," Neil and Marie said, almost in unison.

"Neil, do you have a few minutes?" Hal asked.

"Of course. Come in." Hal followed Neil into his office and closed the door. Hal sat down in the chair beside Neil's desk as Neil made himself comfortable.

"Neil, I just met with a student named Sarah Walsh."

"Oh, yes. I met with her last week. She claims Jason Bennet made a pass at her."

"She said you didn't believe her," Hal said, scanning Neil's face.

"I didn't tell her that in so many words. I *did* tell her she needed to focus on her work."

"She said Jason reeked of alcohol."

"Well, we do know he has a drinking problem. Melanie has asked that I give him a paid leave of absence so he can get dried out next semester." Melanie was Jason's academic department chair.

Hal's face remained expressionless. "Neil, aren't you afraid that we could have a lawsuit on our hands?"

"Well, I suppose that's possible, but really, it is her word against his unless we encourage her and think her story has any credibility," Neil said, looking at Hal for the first time. "Sounds like a drama queen to me." Hal didn't respond.

Hal thanked Neil for his time and returned to his office, furious. He had heard the stories about Jason's drinking. A paid leave for him to dry out? How often had this happened?

Hal paced his office, anger tackling any rational response to the student's dilemma. His mind flashed to a school night when he was twelve. *Studying in his room, he heard his mother on the phone.*

"She was raped," his mother screamed into the phone. "She was raped by her boss. There will be no 'lesser charge.'"

Chapter Sixteen

With phone calls to return and a grant to finish, Hal worked through lunch. Not concentrating, he found himself staring into space once again. The office was quiet. His administrative assistant Joyce wasn't in because she had a medical emergency with her ten-year-old daughter. As he printed a draft of the grant, he reread the letter he'd received the day before.

November 1, 2004

Dear Dr. Doyle:

I joined the firm of Eliot, Winthrop, and McKenzie in 1984 and had the privilege of working with your mother for several years. Your mother was a mentor to me and provided me with a detailed history of how attorneys, including Ruth Bader Ginsberg, used Civil Rights legislation to develop the language and context for litigating sexual harassment and gender discrimination cases.

I have read your oral histories about the Civil

Rights Movement and can hear your mother's voice in the stories you tell. Your mother would be so pleased that you have carried on her passion in your own work.

I will be in Philadelphia for several days in December, December 17–20, and would like to schedule a time to meet with you. Please let me know if this would be possible.

> *Sincerely yours,*
> *Stephanie Winthrop, Esq.*
> *Stephanie.Winthrop@ewm.org*

Hal dialed Stephanie's number and was surprised to reach her on the first ring. Her voice was warm and enthusiastic. They agreed to meet in Hal's office on a Tuesday morning. Hal promised to email her directions to campus.

Leaving the office twenty minutes early to walk to the faculty meeting, Hal took the long way up the hill so he could relax and clear his head. English tea roses, some still blooming, lined the alumni walkway at the bottom of the hill near the library. Hal paused to smell the yellow ones. A purple clematis, wrapped around one bush, seemed to hang on for dear life.

He sat for a few moments beside the reflecting pool, thinking about the many early mornings when Tina would come in from the garden, dirt under her fingernails and smudges on her face. He felt tightness in his chest and a wave of panic came over him. Would he ever stop grieving her? Everything seemed to matter when he knew she was here for him. She helped him see the humor in the tedious politics.

His thoughts returned to Sarah Walsh and what she

had told him about Jason's attack. Neil accepted the College's complicity, protecting Jason.

As he returned to the path, several faculty members from the Fine Arts Department greeted him. Barry Champlain, Chairman of the Music Department, was praising Chelsea for a concert she'd held at Swarthmore College earlier that week.

"So, what are we yakking about today?" Barry asked Hal, a sheepish grin on his face. "I guess it wouldn't surprise you that I haven't looked at the agenda."

"It's fairly light from my standpoint," Hal responded. We have a new track in the MBA—Arts Management—that's up for approval." Hal slowed his pace as the walk grew steeper, allowing the older man to catch his breath.

In the foyer of Franklin Hall, faculty clustered near coffee and cookies. Last-minute discussions about agenda items were laced with the usual complaints about workload and students' inattentiveness.

Bill Stevens, Chairman of the Faculty Senate, brought the meeting to order. Minutes of the last meeting were approved but not until time had been spent discussing the limitations of parking on campus. Lost in thought, Hal missed the approval of the first two items but was brought back to the discussion when the MBA item was brought to the floor. Discussion was brief, with some Liberal Arts faculty claiming there was no place for an Arts Management track in the MBA Program. The new track was approved easily.

As the meeting ended, Hal hoped to slip out and go home without returning to his office, but Neil made a point of drawing him into a conversation about the comments made about the Arts Management track. As faculty dispersed, Hal tried to break away.

Catherine saw the distressed look on Hal's face and was successful in changing the subject. They stopped in the portico for a moment before walking downhill.

"I'm going to see if I can make it to a 6:00 yoga class," she said.

"Sounds good," Hal added. "It's been a long day."

Dusk was falling and the campus looked particularly beautiful, the yellows, reds, and oranges of fall were backdrop to the darkening sky.

"Yes, Hal had a tough morning with a difficult student," Neil said, coming up behind Catherine and Hal on the path.

Hal didn't respond, and Neil continued, "Ah, come on. Don't you want to tell Catherine about the hot babe who was crying on your shoulder?"

Hal stopped abruptly and turned to Neil. "A student came to see me this morning about a serious problem, and she was not crying on my shoulder." His face was flushed, his voice cracking. This morning, he had kept his fury at Neil in check. Now, he couldn't.

"She didn't get what she wanted from me last week, so you were next," Neil continued, not willing to let the subject drop.

"I don't think this is an issue that should be discussed publicly," Catherine interjected.

"The three of us, public?" Neil asked, his voice louder than before.

"Neil, I think others can hear what you are saying," Catherine said softly, facing him as they continued down the hill.

They had reached Tyler Hall, and Hal suggested that

he and Neil continue this discussion at another time. He took several deep breaths as he walked to his car. He'd run a couple miles when he got home.

This is what women live with every day. He thought about the first time he watched his mother shake in a rage about a lost case.

"This motherfucker's going to walk because of a technicality," she said to Uncle Vince. "He's beaten and raped two women. They'll never be free of that, never."

Uncle Vince embraced her and held her close until she was calm. Hal left his perch on the steps and returned to his desk in his room. Uncle Vince knocked a few minutes later.

"Hey, Hal," he said. "I wanted to say goodnight before I go home. Your mother could use a hug."

"Why does she get so upset?" Hal asked. "Getting that mad could make her sick."

"She sees herself in the victim. Feels her pain," Uncle Vince said.

Chapter Seventeen

Catherine slept lightly and awakened twice, screaming. A growling animal chased her down a dark corridor.

She stumbled out of bed and went to the kitchen to put on the kettle. Chamomile tea will calm me down, she thought. As she waited for the kettle to boil, she relived the attack.

As Catherine said good night to Hal and continued down the hall to her office, Neil stepped in front of her. He insisted that she come to his office.

Reluctantly, Catherine followed him and sat down in the chair beside his desk. Dramatically, he dropped his papers and binder on the desk and slouched in his chair. Hands cupped in front of his face, he closed his eyes and took a deep breath. Catherine waited.

When he opened his eyes, he bellowed, "How dare you side with Hal when he's attacking me?"

"Neil, he wasn't attacking you. He was saying he

didn't feel comfortable talking about a confidential matter in public."

"Confidential matter? I suppose the student is always right with you."

"Neil, I don't even know the nature of the complaint, but even if I did..."

"Even if you did, I expect your loyalty."

"What does loyalty have to do with anything?" she asked, exasperated. "Neil, why don't we discuss this when you aren't so angry?"

Catherine's folded hands dropped to her sides, and she started to get up. Standing, she leaned over to reach for the doorknob, and Neil groped her from behind, running his hands over her buttocks and caressing the inside of her thighs. Removing his hands abruptly, he turned her back to face him.

His face was red. Scowling, he pushed her back into the chair. His right hand groped the inside of her right thigh. The expression on his face softened as his hand moved further, grazing the left thigh as well. His fingers kneaded her flesh, and she was unable to move.

"We need to work together." He moved his hand to her face and stroked her cheek. "You do understand, don't you?" Before Catherine could respond, he towered over her and began to kiss her. She pulled away, her nails scratching his cheek.

"You bitch," she heard him say as she ran out of the office. Fortunately, everyone had left for the day. She grabbed her purse and keys from her desk and hurried to her car.

The whistling tea kettle brought her back to the present. She sipped the scalding tea, unable to process what she should do.

6:00 a.m. No sense trying to get back to sleep. She showered, obsessively washing the space under her nails where she had gouged his face. This must stop, she said aloud, rubbing her fingers with a moist towel. She dressed quickly and was in the office by 7:00.

Hal saw her door slightly ajar and knocked gently. "May I join you?"

Catherine smiled and gestured for Hal to sit on the loveseat while she took the chair.

"Catherine, I'm sorry about what happened yesterday with Neil after the faculty meeting," Hal said, his fists clenched, pushing against his thighs. "He was dismissive of Sarah's concern when I spoke with him earlier. Then, to make a joke of it."

Catherine felt a sense of relief as she listened to Hal. She wanted to tell him about what had happened with Neil, but she hesitated. Her stomach was in knots. She hadn't eaten since lunch yesterday.

"Hal, I don't know the nature of the student's complaint," she said, deciding to focus on something she could handle.

"Well, she was accosted by a faculty member, one of her professors, and he was drunk at the time. I'm going to be able to solve the immediate situation and get her into another section, but beyond that, I feel like my hands are tied. This professor is being protected by his chair.

"I'm a dean for God's sake," Hal said forcefully, then paused as if in retreat. "You and I should be telling Neil what needs to be done. If Neil doesn't care, the College should care and be worried about a lawsuit or bad publicity."

Catherine was startled by Hal's anger, and she waited for him to continue. When he didn't, she said, "Hal, there's more. Yesterday, after you left, Neil insisted I join him in his office." She spoke slowly, never losing eye contact with Hal. She omitted nothing, anger seething beneath her quiet, controlled voice.

"I'm going to schedule an appointment with Roslyn. This has to stop." Catherine's eyes dropped to her coffee, and she lifted the mug to her lips with shaking hands.

"Catherine, I don't know if it'll help," Hal said, his voice calmer than before.

"What do you mean?" Catherine asked, thinking about what had happened to Chelsea.

Hal told her the story about his predecessor, Nicole, a woman who had done groundbreaking work as a clinical psychologist while she was teaching at the University of Chicago. She worked with the faculty to develop a new Ph.D. in Psychology which she accomplished within eight months of arriving at the College.

"I was told at my interview that she received a more prestigious deanship at U. C. Davis. That was true. I never understood how Franklin attracted her in the first place. I didn't find out until after I was here that she left because of problems with Neil."

"But she didn't report to Neil? What kind of problems?" Catherine asked.

Hal hesitated. "Catherine, my source is someone I respect, and I can't break their confidence. She left because of Neil, and Roslyn would do nothing to help her. What happened to her is wrong, but no one was willing to rock the boat and take on Neil."

Why was protecting Neil so important? What was he

doing to move the College ahead? Nicole had launched a new graduate program, something the College needed to support its strategic plan and generate revenue. Why would Roslyn tolerate this?

"Does Steve know what happened?"

"I assume he does, but I can't say for sure."

Well, you should know, she thought.

"Catherine, you shouldn't let this go, but please think a little longer before you talk with Roslyn. I'm not giving you the best answer, but it's the only one I have now."

"Hal, this isn't right. The situation with Sarah shouldn't have happened. If it happened to me, to your predecessor, and to Sarah, this is a pattern." Catherine's voice trailed off.

"Yes, you're right. I'd like to see Neil disciplined for what he's done, but I think the best thing you can do now is protect yourself."

Anger and total humiliation were overwhelming Catherine. Protect herself? What kind of fucked-up situation is this? But this was also the advice she'd given Chelsea. Protect yourself. Be on record with the President of the Faculty Senate. Isn't that what she had done all her life? She'd protected herself when no one else would, not her mother, not her father.

Chapter Eighteen

Catherine spent the weekend before Fall Break with her father in Spring Lake. She said little to him about her planned trip to New England with Philip. The incident with Neil made her squeamish about being involved with anyone right now, especially someone with ties to the College. She considered canceling, but then she'd need to explain. She wasn't ready for that.

Philip was out of town during the week, but he called often, asking how things were going among her colleagues at Franklin. Catherine enjoyed his stories about his clients and his travels each week to one of his port cities. He respected her need to spend time with her father on the weekends, so he tried to be back in Philadelphia by Thursday evening so they could have one night together.

The more she saw Philip, the more she missed Peter. Philip was a good date, good company, but she missed the intimacy she had with Peter, an intimacy with a future.

Her father's heart was breaking with the news of

Uncle Ray's death.

"I loved Uncle Ray," Catherine said, wiping the tears from her cheek. "Remember when mother was too drunk to come to my graduation party? He came with you. He made me forget how angry I was at her."

"I remember," Douglas said with a smile. "He was the best friend a man ever had."

I can't imagine how lonely my father must feel, Catherine thought as she walked on the beach Saturday morning after breakfast. Her father and Uncle Ray talked to each other every week and, sometimes, met at a diner halfway between Spring Lake and Princeton for lunch. Their lunch meetings had stopped after Douglas's heart surgery, but Ray called faithfully and talked with her father on the phone.

The surf was rough, and Catherine stopped to watch a lone surfer fight hard to catch a wave and ride it to shore.

The incident with Neil flashed in front of her. She'd never felt such fear, revulsion, like a trapped animal. She knelt in the sand, clutching her thighs, remembering where he had touched her. She placed her hands in the shallow water rolling in gently. "I wish I could wash the whole thing out of my mind," she said out loud. "Wash it all away."

She picked up several shells and, standing, threw one as far as she could into the turbulent ocean.

She wanted to go back to New Hampshire, back to Peter. Childlike, she wanted to run away and live a different story.

There was more to Catherine's relationship with Peter than the romantic times at Lake Sunapee, the crazy sex in unexpected places. Peter understood her tortured relationship with her mother. She told him about the night her mother's diamond had scratched her face.

"But honey, that can't be your fault," Peter said, sitting across from her in the tiny living room, their first apartment. "There may be things buried deep inside of her that she can't comprehend, so she lashes out at you."

"Maybe there's something about me," Catherine said with a wan smile. She needed to talk to her mother and ask questions about her story.

Peter and Catherine had done a lot of hiking when they first were together. Every weekend a new adventure. He'd select the park, and she'd book the inn. But most of the time, after a day of hiking, happy hour became their evening. She'd leave him in the bar and go find dinner on her own.

Peter was sober the entire year that she worked to get tenure at Somerset. The preparation kept her working late into the night. Peter never disturbed her, but he'd offer conversation or a walk in the neighborhood when she needed a break.

A couple weeks before the tenure review, she came home later than usual. Peter was in the living room, reading. A heavenly aroma greeted her as soon as she entered the apartment. Lamb pot roast, one of Peter's favorites.

"What's your secret?" she asked as she sipped the red wine he poured and waited expectantly as he served the pot roast. "You seem so content."

"I have you," he said, spearing a carrot and placing it in his mouth. Their life had a rhythm. Teaching, writing, mentoring students. They talked about buying a house and

making New Hampshire home.

The day she got tenure, Peter took her to their favorite Italian restaurant. As they worked their way through appetizers and salads, he took a small oblong box, wrapped in emerald green paper, from his coat pocket.

"A necklace? Gloves?" she guessed, before unwrapping the box carefully.

"No," he said, patiently waiting for her to open it. Her face fell as she removed an ad from a magazine.

"Dublin. Wicklow. Sligo," she said, recognizing the landscape she knew well. Peter had it all planned: a few days in Dublin, then south to Wicklow and west to Galway and Sligo.

Catherine promised herself she would talk to her mother before the trip. They went to Spring Lake for Easter, arriving in time to attend the Maundy Thursday Service at her father's church. The silence and darkness of the Service gave way to bright lights and sirens screeching in front of her parents' house. Dish towels and potholders were ablaze on the burners when the fire trucks arrived. Her mother giggled, "I've never liked a gas stove."

Douglas put his wife to bed while Catherine and Peter opened all the windows to let the smoke clear.

"I'll still try to talk with her tomorrow," Catherine told Peter as she snuggled under the covers and Peter slipped his arm around her waist. "What story can my mother possibly tell me that explains this nightmare?"

The weekend was part disaster, part resignation. Peter and Catherine came back from a walk on the beach Friday morning to find Douglas pacing in the living room.

"She's gone to her sister's for the weekend," Douglas said, shaking his head. He sat down, studying his hands in *his lap as if they might reveal an answer.*

How can this possibly be about me? Catherine thought. *She remembered the therapy sessions where she described feeling unprotected from her mother's rages.*

"I don't want to blame my father," she had said.

"No need for blame," the therapist offered. "You're not your father. You can be conscious of how you'll do things differently."

Catherine stood in the doorway, looking first at her father and then at Peter.

"I've made so many mistakes, Catherine," Douglas said. "Your mother has felt betrayed at every turn."

"But what about Catherine?" Peter asked, sitting down across from Douglas. "Why this weekend?"

Peter's standing up for her, the way she always wanted her father to take her part.

"She never wanted me to become a priest," Douglas said. "When I felt the call to ministry, we were estranged. I thought the marriage was over, so I never talked with Elizabeth about why my change in direction was so important to me. Holy days like Easter are triggers. Her anger erupts. The drinking starts."

Catherine knew her father was defeated. When the wall went up with her mother, there was no getting around it.

Estranged. She'd never heard this before.

The rest of the spring semester flew by. Catherine won the Lindback Award for Teaching Excellence and finished the revisions for her second book.

They spent three days in Dublin, walking the bustling

streets and talking with strangers in pubs about music and literature.

"Would you ever find a middle-aged guy in an American bar who knew anything about Yeats or Robert Frost or Philip Roth?" Peter asked one night as they walked back to their bed & breakfast.

"The key to the mystery is simple: the Irish still read the primary texts. They read the same books in school, so kids grow up knowing Ireland's story," Catherine said.

"Do you think we'll be good parents?" Peter asked on the next leg of their trip as they stopped to eat lunch at the top of Sugar Loaf Mountain.

"Yes," Catherine said, her heart stirring until open.

"That's all you got? Just 'yes'?" Peter asked.

Catherine reached over and kissed him before she got up and walked to the edge, taking in the green and beige tapestry below, the dappled rockface. She'd be a parent like her Nana, always with a story to tell. Gentle, like her father.

The rainy drive to the Burren area was relaxing. They skipped the walk Catherine had planned and stopped for lunch at the Manley Hopkins Tavern. "He was exiled in Ireland because he preached some heresy the church didn't like," Catherine said.

"Poor man," Peter said, lifting his pint of Guinness. "To your father and his love of a good poem."

"Let's get a walk in before dinner," Catherine said as they checked in at BallyVaughan. They joined a small tour with Sean, a young cattle farmer as guide.

"My grandfather was a cattle farmer," Sean explained. "The way the British parceled off the land, that's all you could do with it." He described long days and nights in the

spring, birthing calves. Still wet from the day's rain, the lush green moss carpet glistened beneath limestone slabs. Tiny wildflowers grew from the fissures in the limestone, light purple Bloody Granesbill, yellow horny rock rose, and blue gentian.

"I want to hike to the top of Abby Hill," Catherine told Sean as the tour ended.

"6:00 a.m. I'll meet you at the Inn," Sean said.

"6:00 a.m.?" Peter asked in disbelief.

"If we make it 5:00, we might see a sunrise," Sean said, turning to Catherine. "Ten pounds. If he comes along, it'll be fifteen."

"Wonderful," Catherine said. "We'll see you at 5:00."

Already light, the sun moved slowly through the cloud cover. The steep climb was under a mile. Catherine breathed in the chilly air as if it was the only oxygen left on earth. The Burren area was a checkered board of greens and browns, while Galway Bay unfolded in deep blues.

"If you look this way," Sean indicated, "you can see where Lady Gregory's Coole Park used to stand."

"Yeats's friend and patron," Catherine offered to Peter. "With a little imagination, we can see the 'nine-and-fifty swans' on the lake." Catherine tried not to dwell on the lone swan, all the others paired off. She loved Peter, but she wasn't sure about mating for life. Her father did, and he's more like the lonely swan, enduring a wife who was never companionable.

"Can you give us a verse or two?" Peter asked in his best Irish brogue.

Needing no further encouragement, Sean began:

The trees are in their autumn beauty,
The woodland paths are dry,
Under the October twilight the water
Mirrors a still sky;
Upon the brimming water among the stones
Are nine-and-fifty swans.

Unwearied still, lover by lover,
They paddle in the cold
Companionable streams or climb the air;
Their hearts have not grown old;
Passion or conquest, wander where they will,
Attend upon them still.

Catherine added her voice to the last verse.

But now they drift on the still water,
Mysterious, beautiful;
Among what rushes will they build,
By what lake's edge or pool
Delight men's eyes when I awake some day
To find they have flown away?

"What were you thinking about when we were on Abbey Hill?" Peter asked as they started the journey to Sligo.

"My father," Catherine answered, glad Peter asked. "My sister and I had a childhood because he was there for us. That scene Easter weekend, fire trucks and all, is his reality. He's not responsible for her behavior, but he lives like he is."

"You can't change it or let it impact the choices you

make," Peter said, glancing at Catherine before he turned his attention to a sharp turn in the road.

"I love you," she said, smiling as she pulled the map of Ben Bulben out of her knapsack. "Are you sure we can do this hike without a guide?"

"Scout's honor," he said.

They started the climb on the mountain's southside. Clouds obscured the peak. They hiked in silence, following the stream, steady breath, rhythm to the gentle rain. The rain stopped before they reached the top, and a slender rainbow was visible over Donegal Bay.

"Yeats came to Sligo as a little boy to visit his grandparents. He kept all this beauty alive in his imagination, believing it was part of his story," Catherine said, wanting the moment to last.

Catherine fingered the shells in her hand. She tossed one gently into the shallow water. Peter, her moment of happiness? She dropped the other shells in the pocket of her windbreaker and headed back to the house.

Chapter Nineteen

Douglas heard Catherine pull the front door shut. A strong wind was coming off the ocean, rattling the shades and curtains in the sunroom. Filling his coffee cup in the kitchen, he paused to take a few sips before walking through the living room, stopping to look at photographs of Catherine and Caroline.

Struggling with the lock, Douglas opened the front door, holding his cup with a shaky left hand. The screen door slowly closed behind him. He reached the railing on the corner of the porch facing the ocean. Coffee splashed, beige against white, as he placed the cup on the railing. The air was moist and cool.

"Rest in peace Ray," Douglas said, eyes opening and closing, tears streaming down his wrinkled cheeks. "May eternal light shine on you." Douglas sipped the hot coffee and strained to see the waves he heard pounding on the shore.

Ray introduced Douglas to Elizabeth. She was

Rosemary's friend. Both Bryn Mawr girls. Best friends, moving in packs as though they were identical twins. But they weren't alike. Rosemary was loud and gregarious with a voluptuous body that spoke a language all its own.

"I could never be like Rosemary," Elizabeth had confided early in their relationship, "but I love her energy. She doesn't seem to care what other people think, but everyone in our class loves her." Ray loved her too.

"Doug," he said. Ray was the only one who ever called him Doug. "She makes me feel like I'm the only one."

"You are the only one right now," Douglas said laughing too hard one early morning after a mixer. "I thought nice girls didn't put out?" Douglas said as Ray described what had just happened with Rosemary.

"They don't," he said, "unless they're sure, and she's sure about me. I have the ring, and I'm asking her tomorrow night."

Ray slid into marriage and claimed nothing changed. She always wanted sex. She always wanted him until one day Ray came home from a business trip and found her in bed, their bed, with another man. He never told Douglas who it was, but Ray cried like a baby, and Rosemary promised she'd never see the man again.

When Douglas told Ray about Grace several weeks after he met her, Ray told him it was just infatuation.

"How do you know that?" Douglas asked, wanting him to listen even if he didn't understand.

"She's beautiful, idealistic. You can't build a life with a woman like that, a life with children," Ray had responded.

Why did Douglas listen to him? Ray's own marriage

was fragile, sewn together with horrible fights followed by passionate sex.

Ray knew Rosemary had been unfaithful many times. The wound went deep, but he loved her. He couldn't make sense of life without her.

Douglas moved to the rocking chair and settled himself on the edge of the seat, feet nailed to the porch floor. Ray got him through the depression after the heart surgery by simply telling him every day, "Hey, Doug, you won't feel like this forever."

Marriage to Rosemary was forever despite its flaws, a forever he wanted. He never understood why Douglas didn't feel the same about his marriage.

A gust of wind caught the screen door. That lock doesn't catch, Douglas thought, beginning to get up and then thinking better of it. His hands weren't steady enough anymore to hold a screwdriver. The wind caught the screen door again, and Douglas breathed in the cool, salt air.

Douglas shifted on his chair and reached for the coffee cup. The saucer slipped off the railing. Looking toward the ocean, Douglas's mind wandered back to 1974.

Douglas slid onto a stool next to Ray and shouted to the bartender for a double scotch. Six years older than Douglas, Ray still had a boyish face and piercing blue eyes. Success with the business kept his spirits high. Fights with Rosemary were only temporary setbacks.

"Doug, it's pathetic that Grace has held onto you for so long." Douglas hadn't mentioned her since she'd written him in January and told him about the breast cancer. Ray

had seemed unconcerned. "She'll get good care," he'd said dismissively. "She's in Boston, and I'm sure family is looking after her." This morning when they scheduled lunch, Douglas told Ray he'd had another letter from Grace, the first one in almost a year.

Douglas didn't let Ray interrupt him until he'd told him about the letter. "She talked about Advent, the Advent we spent together. I had said something to her about God breaking into history." The crowded bar was noisy, but Douglas knew Ray could hear him. He looked at his friend, holding his gaze, as he told him about the letter.

"She remembered the sunrise on Cadillac Mountain... our time together in '68... a tiny sun in the vast, cloudy sky." Douglas hesitated but then went on. "She was writing to tell me it would be her last letter."

Ray seemed unsympathetic. He finished his scotch and ordered another. "Maybe she's finally met someone, come to her senses, and will settle down. It may not be too late. Children may still be possible."

Pathetic... He didn't know Grace, but Douglas had listened to him.

Come to her senses... Ray liked that phrase, but what makes sense about living with a woman like Rosemary who implied you're not enough? What made sense to stay with a woman like Elizabeth who preferred vodka and valium to love and companionship?

The wind off the ocean was too cold, so Douglas went inside and sat down at his desk. Catherine will be back soon, he thought.

Opening the top drawer, Douglas removed the letter from the envelope. It had arrived the day after Ray's death. He read it again slowly.

September 7, 2004

Dear Doug:

Men aren't very good at friendship. We move through life, still scared little boys, afraid we won't be good enough at business, marriage, being a parent.

You, Doug, were always good at friendship. You listened to me. I didn't listen to you when you told me about Grace. I wanted you to be like me, making a marriage successful against all odds.

I'm sorry, Doug. I never understood what you knew about following your heart, real passion.

I've left my daughter a successful business, enough money so she'll never want for anything. I could never tell her I failed with her mother. I was never enough for Rosemary.

Ray

"Rest in peace, my friend," Douglas said as he tore the letter into tiny pieces and threw them into a bag for recycled paper. "Your story lives and dies with me."

Chapter Twenty

Catherine landed in Boston as a severe thunderstorm dumped torrential rain on the city. It was teeming when the taxi pulled up in front of the centuries-old Charles Street Inn. Philip had some work to do with the manager of his Boston office and told Catherine he would meet her at the Inn.

"Mrs. Reynolds, welcome to the Charles Street Inn," the slender man with dark-rimmed glasses at Registration said with a smile. Catherine saw no reason to correct him and followed the bellhop to a room with a canopy bed and fireplace. On the coffee table in front of the fireplace was a bottle of wine on ice and a tray of cheese, crackers, and fruit. A card by the wine read, "I can't wait to see you, my love."

"Madam, can I get you anything else?" the bellhop asked, stiff as a soldier with his hands in his pockets.

"No," Catherine said as she struggled to pull some bills from her purse. "Thank you."

Catherine opened her suitcase on the small rack, undressed, and showered. Settling into the terry cloth robe she found on the back of the bathroom door, she moved to the window as the storm became more intense. After a few minutes, she jumped back as lightning lit up the dark, afternoon sky. She sat down on the couch in front of the fire. Ticking off the things she enjoyed about Philip, she came up short. She'd taken Peter home to meet her father within weeks of their first date. She would have told Peter about Neil. She'd have to tell Philip if the relationship continued, but for now, she'd enjoy her time with him and not think about what happened with Neil.

She went into the bathroom to apply some make-up, but before she could dress, she heard Philip at the door.

Despite his trench coat and umbrella, Philip was drenched. Catherine snuggled into his arms and kissed him lightly on the lips.

"You'll get wet," he said, pushing her away gently. He dropped the umbrella on the floor and laid the coat on the edge of the couch.

"I'd suggest a hot bath," Catherine said, unbuttoning his shirt, "but never in a thunderstorm."

"Never," he said, kissing her neck and moving her toward the king-size canopy. "Making love during a thunderstorm is another matter."

Catherine let the robe drop to the floor. Kneeling on the bed, she undressed Philip as his eyes caressed her body.

Oranges, reds, gold, a lot of gold laced the trees as Catherine wound the Z4 around the coast road. Philip kept the little sports car in the garage adjacent to his Boston office.

"Slow down," Philip warned. "You'll get a ticket."

"I can afford it," she said, playfully running the fingers of her free hand over his thigh.

"Both hands on the wheel," he scolded.

"Now who do you think you are?" she yelled against the wind. "My father. No. My father's more fun. He's the one who taught me how to drive like this."

She slowed to a yellow, then red light. Red to green, she drove through the intersection and pulled over.

"Where're we going?" he asked, relief in his voice that she'd stopped.

"This is a bookstore I like." The sign above the door read "Left Bank." He followed her in, and they went their separate ways, he to fiction, she to "Local Interest."

She leafed through a book filled with photographs of Acadia National Park and Bar Harbor and came upon a photo of Jordan Pond.

"What did you find?" Philip asked, hugging her from behind and looking over her shoulder.

"A memory. When I was little, my father took me to Bar Harbor. We hiked around this pond. I felt very grown-up. Daddy helped me over wet, slippery rocks. After a while, we stopped on a small stone bridge, and he took two apples from his knapsack. Red, shiny. He seemed so happy, telling me about another trip he'd taken to Maine." Catherine paused, and Philip waited for her to continue.

"What is it, Catherine?" Philip asked, cupping her chin in his hand. He kissed her cheek, still red from the sun and wind.

"I'm not sure," she said, hiccupping a bit. "Somehow, I just saw my father in a way I'd never seen him before."

His other trip to Maine was with a woman he loved, someone who made him feel alive, she thought, as she put the book back on the shelf.

Philip paid for the novels he'd found and grabbed the keys.

"I'm driving now," he said, opening the passenger's side for her. Once he shifted into fifth, Catherine took Philip's hand, remembering her father's hands that day at Jordan Pond. Large, strong hands, lifting her before she slipped on wet rocks. Gentle hands around her shoulders as they watched the boats in Bar Harbor. She remembered the look in his eyes that night. He seemed far away, or maybe he was right there with his arm around someone else.

Dusk was settling on Bar Harbor as they turned off Route 3 onto Mount Desert Road.

"Philip, let's go to the harbor before we check in. I want to see the boats before it gets dark."

They parked the car on West Avenue, strolled up the grassy knoll, and found an empty bench. Arms around each other's shoulders, they watched the lobster boats and sailboats bobbing on the water until dusk settled gently.

"Do you ever think about marriage?" Philip asked, caressing her shoulder.

"All women think about marriage," she said evasively, stroking his cheek. As soon as the words were spoken, she regretted them. You should have just said yes, she thought, breathing in the silence.

"I wasn't asking all women," he said as he stood and reached for her hand.

Chapter Twenty-One

Anxious to get an early start on the day, Hal got to the office two hours before his scheduled meeting with Stephanie Winthrop. He had been away at college when Stephanie started at his mother's law firm as an intern. She planned to accept a position at the ACLU. Once she got started, though, she had become interested in the work his mother was doing and stayed on at the firm when she was offered a permanent position.

When Stephanie arrived, they talked easily. Her Boston accent made him long for home.

"My grandfather retired from the firm in 1964, the year your mother was hired. He admired her commitment to social justice, but he also saw her as the future of the firm. I told him when I was nine that I wanted to be a lawyer. That's when he started telling me stories about your mother's work."

"My mother loved working with the interns. She took to you from the beginning. The redheaded firebrand with spunk," Hal said warmly.

Stephanie blushed, crimson rising on her cheeks and neck. "I took John McKenzie's place when he retired."

"I never knew McKenzie and the notorious wife," Hal said, shaking his head.

"Mary McKenzie, the lush with an opinion about everyone," Stephanie said, laughing.

"I would sit at the top of the steps and eavesdrop on my mother's conversations with Uncle Vince," Hal said. "She did a wicked imitation of McKenzie. She saw him as a pawn with whiplash, sucking up to Paul Eliot but sympathetic to Thornton."

"Thornton," Stephanie said with a sigh. "He was marrying his fourth wife when I started as an intern in '83. I can't tell you how many times he hit on me. 'Gender discrimination,' your mother would quip. 'I'm John Thornton. I never discriminate against anything female and still moving.'"

"Sounds like my mother," Hal said. "How's Vince doing?" he added, thinking he should plan some time in Boston and visit him. He stayed in touch by email, but he hadn't seen Vince since Tina's funeral.

"Still going strong. He talks about retirement, but I don't expect that to happen any time soon." Stephanie's speech slowed as she talked about her sense of loss when Hal's mother died. Vince stepped in and provided the support she needed.

"Hal, I learned many things from your mother, but here's the most important. She loved you more than anyone else in her life, but she was married to her work. She was discouraged by the loss of civil liberties during the 1980s and wanted to live to see some of those decisions reversed."

"Yes, I know," Hal said pensively. "I'm sorry to say, though, that even if she had lived longer, she would have been disappointed."

Hal described his three years at Franklin trying to get colleagues in Political Science and History to incorporate some of his work on the Civil Rights Movement and the issue of gender discrimination in the workplace into appropriate courses. He had limited success. A year ago, he had finally received some funding to sponsor a lectureship that explored the Civil Rights Movement's impact on gender discrimination legislation, but it was poorly attended.

Stephanie leaned in, lips pursed, as Hal continued to talk about the lecture series that had not gone well. Even the President was openly hostile to the initiative.

"I came here as a tenured associate professor, and my department chair believed my research was worthy of promotion to full professor, but the tenure committee denied my promotion."

"Hal, there's something I need to tell you that is about your mother's work but also about your own." Stephanie hesitated. She looked toward the pictures on Hal's bookcase before saying more.

Hal said nothing and waited for Stephanie to continue.

She spoke softly, relaying the story as if she was hearing it for the first time.

"Roslyn Ashcroft was the victim of sexual harassment and changing politics at Franklin in the 1970s," Stephanie said. "She was denied tenure, the committee claiming that her teaching as well as her research was inadequate. There was a way, though, for her to get tenure: her academic department chair, Robert DiVos, was willing to fight for her if she would sleep with him. She refused."

"How do you know this?" Hal asked, listening intently.

Stephanie got up and walked to the bookcase. She picked up the photograph of Hal's mother holding baby Hal. Hal followed her with his eyes, finding it incredulous that his mother's work could be this connected to his life at Franklin. His mother knew Roslyn?

"Your mother was a beautiful woman," Stephanie said, looking at Hal and then back at the picture. "The cancer took such a toll on her." She placed the picture on the bookcase and sat down again, crossing her legs and leaning in closer to Hal.

"Roslyn was my mother's contemporary. It's hard for me to picture her as a young woman, so vulnerable. To most of us now, she seems made of steel," Hal said.

"This situation with her department chair may have made her that way," Stephanie said thoughtfully. "President Corbett recommended that Roslyn take a year away from the College, and he promised that when she returned, he would give her an administrative position."

"How do you know all this?" Hal asked again, brow furrowed, hands nervously rubbing his trousers.

"Your mother befriended Roslyn when she worked at the law firm as a research assistant. She and Roslyn had a lot in common in the 1970s. Both were pioneers in professions where women hadn't gone before. Roslyn's research as an anthropologist was groundbreaking, so from what your mother shared with me, the tenure committee's judgment wasn't sound.

"As Roslyn told your mother her story, she became convinced that your mother could win a lawsuit for her."

"What happened? Why didn't she go ahead with the lawsuit?" Hal asked.

"President Corbett convinced Roslyn that the lawsuit would hurt her, and it would destroy the reputation of the College. He promised her not only the job as his assistant but told her he would make her Acting Dean when the Dean retired."

"But that makes no sense," Hal said, shaking his head. "A faculty member who fails to get tenure would never have the respect of the rest of the faculty."

"Well, that's the irony of the situation. The pretext for not giving Roslyn tenure was higher standards. When the President made her Acting Dean, and then Dean, there was some opposition from the faculty, but once they saw what an effective administrator and fundraiser she was, the complaints stopped."

Hal got up and paced the room. Stephanie sat quietly, shifting in her chair, uncrossing her legs.

"Hal, I'm aware of your research because I've followed your career. Your mother would be so proud of your work."

"And Roslyn may not want me to pursue this work," Hal said tersely.

"I don't know that, but I thought you should be aware of her history. There is something else I want to share with you." Stephanie pulled a file and a small spiral notebook from her briefcase.

"Did you know your mother was a writer?" Stephanie asked with a smile.

Hal looked surprised; then, a smile crossed his face.

"Well, she did make up stories for me when I was little. Does that count?"

Stephanie smiled. "Yes. It counts. Two of those stories were published by Harper & Row."

"You're kidding," Hal said. "Why didn't I know?"

"Your mother used a pen name. She didn't think writing children's stories complemented her image as a tough litigator. Anyway, she also was writing about the women who were telling her their stories about sexual harassment. I don't think she ever intended to publish it in any form, but I wanted you to have what she wrote. If you continue to work on oral histories, some of these stories may be of interest to you."

Hal picked up the small spiral-bound notebook and opened it randomly. His mother's small, precise printing covered each page. He ran his fingers over them lovingly. Tucked in the back were several onion-skinned white sheets. Hal smiled as he looked at the typed sheets, remembering his mother's Smith Corona, one of the first electronic typewriters with memory. Without reading a word, Hal looked at each sheet. Hand-written notes covered the margins, sometimes a word to edit or a question that might expand the text.

"I think you'll see as you read this, your mother was reflecting on these stories in light of her own life," Stephanie said. "She was a brilliant, ambitious woman working in a profession where women weren't welcome. Your mother understood the pain these women felt."

Hal closed the notebook and turned to Stephanie. "I can't thank you enough for sharing this with me. What cases are you working on now?"

Stephanie described two sexual harassment cases,

one in the corporate sector and one at a college. Then, she added, "You may be aware of the lawsuit brought against Franklin several years ago. While drunk, a professor sexually assaulted a female student. The College quickly settled a lawsuit in arbitration so no harm would come to the College. The professor's still here."

Hal shook his head in disbelief. Sarah's not the first victim of Jason's inappropriate advances, he thought. I've had my head in the sand. I learned this from someone outside the College. He looked at Stephanie, hoping she could say something that would ease the tightness in his chest.

"I don't mean to sound pessimistic," she said, looking at Hal cautiously, "but in an environment where this type of sexual harassment goes unchecked, there are often more subtle forms of discrimination against women. Are women treated differently than men because they are women? If women are hired at all for important posts, do they get promoted and paid at the same rate as men? Unfortunately, it is hard to prove in a court of law, so most gender discrimination goes unchecked."

Hal was lost in thought... Sarah and the way Neil had talked about her. Jason was still here, protected while students suffered... Catherine and what Neil had done to her.

"I must get into the City for a noon meeting," Stephanie said, getting up and extending her hand to Hal. "Let's plan to stay in touch. I hope you will continue with your research even if you don't benefit from it while you are at Franklin."

Hal closed his door after Stephanie left, shutting out the noise in the busy hallway. He placed the file and the notebook in his briefcase. Joyce was at lunch. He sent her an email saying he would be working at home in the afternoon if she needed him for anything.

Chapter Twenty-Two

Hal dropped his keys on the kitchen counter and took tuna salad out of the refrigerator. He dropped the tuna salad on pita bread, topping it with lettuce and tomato.

Seating himself at the kitchen table, he took a bite of the sandwich before he opened the notebook. He leafed through several pages. One note made him linger longer than the others. It read, "I had never seen anyone so devastated by the loss of a job. No. It wasn't just a job to Roslyn. Her life was research and teaching. Life as she knew it had been destroyed."

He scanned the pages until he saw Roslyn Ashcroft's name several times throughout the pages. His mother knew Roslyn. How is this possible?

Hal reached for a Snapple in the refrigerator and popped off the cap. He read the notebook carefully, cover to cover, not always comprehending all the legal terms and abbreviations. His mother had recorded seven meetings she had with Roslyn in 1974. She had captured the rage

Roslyn felt about what had happened to her in the tenure process, but she also showed Roslyn's fear, her ambivalence about bringing the lawsuit against the College.

Hal took the last bite of his sandwich. Opening the notebook again, he began reading the entries about Roslyn.

February 1, 1974

I was unrealistic about the recovery time after the breast cancer surgery. Three weeks, not one. I reviewed resumes for the research assistant while I was recovering, and Vince interviewed candidates. Roslyn Ashcroft is the new research assistant. She's on leave from a college in Philadelphia. Ph.D. in Anthropology with a paralegal certificate. Three summers working in a law firm. She comes three days a week and has a tremendous capacity to read and synthesize information.

Roslyn will be with us for a year supporting the new gender discrimination cases. Two days into the research on one case—a twenty-seven-year-old plaintiff, allegedly raped by her boss, a prominent banker in Boston—I asked Roslyn questions about the materials she had prepared.

"This is good work," I told her, offering her a cup of coffee as we talked. She relaxed a bit as she sipped her coffee, thinking about my last question. I'd never seen her smile, and her dark expressive eyes seemed sad and guarded. As we discussed the specifics of the case, she shook her head and asked, "Is this everywhere? Are these women believable?" She didn't seem to want an answer. Her mind seemed to be racing. I wanted to hear what she would say next.

She told me what had happened when she got home to Boston. She took a job as a sales clerk at Filene's Basement. She had only been there a few days when her manager pinned her against the wall and started to grope her. She fought him and kneed him in the groin to get free. She never went back.

"I think it is everywhere," I said, seeing the fear and the confusion on her face. "That's why we're working so hard to establish precedents for situations like this so women aren't victimized, don't lose their jobs."

Roslyn shook her head, and we were silent for a moment before returning to the work.

Hal leafed through several entries before he found the next one about Roslyn.

March 6, 1974

I invited Roslyn to have lunch with me. Wind gusts swirled through light snow as we walked around Faneuil Hall before we settled in at a small sandwich shop. Roslyn always seemed so troubled that I didn't want to ask about anything personal. She only seemed comfortable when we talked about work, but I found a way in when I asked her about her work as an anthropologist. Her eyes softened and shoulders relaxed as she talked about her fieldwork in the Congo, Columbia, and Jamaica.

"There was such freedom," she said, "working outside, working with people who weren't asking you to be something you didn't want to be."

"I can only imagine," I said. "My mother sent me to Bryn Mawr so I could be ready for Philadelphia Society."

"Of course," Roslyn said, eyes flashing with anger, "because the only worthy vocation for a woman is marriage."

"So, you had a mother like mine?" I asked.

"I don't know," Roslyn said, looking down at her sandwich. "I was raised by a stepmother. My mother left my father when I was little." I was stunned by this comment. Women like my mother didn't leave a marriage. She couldn't afford to walk away from financial security no matter how bad things were with my father. Before I could think about asking another question, Roslyn went on.

"My stepmother thinks all my years doing research were wasted." Her hands trembled as she lifted her coffee cup and picked at her sandwich. She described Christmas with her father and stepmother.

After the dinner guests left on Christmas, Roslyn and her father settled in the living room. They had helped clean up the kitchen, and once finished, her stepmother went upstairs to change her clothes.

Her father assured her that she was welcome to stay as long as she wished, but the moment of calm was shattered when her stepmother came into the living room and said, "Don't encourage her, Donald. She needs to come to her senses. I'm sure a good secondary school might take her, and it's not too late yet to find a husband." Roslyn mimicked her stepmother, free of anxiety for a moment.

"I can take you to my hairdresser," she continued, placing her hands on her hips and looking stern. "Get a haircut that makes you more attractive... and a manicure. You're thin enough that you can buy some tailored skirts. They'll accentuate your legs.

"I can help you with all this now, but in another year or two, it'll be too late." After she mocked her stepmother's defeated look, we both had a hearty laugh.

"When I was sixteen, I came home and told my father I wanted to be an anthropologist like Margaret Meade. I told him about my teacher in History who talked about Meade's research. My stepmother was in the kitchen, getting ready to serve dinner. Before I could finish, the kitchen door swung open, and my stepmother slammed the casserole dish down on the wooden trivet. Bubbling creamy sauce over chicken splattered on the tablecloth and splattered on my hand. I jumped back and wiped my hand with the linen napkin.

"Where do you get these ideas?" she screamed at me.

"My father started to answer, not seeming to comprehend her tone and her attitude toward me. "Her History teacher, dear."

"What kind of nonsense are these children learning?" her stepmother asked, incredulous. "Margaret Meade shouldn't be discussed in History class. She has outrageous ideas about childrearing. She's a freak... three husbands, acts like a man. Is that how you want to end up? If you won't talk some sense into her, Donald, I will." Roslyn's sense of humor surfaced as she mimicked her stepmother again, but the reserved demeanor returned as she finished the story.

"My mother and your stepmother have so much fear," I said.

"And so much control," Roslyn said. "I don't know why my father puts up with her. I told him I couldn't stay with them. I know it hurts him, but I had to stand up for myself."

"You did the right thing," I said signaling the waitress that I wanted the check.

Stephanie is right. This reads like an oral history. His mother captures how Roslyn feels, how she pushed against social norms. Hal scanned several entries about the Wentworth class-action lawsuit before he came to another entry about Roslyn.

March 9, 1974

Roslyn left a message this morning saying she wouldn't be in because she is ill. She said she'd make up the time another day. I called in the evening to see how she was doing. She said she'd seen a doctor and hoped to be back in the office the next day. I assured her that if she needed more time, she should take it.

April 1, 1974

Radiation. Mornings are difficult. I go in late if at all.

Last night, I was working in the office. Hal was staying overnight with a buddy, so I lost track of time. About eight o'clock, Roslyn came in to ask me some questions. She looked pale, skin drawn and eyes bloodshot.

"Are you feeling ill?" I asked.

"I didn't mean to be dishonest, but it wasn't a doctor. It's a therapist I'm seeing."

I assured her that this was fine, and she could tell me as little or as much as she wished. She sat down and started to talk. At first, she didn't look at me. Her voice was soft, unsure, but as the story unfolded, she became more confident, anger giving her words vitality. She told me about the tenure decision.

She said she couldn't move, couldn't process any of what was happening. Five years of graduate school... seven years of teaching and research... and for what? The decision was swift and cruel.

Her research was inadequate for tenure. All those years in the field... not adequate.

The dean told her that her teaching evaluations were negative. She hadn't engaged students. She was physically sick for three days, unable to handle any food.

Roslyn lifted her head and looked at me. She seemed to be searching for something in my face. Acceptance? Understanding?

Several weeks before the tenure decision, her department chair had made it clear to her that there was a way for her to get tenure. Roslyn's sense of humor returned as she described the department chair.

"A wizened man, he was," she croaked, the light returning to her eyes, "called me to his office a week before the tenure review. His hands crippled with arthritis, teeth yellowed by tobacco, he offered a simple proposition.

"Sleep with me, Roslyn," he said, rubbing his hands on his corduroy thighs. "I'll make the tenure vote go your way." She had refused. Repulsed by his proposition, she told a colleague in the History Department. Her colleague told her that he'd done this many times before, mostly to students. About a decade ago, a student got pregnant and left in the spring of her junior year. He wasn't even reprimanded, although his wife left him.

The president called her the day after the tenure decision and asked her to meet with him. He gave his condolences for the failed tenure bid.

She asked if he thought it was a fair evaluation. His reply was ambiguous.

"Yes and no," he answered, looking out the window, seeming reluctant to look at her. "Five years ago, you would have received tenure without a fuss, but the dean is pushing for higher standards, and frankly, student complaints have become more of an issue."

He suggested that she take a year off and told her he would make a place for her in his office as his assistant. He offered to make some calls for her about teaching opportunities.

She told him she was going to Boston to live with her father and would find some other kind of job for a while.

I got up and came around the desk to sit in the chair beside her. I told her she had a case. I'd help her in any way I could.

She nodded. "Working has helped," she said quietly. She said she had so much to process, to sort out.

I nodded and told her to talk with me again when she was ready.

Hal went to the refrigerator for another iced tea. It was hard for him to imagine Roslyn so young and vulnerable. His mother must have realized how fragile she was. Were they friends? Hal didn't remember his mother having friends. Tina had lots of girlfriends... met them for drinks or dinner. His mother never did, at least as far as he knew. She was always working and looking out for him.

Hal returned to the journal and found the next entry about Roslyn.

May 5, 1974

I invited Roslyn over for Sunday dinner. It's the one day of the week I made a nice dinner for Hal. Weekdays are always rushed if I get home for dinner at all. Most nights, Hannah cooks for him.

Despite Roslyn's reserve around me, she was warm and talkative with Hal. While I was getting the lamb and vegetables out of the oven, I heard Hal's laughter and his heavy tread on the steps.

"What's he up to?" I asked, placing the platter on the dining room table and inviting Roslyn into the dining room.

"He was talking about his Geography class," Roslyn said as Hal came into the living room and placed his Geography textbook on an end table.

"You two can look at that after dinner," I said, placing a plate of lamb, carrots, and onions in front of Roslyn. Without hesitating, Hal started to ask Roslyn questions. She patiently answered each one.

Hal vaguely remembered this. He didn't remember what he talked about with Roslyn, but he remembered she was smart like his mother and treated him like an adult.

May 25, 1974

Paul and Lucille Eliot offered me their cottage on the Cape for the Memorial Day weekend. I asked Roslyn if she would like to join us. She will on Saturday after she spends some time with her father.

Roslyn was missing all that was familiar to her. Her eyes were vacant and her gaze far away when she talked about leaving Philadelphia in December. She'd brought only what she needed for the Christmas holidays, packing everything else and leaving it in storage.

"It was unreal," she said. "Why did this happen to me? I

played by everyone else's rules... always the 'good girl' until the end. How could that ugly man—body odor and hacking smoker's cough—think any woman would want him to touch her? Maybe other women let him. Maybe they had encouraged it. They were tainted, but I wasn't."

I didn't want to interrupt her train of thought, but I was disturbed by her take on "other women." Where did this come from?

May 26, 1974

When Hal got up, I made a big breakfast... pancake, sausages, and eggs. Roslyn chatted with Hal about his schoolwork, his new interest in soccer. They left me to do some work while they walked on the beach, collecting shells.

Later in the day, Roslyn and I sat on the beach, bundled up against the cold wind coming off the ocean. Hal played catch with two other boys near the water's edge.

Roslyn was more talkative than usual. She seemed to have made some decisions about her life. I hoped she was going to talk to me about her case, but instead, she talked about her sessions with the therapist.

She paused and looked at me closely. She said the therapist helps sometimes, but he's also like her stepmother. "He wants to fix me. He thinks marriage will do the trick."

"You can get another therapist," I said, appalled that a professional was telling her this. "You have a case against the College. You can fight this."

I wanted to fill the empty space, to say something more, but what could I say?

"Too many gray areas," she said to me, looking at me appreciatively. "I'm not a crusader. I'll never change the world. President Corbett told me that a lawsuit will only hurt the College, and it won't change people like Bob DiVos."

"President Corbett is right about DiVos," I interjected, "but a lawsuit might deter another lech in the future."

Roslyn had made up her mind. I knew I couldn't do anything to persuade her.

Hal put the notebook down and looked out the kitchen window. Dusk spread across the sky, casting shadows on the trees in the backyard. This made sense. Roslyn came back to Franklin and played a different role. Protected by Corbett, she kept her distance from anyone who could hurt her or love her. Was this why she was so cold? People at the College talked about her, saying she didn't have any friends, but she was respected, even revered for her work as Dean and now as President.

Hal's mother had followed Roslyn's career. Newspaper clippings coincided with the notes on the last page of the notebook.

December 6, 1976: Corbett's Assistant Becomes Academic Dean at Franklin

April 4, 1978: President Corbett Dies; Dean Ashcroft Becomes Acting President

May 1, 1980: Presidential Search Committee Selects Ashcroft

Hal put on his running clothes and took a long jog around the neighborhood. This doesn't justify Roslyn's behavior, but it explains it. Roslyn bought into the system, a system that gives men power, no matter what. So much of his mother's work shows the ambiguities of these cases. Women who want to stand up for themselves are often labeled malcontents.

Hal needed to talk with Catherine and tell her Roslyn's story.

Chapter Twenty-Three

The Christmas party at the President's house was semi-formal, so Catherine wore a red silk dress with matching pumps. When Philip arrived at her house before the event, she already had her coat on, ready to leave.

"No time for a glass of wine?" he asked, kissing her gently on the lips.

"Not tonight. This is my first time dining at the President's house, and I understand that she wants all the trains to run on time." Roslyn had praised Catherine for the successful trip to Boston, giving her positive feedback she'd heard from alumni about her presentation and the warm connection she'd already made with the alumni chapter. Hal's comments about Roslyn not supporting Nicole were in the back of her mind, where she needed to leave them for now.

Philip parked across the street from Roslyn's house White candles burned in each window, and an eight-foot tree graced the foyer. The tree was decorated with old-fashioned ornaments—dolls, candy canes, bells, and miniature Santa Clauses. Roslyn greeted them at the door, wearing a black, knee-length dress. The jacket to the dress was trimmed with emerald-green sequins. Catherine was always amazed at how sexless Roslyn could look even in the feminine outfit she was wearing tonight. Normally, she wore suits—slender skirts, blouses buttoned to her throat, and tailored jackets that hid her thin torso. Her legs were lean and shapely, but any hint of sexuality was lost as the eye traveled to the heavy, orthopedic shoes. Tonight, though, she had on simple black pumps with a dainty strap.

She brushed Philip's cheek with a kiss. "It's always good to see you." Roslyn showed no sign of surprise that Catherine was with Philip and greeted her with a ceremonial embrace.

Roslyn moved to greet the next guest, and Catherine and Philip moved into the crowded living room.

A bar was set-up in the corner of the living room, and Hal moved slowly around groups of chatting colleagues to reach it and get a second glass of wine. Tina loved occasions like this, he thought, as he made small talk with the bartender. Getting dressed up and drinking someone else's wine always appealed to her.

Hmm. The pinot grigio was excellent... crisp with a hint of apple and pear. Hal loved fine wines and would often surprise Tina with an expensive bottle on a special occasion or a Friday night.

Jeff Watson, Chairman of the History Department, joined Hal at the bar and introduced his wife Kristin. Kristin described her work as a child psychologist and referred to several articles Tina had published.

"Yes," Hal said. "I think if she'd had more time, she would have moved into work with adolescents and young adults exclusively. She had also talked with Melanie about teaching a graduate course here in Adolescent Psychology."

Hal continued his conversation with Jeff and Kristin but spotted Catherine across the room. She was with Philip Reynolds. An empty suit, Tina would have called Philip. But it wasn't really his concern, was it? She's my colleague. Maybe he's a good match for her, or maybe she needed a date for this dinner. Yes. He should have brought someone as well... stop standing out as the lonely widower.

Hal watched Roslyn circle the room. Regal almost, he thought, noticing her artificial smile and imagining the small talk bestowed on every guest. The young Roslyn was gone... the woman his mother brought to life in her notebook. Is this what happens to all of us if we give in to these politics?

The waiter asked that everyone take their seats, and Hal moved across the room to the table where he would be seated with Catherine, Neil and his wife, and two trustees he knew well from work on the Capital Campaign. Hal said a cordial hello to everyone at the table as he was seated. He tried to catch Catherine's eye to see if she was uncomfortable with this seating arrangement. She must be better at play acting than he thought. She appeared nonplussed to be seated so close to Neil.

Catherine gave Hal a warm smile as she took her seat between Neil and Philip. She leaned in to say something to Philip, conscious that her back was to Neil. With the tilt of her head and her rigid body language, she hoped Neil got the message she didn't want to chat with him.

Neil's wife Mary Anne was considerably younger than Neil with dark hair, brown expressive eyes, and a loud grating voice. She talked incessantly about their two small children, which seemed inappropriate for the occasion.

"So, Catherine," she yelled across the table, "how are you settling in at Franklin?"

"Very well, thank you," Catherine replied.

"Well, it certainly hasn't taken you long to get your hooks in a Trustee."

Catherine was speechless, but Philip replied with humor. "Mary Anne, Catherine doesn't have hooks, and I'm no longer a Trustee."

The other two couples at the table looked uncomfortable and changed the subject.

Mary Houston's husband Roger said, "Catherine, Mary tells me how glad she is that you're here. She's so pleased about the way you are getting alumni involved with students."

"Thanks, Roger. I think we have a program with a lot of potential. Alumni and alumnae seem more than willing to help out, and I think it's a good way to get some to campus who've not been engaged."

David Thurston's wife Cecilia, who was in her early seventies, added, "I'm an alumna, Catherine, and I would be happy to get you connected to some of my friends who would be good candidates for the program. I was at Franklin at a time when women were not encouraged to do anything but find a husband. I am pleased to say that many of us have been successful with careers."

"I look forward to talking with you, Cecilia. Our students need role models who make career and family work, not just the women but also the men."

"I would agree," Philip added. "Students need to hear our stories, so they see that there are options, and there are always choices along the way."

Philip looked up and saw Roslyn standing behind him.

"Madame President, you snuck up on me," Philip said flirtatiously, getting up as he acknowledged her.

"Yes, but I didn't want to interrupt." She patted Philip on the shoulder. "I'm glad you and Catherine have connected." Roslyn spoke with Neil briefly and continued to circulate around the crowded room. Hmm. She said nothing to me. Does Roslyn just see me as Philip's date?

Mary Anne said little and continued drinking at a steady pace. Neil seemed to ignore her, which was evident to everyone around the table. Roger asked Hal about his research on the Civil Rights Movement. Catherine strained to hear what Hal was saying, but the din of the room made this impossible. She needed to reconnect with Hal. She hadn't asked him about his class since the first few weeks of the semester.

As dessert and coffee were served, Roslyn stepped to a small podium that had been placed near the doorway.

"It's always my pleasure to welcome all of you to my home during this holiday season. As in years past, I want to say thank you to our faithful trustees and our hard-working Executive Administration for all you do on behalf of the College. Tonight, though, I also want to announce a special gift to the College." Roslyn paused, and a slight murmur spread through the room.

"As you all know, Anne Peterson Reynolds, Class of 1976, died tragically in a car accident. She was active in the Alumni Association, and her two children, also graduates of Franklin, carried on her service and commitment to the College. Her husband Philip has donated $5 million to start a scholarship in her name. This scholarship fund will benefit students entering Franklin beginning in the fall of 2005."

A round of applause began slowly and grew as Philip joined Roslyn at the podium. Philip took an envelope from his pocket and handed it to Roslyn. On cue, a photographer appeared and snapped several pictures of them shaking hands. The announcement took Catherine by surprise. She scanned the room and surmised that others were surprised as well. She saw a dark look pass over Hal's face as he clenched his linen napkin until his knuckles looked white. What was the matter with him? she wondered.

As Philip took his seat, Roslyn wished everyone a Merry Christmas. Most came over to thank Philip for his generosity, but Hal was the first to leave, saying good night to Roslyn and getting his coat. Steve brusquely shook Philip's hand and followed Hal.

As Catherine and Philip left, a light snow was falling, and the Christmas lights from the house made everything look magical.

"Oh, everything looks beautiful," Catherine said, exhilarated by Philip's generosity. She wanted to kiss him but thought better of it and took his hand instead.

"Yes, it does," said Philip as he opened the car door for Catherine. As he slid in next to her, he took her hand very gently.

"May I take you out for a nightcap?"

"I have a better idea. Take me home, and I will give you a glass of port or a cognac."

Catherine was feeling the warmth of the red wine she

had had with her filet and the exhilaration of being with Philip. She said, "Your gift is magnificent."

"It would make Anne so happy," he said, stroking her fingers. "She loved her time at Franklin and was so happy that our children attended as well." She heard his voice catch when he said Anne's name.

When they arrived, Catherine didn't wait for Philip to get the door for her, and she slid slightly on the snow and ice accumulating on the driveway.

"Watch your step, Catherine," Philip warned.

Brushing the melting snow from her leg, she opened the door and was greeted by Molly and Maggie. She picked up Maggie, and the cat kissed her cheek. She put Maggie down, and as Philip helped her remove her coat, he brushed against her breast.

She put her cold hand on his cheek.

"Port or cognac?"

"Port," he said.

She poured two glasses and moved toward the fireplace to start a fire. Philip took a sip of the port and moved toward her, handing her several logs from the bin.

"How did I do tonight, Dr. Finley?"

"You were wonderful," Catherine said, "saving me from the dragon lady. Have you met her before?"

"Yes, and she's always as charming as she was tonight."

"I'm sorry to hear that."

"Yes. You are not her first victim. Steve brought a date to another affair. She was all over her."

"Poor Steve."

"No, he handled it very well."

Catherine took another sip of port and held it for a few

seconds in her mouth. As she swallowed, she reached over and caressed Philip's thigh.

"Did I just imagine that?" he asked playfully as Catherine moved closer and kissed him on the lips.

"No, I didn't imagine that," he said as he took her in his arms, kissing her hard on the mouth and allowing his tongue to probe her lips and make its way into her mouth. She moved closer, spreading her legs slightly. He ran his hand up her warm thigh, fingering the lace at the top of her stocking.

As he started to unbutton her blouse, the encounter with Neil went through her mind. She stiffened and pulled away.

"Catherine, what is it?" he asked, tenderness replaced with exasperation.

"I'm sorry, Philip," she said. "It was a lovely evening. I appreciate your taking me to the dinner, but I need to call it a night."

"Okay," he said, looking disgruntled. "Suit yourself." Without a word, he pulled his coat from the coat tree and left.

She sat, sipping the port, remembering Neil's hands on her thigh, kneading her flesh like dough. She'd had the nightmare again last night, his tongue in her mouth, choking her. She woke up in a sweat, tasting blood.

She thought about Chelsea and what she was carrying now because she never came to terms with Neil's assault when she was in college.

This can't go on. It's controlling my life. If I can't stand up for myself, how will I ever standup for Chelsea or any of the students?

Chapter Twenty-Four

Catherine's stomach was in knots. She hadn't met with Neil since the attack. Sometimes, she imagined he would be so embarrassed by what he'd done that he would be reserved and act as if nothing happened. But knowing what he'd done to Chelsea, who was she kidding? Hal's information about Nicole, the incident with Jason and the graduate student... She took a deep breath. Her legs trembled and her palms were sweaty. Why hadn't she called in sick so she could avoid seeing him until after the New Year?

Catherine collected her materials for her meeting. Bette didn't look up from the spreadsheet she was studying as Catherine left the office.

Marie was not at her desk when Catherine arrived at Neil's office, so she knocked on the open door and went in. Neil looked rested in a three-piece suit with a pocket watch hanging from his vest.

"Good morning. I trust you had a good weekend," he

said, looking at the computer screen.

Catherine had learned not to fall into conversation with Neil about her personal life. "Yesterday was my weekend, the first day in weeks that I really took a day off. The laundry's done, you know, all the important things."

"No, I wouldn't know. I'm lucky enough to have a wife," he said, looking at Catherine.

There's the trap, she thought. "I was able to finalize these budget recommendations while I was working on Saturday," Catherine said, placing the spreadsheets on Neil's worktable. Neil placed his reading glasses on the table and sat down across from her.

"Come, come, Catherine. You don't think you're going to move on as if Saturday night never happened."

"Yes, I am," she said, looking at Neil with no expression.

"No comment about my charming wife?"

Catherine could feel the color coming to her cheeks. Was there a graceful way to get around this conversation?

Neil got up and closed the office door. "Our children are young, so I don't feel I can divorce her now, but I'm getting to the end of my rope. She disgraces me publicly all the time like she did on Saturday night, but if I don't bring her to functions, people talk."

"Neil. I'm sorry. Perhaps, we should just focus on our work."

"Focus on our work? Who do you think you are, Joan of Arc? I've told you before: I expect your loyalty. If I need to talk about a pressing problem at home, I expect you to listen."

Loyalty. That word again, as if there was something between them. This is a working relationship, not a friendship. Catherine wanted to scream, but she was silent. Why was she incapable of speaking up for herself?

He was pretending that he had done nothing wrong, but it wasn't out of embarrassment. Catherine rose from her chair and began to gather her papers.

Neil lurched at her, grabbing her wrists. "Where do you think you're going, Catherine? I'm the boss, and I'll decide when you're leaving."

"No, you won't." Catherine pulled away from Neil, her nails grazing the gold cufflink on his right sleeve.

"Let go of my wrists. I don't think you want to make a scene here as well."

Neil clasped her wrists harder, moving even closer to her until his lips were on her mouth. He thrust his tongue into her mouth and kissed her hard. She bit his tongue and pulled away from him. Neil raised his hand to his mouth, blood trickling onto his fingers.

"You bitch," he yelled. "You made me bleed."

"Neil, let me be perfectly clear with you. This will never happen again, or it'll become a matter of record."

"Are you threatening me?" Neil asked, incredulous.

"Yes, I am." Catherine left the office and quietly closed the door behind her. Marie was at her desk but didn't look up as Catherine passed. Catherine stopped in the women's restroom before returning to her office. She wasn't ready to have anyone on her staff know about this.

Her face was flushed. She tasted blood. She rinsed her mouth with cold water and splashed water on her face. Breathing deeply, her hands shook as she braced herself against the sink.

What is wrong with him? What's wrong with me? I'm being logical, and there's nothing logical about this. He attacked Chelsea when she was a college student. He feels entitled.

Catherine returned to her office and asked Bette to hold her calls. She closed the door and worked on several projects that kept her mind off what just happened.

Her hands shook, and she couldn't concentrate. After some thought, she picked up the phone and called the President's Office. She asked Michelle for an appointment with Roslyn. She thought about what Hal said: Roslyn wouldn't protect her, but she needed to be on record about what had happened.

She left the office early, deciding to do some Christmas shopping, a welcome distraction. As she pulled out of the parking lot, her cell phone rang. It was Philip.

"Catherine, I have left you three messages. Are you ignoring me?"

"No, Philip. I'm sorry. My cell phone wasn't on today." She could feel her irritation growing as she listened to his voice. "I'm heading out early to do some shopping."

"May I join you?"

Catherine hesitated before answering.

"I'll take that as a no. What about dinner?" Philip said.

They agreed to meet in Chestnut Hill for dinner after Catherine finished her shopping.

When Catherine arrived at the small, crowded restaurant, Philip was seated at the bar, nursing a glass of scotch. He got up and gave her a kiss on the cheek. Catherine asked the bartender for a glass of pinot grigio. She pulled her stool closer to him, so she wouldn't have to shout over the din.

"How are things at the College?" Philip asked.

"A little strange. I had a meeting with Neil this

morning about some budgets for next year, and I couldn't get him away from the topic of Saturday night. I'm really not interested in his dilemma with his wife." Why was she hesitating? She should tell him what happened.

"Well, that doesn't sound very kind, Catherine," Philip said, taking another sip of the scotch.

Catherine looked at Philip closely to see if he was serious or not. He seemed to be relaxed, enjoying the moment, but she could feel the anger growing in her. She hesitated and then described the incident after the faculty meeting when Neil accused her of being disloyal... then began to caress her.

"Today was even worse. He grabbed my wrists and thrust his tongue in my mouth."

Philip, looking nonplussed and asked, "What are you going to do?'

"I don't know." Her voice was shaking, and she cautiously sipped her glass of wine. Catherine held Philip's gaze, showing none of the anger she felt.

"Well, I wouldn't make a federal case out of it. It sounds like the guy is having a difficult time at home. He's just looking for a little support."

Why don't I walk out of here right now? she considered. If he weren't associated with the College, I probably would.

"Why don't we ask for a table? I need to eat something," Catherine said, gesturing to get the bartender's attention. Eat something and get this evening over and done, she thought.

The rest of the evening was awkward, and Catherine said little. Philip asked her to have dinner with him and his two children over the weekend. Catherine declined, telling him Judy was coming in. She was glad for this excuse. She would have declined anyway, and she didn't have the energy right now for a confrontation.

As they left the restaurant, Philip asked if there was a night he could take her and Judy to dinner.

"Philip, I really don't want to discuss this here on the street, but I just told you something very troubling, and you aren't the least bit concerned."

"Catherine, I'm sorry. I didn't feel comfortable talking about it in the restaurant. I'll follow you back to your house, and we can talk there."

"Okay." She could feel some tension drain from her body, but she was still shaking.

They sat facing each other on the couch, and she told Philip more about Neil's assault. He was quiet, looking at her intently.

"Catherine, I don't know what to tell you. Maybe you need to find another job." His tone was flat. He drummed his fingers on the arm of the couch, looking away from her.

"Why should I find another job? *He's* the one who's acting like a crazed animal."

"Catherine, I know you're upset, but..."

"Why aren't *you* upset? Can you even imagine treating a woman like this?"

"No, but I've never had to..."

"Had to?" She got up and paced the room. She stopped abruptly and looked down at Philip.

"Philip, please go. I need to think this through on my own." He walked to the door without objection and she closed it gently behind him. Maggie looked up at her from the arm of the couch. Catherine stroked the cat. "That man's an asshole. We're better off without him."

She went upstairs and ran a bath. The hot water and the lavender bath oil calmed her. Exhaustion eventually made sleep possible.

Philip left two messages on her cell phone the next day, apologizing for the way he responded to her situation with Neil. He sounded so sincere. But why wasn't he angry? He has a daughter. What if something like this happened to her?

When he called again on Thursday afternoon, he apologized again, and she halfheartedly accepted the apology. She invited him over Saturday night for a light dinner with Judy. She thought about mentioning the tree she and Judy would trim on Saturday but decided against it.

"I'll look forward to seeing you then. I love you, Catherine."

Catherine felt numb. She didn't find Philip convincing, but she didn't want to give up on the relationship yet. Another failure would be too much right now, she thought, remembering the painful weeks following her break-up with Peter.

Before she left work, Catherine printed the listing for a home she wanted to look at with Peter. A hundred years old, it needed a little work... a new kitchen and a lot of paint, but the woodwork and the hardwood floors were perfect. Three bedrooms and a bath on the second floor, and a third floor with two small rooms under the eaves. A study for each of them.

Home, she thought as she got in her car and drove to

their apartment. A home different from the one she knew growing up. Peter wanted that too. Laughter. Openness. No silences drenched in alcohol. Their children would feel safe, happy.

She parked on the street. A red Honda was in the driveway. She didn't know anyone with a red Honda. Catherine closed the front door quietly, dropping her book bag and purse on the chair in the hall.

She heard a woman's laughter and water running in the shower. She walked up the stairs slowly and stopped at the bedroom door. A naked, soaking wet woman was riding Peter, smoking a joint. Playfully, she'd bring the joint close to his mouth, then pull it away.

Thirty seconds, maybe not even that long. They didn't notice her presence until she went into the bathroom and turned off the shower. Naked Peter stood in front of her.

He started to speak, but Catherine cut him off.

"Get out," she screamed. The sound of her own voice surprised her. A wave of nausea came over her. Swallowing hard, she said, "Take a change of clothes. We'll find a time when you can come back and get your things when I'm not here."

"Just like that?" Peter asked, the color drained from his face.

"Just like that," Catherine said, pointing to the naked woman pulling on a sweater and sweatpants. "Just like that," Catherine repeated in a whisper. She closed the bathroom door and threw up.

Chapter Twenty-Five

Catherine took the shortcut uphill, avoiding the biting wind. She tried to get control of her shaking hands as she turned the enormous brass knob on the front door of Franklin Hall.

Roslyn's assistant wasn't in yet. Catherine looked at her watch. I'm five minutes early, she thought, taking a deep breath. As she exhaled, the door to the President's Office opened. Roslyn looked rested in black slacks, an emerald green blouse, and black jacket.

"Good morning, Catherine," she said smiling broadly. "It must be good to have your first semester behind you."

"Yes, Roslyn, it is."

Roslyn motioned for Catherine to take the chair in front of her desk, then slid deftly into the mahogany one behind it. She glanced briefly at her computer screen, waiting for Catherine to speak.

"Roslyn," Catherine said, leaning forward in her chair, "I'm sorry to bother you with this, but I've had two run-ins with Neil."

"Run-ins?" Roslyn repeated, sounding incredulous. "Has your collaboration with Hal upset him? Hal may have told you that Neil was unhappy when I said Hal would continue to report to Steve. I may make that change at some point..." Her voice trailed off. Her mind seemed to wander away from the conversation.

"No. It isn't about the collaboration with Hal. Hal and I have a three-part plan for program development we'll be sharing with Steve and Neil in January. I've kept Neil apprised, but frankly, he's shown little interest." What am I saying? Catherine thought. I have a boss who's disinterested in the work that's moving the College forward. Isn't that a problem in itself?

"Well," Roslyn said, seeming to show no concern about what Catherine had just said, "he has a full plate, and he knows you're capable. I imagine his attention's on other things."

"Yes," Catherine said, unable to repress a nervous laugh. "His attention is elsewhere. The run-ins I'm referring to are his physically attacking me, grabbing my wrists, sticking his tongue in my mouth."

Catherine realized she'd gotten to her feet and was shouting at the President.

"Roslyn, I'm so sorry," Catherine said, sitting down and willing her hands to stop shaking.

"Clearly, you're upset, my dear," Roslyn said. She picked up the phone and asked Michelle to come in. She immediately appeared in the doorway.

"Please get Catherine a glass of water," Roslyn ordered. Without saying a word, Michelle turned on her heels, left the room, and returned promptly with the water. Catherine sipped from the glass, waiting for Michelle to close the door behind her.

"Now, my dear," Roslyn continued, "we can't let this upset your work."

Catherine was screaming inside. Stop calling me *my dear*. I'm not a child. You're a college president, for God's sake, not a headmistress at a girls' school. She looked at Roslyn and saw the deep lines in her face. Under the lined skin, she saw no emotion.

"No, we can't," Catherine said. "You need to tell him that this behavior has to stop."

"Well, of course, I can do that, dear," she said. "I'll chat with him after the Christmas break."

Chat with him... *chat with him* was reverberating in Catherine's head. You need to understand how serious this is. Even if you don't care, the ramifications for lawsuits given what's happened to Chelsea, Nicole. Roslyn's gaze had wandered to the computer screen. Catherine felt her composure returning as Roslyn turned to look at her.

"Roslyn," Catherine said. "I know about Nicole." She held Roslyn's gaze, waiting to see if there would be any response. There was none.

"Nicole. What has this got to do with Nicole? She left to take..."

"She left because of what happened with Neil," Catherine said, standing slowly and looking down at Roslyn behind her desk. "I hope you won't wait until after Christmas break to speak with him."

Catherine didn't wait for a reply. She moved toward the door, looking back for a moment to see the shocked look on Roslyn's face. Michelle looked up as Catherine passed her desk.

"Have a wonderful holiday," Catherine told her.

"You do the same, Catherine," she replied. As Catherine left, the doorstop caught in the door. Catherine heard Roslyn scream, "Michelle, get me Philip Reynolds on the phone." Catherine left the building quickly and walked slowly downhill.

Her mind was racing. Why the hell is she calling Philip? What does she know about us, other than we were together at the Christmas party? What's between those two?

Staff in Tyler Hall were talking about the upcoming holiday break. Catherine could feel her stomach lurch, and she didn't look at Bette as she passed her desk. I must calm down, she thought, and just get through today.

Bette gave Catherine a warm good morning and said, "Everyone's in early today, hoping the boss is feeling generous and will let us leave early."

"Good morning," Catherine said from behind her partly opened door. "I intend to do just that." She closed her door and sat down to send the email about leaving at 3:00.

Catherine stared at the computer screen. "I don't know what to do with any of this," she said out loud. "I never should have taken this job. I should have listened to my gut, stayed in New Hampshire another year..."

There was a knock on the door, and before she could respond, Hal opened the door slightly and asked if he could come in.

"Yes, of course," Catherine said, realizing she hadn't checked her make-up after walking downhill in the biting cold.

"Is something wrong?" Hal asked, smile fading to a

frown as he realized he was intruding.

"Please come in," Catherine said, getting up from behind the desk. She needed to talk with him now. He had been right about Roslyn.

Hal sat down on the loveseat, and Catherine came from behind her desk to sit in the chair next to him. He ran his fingers through his thick hair. She looked at Hal's earnest face and noticed something she had not seen before, vulnerability. He looked concerned, leaning in, indicating he had plenty of time to listen.

"I went to Roslyn this morning about Neil. You were right. She doesn't see the gravity of the situation, or if she does, she's not admitting it. She said I shouldn't let this interfere with my work. Hal, this is 2004, and a college president is not outraged by what happened to me, what happened to Nicole."

Hal looked at Catherine.

Rage erupted in her. "Why aren't you saying anything?" she asked, getting up from her chair and walking to the window. The playing fields were shrouded in snow.

"You told me about Nicole. Was I supposed to keep quiet? Become part of this secrecy? As I left Roslyn's office, she screamed at Michelle, telling her to call Philip Reynolds. What is *that* about?"

A frown deepened on Hal's face when she mentioned Philip. "Catherine. I'm sorry. I'm just trying to gather my thoughts.

"I know this may sound strange," Hal said, "but when you told me about what happened with Neil, all I could think was that my mother would know how to handle this. This is what she believed thirty years ago could be changed, and nothing has changed. In some ways, I think things have gotten worse." He leaned in again, running his hand through his hair.

There it was again. His hesitation. Then, total honesty. Did he get this from his mother, the woman he adored? Catherine left the window and went back to her desk. She picked up a pen and turned it over in her hand.

"A woman from my mother's firm came to see me last week. My mother was her mentor, and she is aware of my research. I shared with her how my efforts to get the civil rights and gender discrimination colloquium were thwarted by Roslyn. She shared with me that my mother knew Roslyn. Roslyn told my mother about her own case of sexual harassment."

"What?" Catherine asked, incredulous.

"Yes. Roslyn was harassed when she was trying to get tenure." Hal ran his fingers through his hair again, looking down and then, up directly at Catherine. "Here's what I mean that things have gotten worse." Catherine didn't move, waiting to hear what else Hal would say.

"I don't understand. If Roslyn went through this, why is she denying that this is happening to other women?" Catherine asked.

"It's complicated. Her mother left her father for another man. My mother's notes indicate that Roslyn believed that women like her mother were bad and brought on things like this."

Catherine got up and paced to the window and back. "What does her mother's behavior have to do with Roslyn being propositioned by her department chair?"

"I'm not a psychologist, Catherine, so I'm not sure I understand it all, but Roslyn came back to Franklin, first as assistant to the President and then as Dean and President. She seems to have buried a past that is too painful to confront.

"Catherine, you did the right thing. I would suggest you put the conversation with Roslyn in writing today and send it to her. Let her know this is a matter of record now. Because of what I know about Nicole's situation, I can support you."

"I appreciate your support," she said as Hal got up and left.

Catherine walked back to the window and ran her fingers over the cold glass. Roslyn propositioned by her department chair. She lied about her transition from faculty to administrator. No. That's not fair. She told her story in a way that made it bearable. How many women have been harassed, raped, and were never able to talk about their stories? Stories suppressed by fear and powerful people.

Roslyn talked about President Corbett being such a wonderful mentor. Maybe, but he also needed Roslyn's silence.

Catherine wondered if Hal's mother had ever talked with Roslyn about a settlement, a way for Roslyn to move on from Franklin and start again. Probably not. Roslyn glowed when she talked about the College. It was her life. Buried, the harassment becomes just a bitter memory.

Did anyone remain at the College who knew Roslyn's secret? It happened thirty years ago. Maybe no one. Roslyn's younger self gone. Catherine saw a glimmer of that young Roslyn the day they had tea and chatted like colleagues.

Chapter Twenty-Six

The house was still when Catherine awakened. She made her way downstairs quietly, not wanting to disturb Judy. Snow was falling steadily; high winds caused it to gust along the window ledges. She fed Molly and Maggie, stroking Maggie gently as she ate. Then she made coffee, leaving Judy a note that she was going to the firehouse to get the tree. She selected a Douglas fir, just under seven feet, and the two young men loaded it into their pick-up truck.

By the time Catherine returned, Judy was dressed and drinking coffee in the living room.

"I would have gone with you," Judy said.

"No need," Catherine said. "I have some good muscle here."

The men stood the tree in the stand and got it straight on the first attempt.

After a second cup of coffee, Judy went to the study to finish grading.

Catherine felt an incredible contentment as she brought the ornaments from the basement. She would take her time, getting the chili made and the salad prepared for their early dinner while Judy finished her work.

Her mind wandered to a childhood Christmas that she remembered as exciting but filled with tension. Her contentment disappeared as the gloomy memory took hold.

It was Christmas Eve. Uncle Ray, Aunt Rosemary, and Karen were there for dinner before church. Caroline and Catherine were dressed in velvet dresses, one red and one green. Their mother was dressed in an emerald green satin, knee-length dress. Majorcan pearls lay around her neck and graced her ears. Her father was already dressed for church, white cleric's collar and black suit. He and Uncle Ray were engrossed in a conversation. Uncle Ray seemed to gulp the red wine that her father sipped pensively.

Aunt Rosemary was more loquacious than ever. Mother had a pained expression on her face as she listened passively.

Uncle Ray's voice rose above his wife's din as he talked with her father about a new business project. On reflection, though, Catherine realized that her father was more interested in the characters in the story than he was in the project. *A builder in Havertown with a booming business needed advice about managing a growing workforce.*

Mother encouraged everyone to take a seat at the table. Her father said the blessing, but he didn't sound happy like he usually did on Christmas Eve. Karen, Caroline, and Catherine talked about what they wanted for

Christmas, but no one seemed to be listening.

Her father wasn't home after church to read "'Twas the Night Before Christmas" like he always did. Mother read to the girls instead. Something didn't seem right. Catherine lay awake a long time after her mother left the room and Caroline was fast asleep. About 3:30, she heard her father's car pull into the garage and heard his soft tread on the carpeted stairs.

Catherine pretended to sleep as her father gently kissed Caroline goodnight. "Sweet dreams, beautiful girl," he said, pulling the covers up over her red flannel pajamas. He kissed Catherine on the forehead and said, "Sweet dreams, Catherine. I'm sorry I wasn't here tonight to read the story." As she drifted into sleep, she heard her parents' voices, angry and threatening.

"You're a hypocrite," she heard her mother say. "If people knew the truth about you, you'd never get a call, not to any church."

What had made her mother so angry? What was so important that her father wasn't home on Christmas Eve?

Catherine's thoughts were interrupted by her ringing cell phone.

"Good morning," Philip said when she picked up. And then, there was a pause.

"Hi," Catherine said, the memory of Roslyn telling Michelle to get Philip on the phone kept her from saying much more. "Judy got in last night, and I'm getting the decorations out for the tree."

"Good," he said, his tone distant and strange. "Catherine, I won't be able to make it for dinner tonight."

"Really," Catherine said, sarcasm taking over any other emotion. "What could be more important than dinner with me?"

"Look, Catherine," Philip said.

"Look, Philip," she shot back. "Let's work on the truth here. Why aren't you coming to dinner tonight? Does it have anything to do with the phone call you received from Roslyn on Friday?"

"How did you know about that?" he asked, sounding perplexed.

Catherine kept silent.

"Catherine, this isn't working out. I've enjoyed our time together, but..."

"But what?" she asked, feeling her voice shake.

"You're making a lot of people at the College uncomfortable, and I feel uncertain about continuing this relationship under these circumstances."

"These circumstances... a lot of people..." She was shouting just as she had done in the meeting with Roslyn. "You mean Neil and Roslyn are *uncomfortable*?" She spit the word as if it was vinegar.

"You're making a fool of yourself. Neil's attracted to you, yes, but use it to your advantage."

"Use it to my advantage. What does that mean?"

"Well, you certainly slid into bed with me easily enough. Why should Neil think it would be any different with him?"

"You and I were in a relationship when I slid into bed with you," she spit back at him. "Clearly, I misread you, Philip. I thought you loved me." The moment she said it, she regretted it. How naïve!

"What does a woman like you know about love?"

"What does *that* mean? A woman like me?"

She heard the line go dead. She sat down on the couch, still looking at the phone when Judy came into the living room.

"I finished posting my grades," she said, and then saw Catherine's face, her shaking hands. Before Catherine could say anything, Judy sat down and put her arm around her friend. After a moment, she got up and poured a glass of water from a crystal pitcher Catherine had placed on the piano. Catherine took the water and sipped it, breathing deeply.

Catherine spoke slowly, measuring every sentence, wanting Judy to listen, to understand. She thought she knew Judy well enough to know that she wouldn't be upset, she'd be angry, if she were harassed. Catherine told Judy about both run-ins with Neil, emphasizing the stand she took with him in the second attack.

She then described her meeting with Roslyn. As she relived it, she could feel the anger washing over her like an enormous wave.

"Good for you," Judy said, getting up from the couch to pour herself a glass of water. "These bastards need to know that this behavior has to stop." Judy pushed up the sleeves on her sweater before picking up the glass of water and settling into the ottoman, facing Catherine.

"She denied the part about Nicole," Catherine said, taking another sip of the water. "She said she had left for a prestigious deanship at U. C. Davis."

"But you're on record, and she knows that you are aware of the true circumstances," Judy said like an attorney stating the case.

"I don't know the specifics of what happened to

Nicole," Catherine said, looking at Judy carefully, "but Hal does. He says he'll support me and be able to share what happened."

Catherine gazed at the tree. She had been so excited about spending Christmas with Judy, but now she was exhausted and angry. She wished she'd never left her position in New Hampshire. She wished she had never gone out with Philip.

"Catherine?" Judy asked, breaking the silence. "Who was that on the phone?"

"Philip," she said, overwhelmed already with what she was about to say. "Roslyn told him about my allegations against Neil. He dumped me."

"This is more twisted than even I could imagine," Judy said, her eyes flashing anger and then softening when she saw Catherine's distress.

Catherine laughed. "In a twisted way," she said trying to mimic the way Judy said *twisted*, "that makes me feel a little better."

"A little better," Judy said. "It ought to make you feel a lot better. These assholes get away with this kind of shit because it's unbelievable. Dean gets involved with College Trustee."

"Former Trustee," Catherine corrected.

"Academic Vice President hits on Dean," Judy continued. "Dean tells President. President calls in Trustee to do what? Break up with Dean to silence her?"

"You're right. It's unbelievable. When I told Philip the other night what Neil had done, he suggested that maybe I should get another job, but I have no intention of doing that. I'm going to find a way to get through this with my professional life intact."

"Catherine, I think you should do that, but if you decide you don't want to work in this type of environment with these screwed-up assholes, don't be hard on yourself for deciding to leave."

Judy sat quietly for a moment before she said, "Catherine, spend as much time as you need talking with me about this or thinking about it, but don't let it ruin this Christmas with your father. It may be his last."

"Good advice," Catherine said, getting up and going over to give Judy a hug. Judy stood and embraced her.

"It sounds like you have a real ally in Hal when you have to get back to work. I think that will be an enormous help," Judy said.

Ally was a good word to describe Hal. He kept his distance from the politics but was honest with her about how he struggled with them. She trusted him. The information about Roslyn's past was as baffling to him as it was to her, and she knew he was processing it slowly.

Judy and Catherine worked silently. Unwinding strands of lights, Catherine began wrapping them around the tree. They worked in rhythm, passing the clumps of lights from one hand to the other. Then they began to take ornaments from the boxes, randomly placing them on the tree. Small nutcrackers, bears, and Santa Clauses, ornaments with dates marked on them from previous Christmases.

Catherine unwrapped the porcelain Snow White with her yellow skirt and blue bodice with yellow trim. Mother gave us Snow White and the seven dwarfs the same Christmas she took us to see the Disney film. Her first trip to the movies. Maybe Caroline has the dwarfs.

Catherine passed the angel to Judy to place at the top

of the tree.

The smell of the chili drew them to the kitchen. "Let's turn this off and take a walk. We'll work up an appetite," Catherine said.

"I have one now," Judy said." I do need the exercise, though. I haven't been working out this semester. I've been living on Stouffer's and peanut butter cups."

"Be careful," Catherine warned as they made their way up the steep path that led to the covered bridge. "We'll have an easier trail on the other side."

Catherine slowed partway, giving Judy a chance to catch her breath. Snow crunched below their feet, and the sun shining through barren trees illuminated the blue-green stream below.

They walked without speaking for a while, an occasional biker whooshing by, disturbing the silence.

"Philip and I had a good time in New England over Fall Break, but he's not Peter," Catherine said as much to herself as to Judy. She didn't need to disclose much detail. Judy had listened to it all before.

"Philip. Good sex. Decent company. No intimacy," Judy said as though she were reading a grocery list.

Not far from the truth, Catherine thought. Everything about him was tainted by the conversation they had earlier today. His comment, *What does a woman like you know about love?* ran through her mind.

Catherine could feel Judy's comforting arm around her shoulder as she navigated a cluster of boulders. "Maybe Peter wasn't the love of your life. He may still be out there," Judy said gently.

"Here's a thought. The Finance professor. The

wealthy businessman, former Trustee... a fitting companion for the young, accomplished dean. You know what this sounds like to me?" Judy asked.

"What?" Catherine asked, not sure she wanted an answer.

"Your mother's recipe for happiness, not yours," Judy said. "Why not keep your eyes open for someone who can be your best friend?

"I asked my mother once," Judy continued, "how she knew dad was right for her. She told me he was her best friend, a little shy at first before he became her lover."

"Your mother sounds so healthy. I don't think my mother ever loved my father. She loved alcohol more than any of us," Catherine said.

"She may not have been able to come back from that," Judy said.

Catherine looked at her watch and suggested they turn around.

"I'm smelling the chili," Judy said as they drove home. "I'm starving."

"It tastes as good as it smells," Catherine said.

They left their boots at the front door while Judy went upstairs to get her shoes. After Catherine hung their coats in the closet, she turned on the Christmas tree lights.

"We did a great job," Judy said from the steps.

"You were a million miles away. I didn't want to interrupt what was going on there. Are you thinking about work?" Judy's voice brought Catherine's attention back to the road as they headed for Spring Lake.

"I'm sorry," Catherine said. "No. I was thinking about some of the conversations I've had recently with my father." Catherine paused for a moment as she shifted into fifth.

"Remember when we were in Boston this summer, and I was telling you about how he talks about the past and his marriage to my mother now like I'm an adult, not just his daughter."

"I remember," Judy said.

"I've been reliving a lot of my memories of their fights. It's all fragmented and leaves me with lots of questions."

Catherine's thoughts turned to Spring Break, her junior year in college.

The beach was empty. A cold wind blew as she crossed Ocean Avenue.

No cars on the street. Climbing over the dune, she took in the pounding surf. It was her hardest semester in three years at Smith. She shouldn't have left the Biology requirement until this year... and the Philosophy minor was only a good idea before she knew she had to take Logic.

She took off her shoes and walked on the wet, hard sand. Coming home was a mistake. She should've stayed at school or gone home with friends who had parents that got along.

Daddy's weak, she thought. He puts up with her drinking. He ought to have more control.

She stopped for a moment, reaching down for a conch shell that rushed into shore on a wave. She picked it up out of the foam. Cold, biting, frigid water.

The shell was broken. Its interior was pink, marked with dark veins that made the pink seem brighter somehow.

She held it up to her ear and listened. She heard her

grandmother's voice.

"It's the sea, Catherine," her Nana said, holding the conch shell up to her ear. "Do you hear it? God put something big in something small."

"No," she squealed. "No." She was four.

She looked at the shell's interior, chipped, battered, broken.

"Your mother needs our love," she heard her father say.

"And what about us?" she'd responded at ten, stamping her foot and screaming at her father. "What about us?" She put the shell to her ear, listened to the ocean, and heard her Nana's voice again.

"Do you hear it, Catherine?" Nana asked. "God put something big in something so small."

"I hear it Nana," she yelled into the roaring surf. "What does it mean? Daddy prays ... looks embarrassed because of her drinking. People make fun of him... the priest with a drunk for a wife."

I wish I hadn't come home, she thought, tossing the shell as far as she could... away from the shore... away from her... away from the pain.

She sat on the cold, hard sand, losing track of time. The wind changed, and the surf kicked up.

The conch shell washed up again pink, shattered side up. She held it to her ear again. "God put something big in something so small," she heard her Nana say once again.

"Tell me what that means," she shouted into the roaring surf.

Catherine let go of the memory. As they got closer to the shore, the wind kicked up and the temperature began to drop.

"This weather's so unpredictable," Catherine said.

"Thankfully, we won't have to worry about it once we get there."

Catherine turned onto Third Avenue, and the car slid a bit. "Almost there."

She pulled up in front of her father's house. A Christmas tree graced the foyer and candles cast light from every window, upstairs and downstairs. The front door opened, and Catherine caught a glimpse of her father and his friends.

"We can get our bags later when I put the car in the garage." Catherine ran to the door and embraced her father. "Merry Christmas," she said.

"Merry Christmas, Doll," he said, placing a kiss on her cheek. Douglas held the door and Judy and Catherine came into the foyer.

"Ruth and Al, it's so good to see you." Catherine gave each of them a big hug. "I want you to meet my friend, Judy."

"It's wonderful to meet you," Al said, offering a warm handshake. Ruth gave Judy a hug.

"Please come in out of the cold," Douglas commanded. "I've talked Al and Ruth into staying for dinner."

"Great." Catherine looked through to the living room. A fire was blazing in the fireplace. She took in the Christmas decorations. A beautiful ceramic crèche made by a man in her father's church in D.C. and old-fashioned stockings, embroidered by hand, with her name and her sister Caroline's name on them, hanging by the fire.

"You've outdone yourselves," Catherine said.

"I give Ruth a lot of the credit," Douglas said. "She was

able to remember exactly where your mother placed everything.

"Allow me to get everyone a glass of wine, and then I have a real surprise for dinner," Douglas said, moving slowly toward the kitchen.

"Oh. Does this mean we are going to need to order pizza?" Catherine said, smiling at Al, who had seated himself on the couch.

"Hopefully not," Douglas said as the women followed Al and sat down in the living room. "I've made my mother's macaroni and cheese, with a little help from Ruth." He winked at Ruth. Along with macaroni and cheese, Douglas had made a green salad and cauliflower au gratin. Dessert was Ruth's cheesecake topped with blueberries.

"Everything was delicious," Al said as he took a bite of cheesecake.

"It was, Dad. I'm really impressed." She was surprised as well. Christmas seems to have given him a new lease on life. Perhaps, he's come to terms with Uncle Ray's death.

They moved to the living room, and Catherine opened a bottle of port. Al got the fire going again, and they sat admiring the decorations.

"Wouldn't it be fun," Catherine mused, "if we could all be kids again for just one Christmas? I have such fond memories of Daddy reading us "'Twas the Night Before Christmas" and tucking us in on Christmas Eve. Then, we would try hard to go to sleep, but usually Caroline and I would lie awake whispering about what Santa might bring. I remember the Christmas when I was five and Caroline was seven. She told me that she no longer believed in Santa Claus. I was horrified. I made sure that

Mom and Dad knew that I still believed."

"I remember," Douglas said, a grin brightening his wrinkled cheeks. "That Christmas I got a note along with Santa Claus."

Catherine looked over at Al. He was nodding off in his chair.

"Maybe you should get your belovéd home," Douglas said to Ruth. "You've both put in a long day, and I can't thank you enough."

Ruth patted Al's arm to awaken him. After Ruth and Al left, Judy decided she would turn in for the night.

"Judy, I am so glad you were able to join us for Christmas," Douglas said.

"I'm glad to be here," Judy said, crossing the room and giving Douglas a hug.

Catherine said good night to Judy and returned to the living room. Her father had poured glasses of port. Catherine lifted hers off the table and sat down on a cushion in front of the fire. They were silent for a while until Douglas lifted his glass, took a sip, and asked Catherine how she was feeling about her new position.

"I like Franklin, but I'm already seeing some negative things about my boss and the college politics that are troubling." Catherine had no intention of telling him about what happened with Neil even though she was unable to get the scenes with him out of her head. Anger kept erupting when she thought about Roslyn's response.

"You mentioned that in one of our phone conversations." Douglas said. "I'm afraid that the politics are everywhere. The issue becomes whether you can accomplish your goals and the broader goals of the College and manage the politics. It's also important," he added, "to take care of yourself."

Catherine got up from the cushion and sat down in the chair next to her father. She leaned in towards him and said, "You always put things into perspective for me, Dad, without belittling my concerns. I wonder if you kept that balance in your own life?"

"How do you mean?" Douglas asked

"You've told me a lot of things lately about your relationship with Mother. I know how you felt called to the urban ministry in Washington, but you gave that up for her and took the church here in Spring Lake. How would it have been if you had followed your own desires?"

Douglas was silent for a moment. He studied the glass of port in his hand and took a sip before responding. Catherine was fearful that she had said too much, but she decided to wait and hear what her father had to say. He took another sip and gazed into the fire. He looked like he was miles away.

Her father repeated what she had heard before: his regrets about neglecting her mother while he and Uncle Ray were growing the business.

"Things only got worse when I began talking about going to seminary." Douglas stopped, a pained expression on his face.

"Dad, you don't need to go on."

"I want to talk with you about this, so you will understand your mother better... so you'll understand why she was so hard on you."

Douglas gazed into the fire. She could only imagine what was going through his head. Guilt? Regret? But why now? She asked him when she was a teenager, and he didn't tell her. When Peter confronted him and asked what mother's meltdown on Holy Thursday had to do with her, he didn't answer.

Catherine sipped from her glass, uncomfortable about what might come next. She put her glass on the end table and shifted nervously in her chair.

Douglas looked at Catherine cautiously before saying, "While Ray and I were in business together, I met someone else."

"Was her name Grace?" Catherine asked, holding her father's gaze.

"Yes. How did you know that?" The look of surprise on his face made him appear younger somehow, closer to the young, healthy father she remembered from childhood.

"I used to hear you and mother fighting. Things would grow quiet or you would whisper after she mentioned her name. Catherine took a sip from her glass and asked, "What was she like, Daddy?"

"I met her the night before the March on Washington, the summer after she had finished law school. She came from an Irish Catholic family in Philadelphia. She'd received a scholarship to go to Bryn Mawr, so her parents reluctantly let her go to college. She studied literature, and her parents assumed she would be a teacher. I'm sure she would have been a wonderful teacher, but she wanted nothing to do with this plan. She got a scholarship to go to law school at Penn."

"Dad, you're reading her resume. What was she *like*?" Catherine asked.

Douglas sighed and got up, his hands shaking as he reached for his glass.

"She was everything your mother wasn't."

He walked to the window, his back to Catherine.

"She was a brunette—black Irish—with incredible spunk. Her eyes were green, and she had a wicked sense of humor. She had more energy than I ever did, and I was as much attracted to her intelligence as I was her beauty." Douglas took a few steps toward the chair he'd been sitting in and stopped.

He looked like he was close to tears, frozen where he stood.

Catherine said, "You don't need to tell me more if this is upsetting you."

"I want to tell you, Catherine, so you can understand better about our marriage. So, you can understand that no failed marriage is ever just one person's fault."

I shouldn't put him through all this, she thought. It's been a good day, but he must be exhausted. She got up and took the glass from him and placed it on the table. He moved slowly toward his chair and sat down.

"Daddy, did you ever think about leaving mother for Grace?" Catherine liked saying the name, already trying to picture her young, shy father with this beautiful woman.

"I'm sorry to say I did. I was already thinking about going to seminary when your mother found out about Grace. She threatened to go to her father and tell him about my infidelity. To add insult to injury, I told her I didn't care if she did. I wanted to move in a new direction, so quite honestly, I didn't care. Your Uncle Ray helped me see that I was just infatuated with an ideal and got me back on track."

"What do you mean, back on track?"

"I wanted someone to share my passion for politics, my interest in urban ministry. Ray pointed out that I would never find this in a woman who wanted to have children."

"He may have been wrong about that, Dad."

"I don't know, Catherine. It was a different generation than yours. Many of the women I met in the Civil Rights Movement wanted to change the world, overturn traditional roles, and make things different. I admired all that, but I also wanted to have children. I wanted to have many children, but the peace your mother and I made did not last long."

"And what were the terms of the peace accord?" Catherine asked, shaking her head. "Peace at any cost for you?"

"Yes and no," Douglas said, reaching for his glass and then leaning back in his chair. His face was ashen, and his right hand shook as it fell to his side.

"Maybe we should call it a night. You look exhausted," she said.

"I think you're right. I'd like to continue this conversation another time when it's not so late." Douglas placed his left hand on the arm of the chair and pushed himself up slowly. He shuffled to the fireplace and closed the doors. One small flame flickered on the log. Catherine got up and moved close to her father. She stroked his right arm. Her eyes smiled at him as a wave of emotion made her sigh deeply.

"You've always told me not to look back and have regrets. You've told me to look ahead and build on what is good, forgiving myself for the things that didn't work. I hope you can do the same."

Catherine took her father's hands in hers. He didn't have much time for looking ahead.

He must have read her mind because he said, "I've made many mistakes. I never made peace with your mother. It's taken a toll on us."

She squeezed his hands and said, "I don't know what that means for you, Daddy, but I love you. In one way, it's good to know you're human."

"Human and capable of doing great harm to people I love," Douglas said. He let go of her hands and pulled a linen handkerchief from his pocket. He wiped tears from his steel-blue eyes and placed the handkerchief back in his pocket.

"That harm can never outweigh all the good that you've done."

"That's what we can hope for as we look back on our lives." Douglas gave Catherine a kiss on the cheek and climbed the stairs to bed.

"Sleep well," Catherine said. "I'll see you in the morning."

Catherine climbed the stairs slowly after she heard her father close his bedroom door. She pulled on a nightshirt and curled up on top of the comforter.

She was four, awakened from a dream and padding downstairs to the kitchen to get a glass of water. After getting the water, she saw the light was on in the study. Her father was sitting at his desk, tears rolling down his face. A book of poetry lay open in front of him.

"Daddy, why are you crying?" she asked, walking over to him. He reached down and took the glass of water from her and placed it on the desk. She climbed up into his lap.

"Sometimes, Doll, Daddy gets sad."

"Did someone make you sad?" Catherine asked.

"Yes, but she didn't mean to. We were friends. She had to go away." Douglas nestled his chin against her hair.

"Well, maybe you should go and visit her. I bet she misses you too."

Douglas stroked Catherine's hair and held her close. "I don't know, honey."

Catherine kissed her father on the cheek, slipped off his lap, and went back to bed.

Now it seemed clear. He was talking about Grace. He seemed so full of doubt. Was he worried that Grace didn't love him?

My father... in love with another woman when I was a little girl. No wonder he couldn't make his marriage work. Someone else was on his mind, keeping him up at night.

Chapter Twenty-Seven

Douglas pulled on his pajamas, each button a challenge for his arthritic fingers. He pulled back the sheet and comforter and sat on the edge of the bed. His life here in front of him, he thought, looking at the photographs displayed on the dresser. Elizabeth had arranged them carefully... Douglas with his mother on the beach in Cape Cod... his parent's wedding picture... Elizabeth's father and Suzanne on their wedding day... baby pictures of Caroline and Catherine... Caroline and David on their wedding day.

"But you're not here, my love," Douglas said as he walked beside this sea of faces. "You're not here, the one I hold in my heart."

Grace came to Philadelphia that Christmas her father was dying... 1968. Douglas's heart was still filled with the time they spent together in Bar Harbor. He met her in the diner on Germantown Avenue after church on Christmas

Eve.

"*Thanks for meeting me,*" *she said.*

He sat in the booth beside her, holding her hand. Her face was drawn, tears had smudged her mascara. He dipped his napkin in a glass of water and washed the mascara from her cheek.

"*He doesn't have much time,*" *Grace said.* "*He's asked that Father O'Donoghue be with him at the end.*"

"*Of course,*" *Douglas said.*

"*Father O'Donoghue has been good to our family over many years. He baptized all of us, married my brothers. He even knows about Theresa. Theresa is the woman I told you about that my father has been involved with for so many years.*"

Douglas looked at Grace's face and saw all her questions, all her fears. He'd never seen her fear before.

"*Do you believe in heaven, Douglas?*" *she asked. He loved the way she said his name firmly, softly.*

"*I do, Grace,*" *Douglas said with more certainty than he possessed.*

"*Will my father go to heaven, even with all of his sins?*" *Her voice was the voice of a child, asking for answers from someone wiser.*

Douglas's eyes fell on a favorite picture: Caroline and Catherine, arms linked, on the day of Catherine's First Communion. He sat down on the bed, remembering the awful events of that day

"*Douglas,*" *his mother exclaimed,* "*these skirts are too short. If Elizabeth has no sense, even more reason you need to have some.*"

"Mother, it's the style. She's only twelve," Douglas said, feigning exasperation.

He snapped the picture while his mother looked into the living room from the foyer. She smiled, despite her disapproval of the dress.

"Elizabeth, we need to leave. I need to meet with the communicants before the service," he called up the steps. There was no answer. He took the steps, two at a time, fearing the worst.

Elizabeth sat at her dressing table, mascara brush in her right hand, a glass of scotch reaching her mouth from her left hand. Douglas closed the bedroom door.

"You're a disgrace," he said, taking the glass of scotch and putting it on the windowsill, out of reach.

"I'm not that drunk yet," she said, continuing to make-up her eyes and give her cheeks one last burst of color.

"Are you doing this to spite me, or is this about Catherine? This is a big day for her."

"Do you really think she cares about any of this nonsense?" Elizabeth asked, slipping into black pumps. Douglas recoiled from her penetrating gaze, her cold cynical eyes dismissing the faith defining him.

"She cares, Elizabeth, and I'll not have you disgrace this family. We'll see you after church."

Douglas looked at Elizabeth, remembering her before alcohol, before Grace. As he closed the door behind him, he heard a crash, glass breaking against the door. He kept moving away from Elizabeth toward his girls.

His mother and the girls were already in the car. He slid into the driver's seat and looked at his mother, her face tense, her hands folded in her lap.

"I'm sorry, girls. I'm sorry, Catherine," Douglas said

as he scanned the back seat. "Your mother's sick."

"Stop saying that, Daddy," Caroline said. "She's not sick. She's drunk." Caroline looked at Catherine and said, "Don't cry, Catherine. Nana will take us to lunch after church, won't you Nana?"

His mother turned and gave the girls a nod. They drove the short distance to the church, and he took Catherine's hand as Caroline and his mother entered the sanctuary.

Catherine pulled him close to her. Douglas crouched down so his face was level with hers. Her nose grazed his as she whispered in his ear, "It's not your fault, Daddy. It's not your fault." She squeezed his hand and kissed his cheek, letting him go gently as she went off to join the other children.

Find the words. Find the words. Catherine doesn't judge you. She doesn't believe what his father-in-law believed... that Elizabeth's problems, her pain, was his fault. Douglas looked again at Catherine and Caroline's picture on the day of Catherine's First Communion.

Douglas knew the service by heart, but that morning, he stumbled over the familiar words.

"This is the Body of Christ, broken for you. This is the Blood of Christ, shed for the remission of sins.

"I am the Good Shepherd. The Good Shepherd gives his life for his sheep," he recited, feeling emptiness, a hollow voice touching each congregant as they came forward to receive the elements.

His homily was blessedly short that morning. The girls joked about it at lunch. Caroline, mischievous, mimicked him, trying more than she usually did to cheer up her sister.

Wagging her finger at us, Caroline exclaimed, "The crowd greeted Jesus with 'Hosanna! Blessed is the one who comes in the name of the Lord!' Like a New York-style ticker-tape parade for a retiring warrior or politician, the crowd adored him. Within days, they called for his death.

"This is the Word of the Lord," she repeated slowly.

"Thanks be to God, we think," Catherine and Caroline said in unison, overcome with giggling they couldn't control.

The girls continued to laugh as their Nana ordered chicken salad and oysters.

"Do you ever order anything else?" Caroline asked, taking a bite of her cheeseburger.

"Pot calls kettle black," Nana said, winking at Douglas. Laughter and the lightness of the conversation relaxed him.

A cold wind caught the car door as he held it for his mother. Palm Sunday, a day of triumph. First Communion, a special day for his little girl.

The wind caught his mother's hat as she stepped from the car. Douglas reached out to catch it.

"Dad," Caroline said. "We're going to change and go over to see Karen. Aunt Rosemary invited us."

"That's fine, honey," Nana said, taking her hat from Douglas's hand with a smile. "We'll join you later for dinner."

Douglas hung up his mother's coat and sat down on the couch next to his mother's chair, his collar and prayer book beside him. His mother sat down and picked up her knitting.

"This is the Body of Christ, broken for you." He took a

deep breath and closed his eyes. "This is the Blood of Christ, shed for the remission of sins."

Douglas opened his eyes and looked at his mother's worried face. He heard Catherine scream.

He took the steps, two at a time, water running, the sound cutting through the afternoon stillness.

Caroline ran from the bathroom. Catherine knelt by the tub, water and blood touching her outstretched hands.

Body and Blood. The Good Shepherd gives his life for his sheep.

"Oh Grace," Douglas said, getting up from the bed and holding the picture of Caroline and Catherine. "Why couldn't they have been your daughters? We could have celebrated those special days with them. All your questions about God... All of mine... We could have asked them together."

Douglas opened the bedroom door carefully, not wanting any noise to awaken Catherine or Judy as he moved slowly down the steps to the study. He turned on the banker's lamp on his desk and moved toward the iron box. The clock on his desk read 3:07 a.m. He lifted the box to his chair and opened it with the key from the tray in the middle drawer of the desk. He caressed the bundle of letters tied with the green ribbon and located the large envelope.

He opened it. Inside were two pictures. He left his wedding picture in the envelope, taken on a beautiful sunny day in Princeton, and removed the picture of Grace in an emerald green dress. He laid the picture on his desk and sat down.

Her voice again... "Douglas, will my father go to heaven, even with all of his sins?" He felt her hand in his and wanted, needed to answer her question.

"Sins, Grace?" he asked, looking at her closely and squeezing her hand. "Your father, we all leave our sins at the foot of the Cross. I hope he hasn't been carrying them all these years."

She stroked his hand, sending electricity through his body.

"You're a good priest, Douglas," she said. "It makes sense when you say it."

The waitress came and filled their cups. Douglas ordered some eggs and toast for Grace. He knew she hadn't been eating.

"Douglas," she said. "Tell me about Advent." Her hand slid away from his as she took a piece of toast.

"How do you mean?"

"The Christmas I believed we'd be together always, you taught me about Advent."

Her words cut through him like a knife. So there had been a time when she believed they were possible, and he had ruined it.

Douglas looked at her picture, her beauty captured in a moment of happiness.

"Yes, I remember, Grace," Douglas said running his index finger over her eyes, her nose, her bright red lips before he placed the picture in the envelope and returned it to the desk drawer.

Douglas shuffled across the living room and climbed the stairs. There was a piece of purple ribbon streaming from his left fist. He placed the key on the dresser and sat on the edge of the bed. He heard her voice again as he stared at the pictures on the dresser.

It was 1963. Elizabeth was up with Caroline in the night, walking her back and forth in the nursery when she cried. After church that December, Douglas drove to Grace's apartment in the large stone house. She had coffee ready, having had hers, already up for hours reading, working.

"What's this?" she asked, as she took his coat. Douglas placed the pine boughs arranged in a circle on the tiny, square kitchen table. The bag of candles was still in his hand as he reached out to kiss her cheek.

"It's an Advent wreath," he said, taking the candles from the bag and placing them on the wreath, three purple, one pink.

"Advent is the period of waiting before Christmas, waiting with anticipation for God to break into history." Douglas sat down at the table and lit a purple candle. Grace stood beside him, her hands resting lightly on his shoulder.

"God breaking into history," she repeated.

"Yes," he said. "I believe the main purpose of the Incarnation was to provide hope... hope that human existence has meaning, that our lives have purpose beyond our experience, hope that what we contribute can create new beginnings.

"Advent looks forward to the birth of Christ, but it also reflects on the struggles of the oppressed people of Israel. These stories reveal God's willingness to work in and through each of us."

Grace pulled out the chair next to Douglas and sat down. "So, this is where you get your hope that we can change society," she said, taking his hand.

"Yes," he said. "We may never see the results of the change we help to create, but we have faith that it will matter."

Douglas went every Sunday in Advent to see Grace. When he arrived the second week, Grace had placed a copy of a family Bible next to the Advent wreath.

"You can read from this," she said, touching the worn leather cover. The Bible lay open to a passage from Micah that Douglas had quoted the week before:

And what does the LORD require of you?
To act justly and to love mercy
and to walk humbly with your God.

Douglas arrived the third week with his copy of Hopkins's poems. He read "God's Grandeur" and a passage from Romans.

"Redemption, my love, isn't just about individual sin," Douglas said.

"That's not what I learned growing up," Grace said. "I was a little girl making stuff up for confession."

"Perhaps the broader message was there, and you weren't paying attention," he scolded.

Douglas took her hand. "God wants to redeem all Creation, creating a new heaven and earth. That's why there's so much cause for joy."

Grace lit the three purple candles, and they sat for a few moments quietly, her hands covering his.

Chapter Twenty-Eight

Catherine awoke and looked out on a still, dark morning. Too early to get up, she hugged the down comforter around her. The house was still. Not sleepy, she decided to take a run on the boardwalk. She put on several layers and her sweatpants. The thermometer on the back porch read 32°F. Catherine left her father and Judy a note: "Be back in an hour. – C"

She ran the three blocks to the ocean, the cold air enveloping and invigorating her.

The sky over the ocean was a canvas of pinks and yellows. The sun was trying to peek through the light cloud cover. The boardwalk was wet and slippery. She ran faster, thinking about her father.

No wonder her mother had been so adamant about her daughters marrying the right man. Her mother married the well-bred man who knew how to make money, but then, he became someone else. Caroline had done the right things... married the Harvard man with money and a fast track job on Wall Street. Catherine had become her father, more concerned about ideas and people than making money. No wonder her mother resented her so much. Or worse, perhaps her mother saw her as a woman like Grace.

Catherine reached the end of the boardwalk. A light snow was falling, mixed with sleet. Leaning against the railing, she raised her head and closed her eyes. The cold moisture stung her face. She'd spent her life trying to make sense of her parents' story only to find out now that important chapters had been missing.

She opened her eyes and turned around. Gray clouds, like wisps of smoke, were moving in from the west. The town was not yet awake, and the ocean rolled in gently.

As she returned to the house, she noticed the light in the study. Opening the front door carefully, she called out, "Daddy, are you up already?" He probably wasn't sleeping and came down to read. Catherine opened the door slowly and came into the empty room. She turned off the banker's lamp on his desk and went upstairs for a shower.

Catherine worked quietly, placing Christmas presents in neat piles in the living room. No wonder her father hadn't slept, she thought. She'd kept him up talking about things that upset him. Grace. The name suited her. She was a gift to my father... an unwarranted favor. Grace.

My father was in love with her... Grace... He let her go for a dead marriage. She wondered if he talked with Uncle Ray about her again. Probably not, especially after Uncle Ray said he wouldn't be able to have children with a woman like that. Catherine placed a beautifully- wrapped package on her father's recliner. With Love from Ruth and

Al, the card read. Probably a sweater.

Did she ever have that kind of passion, love, for anyone? For Peter? Would she have made him happy, so he didn't need anyone else?

Catherine's thoughts were interrupted when Judy came down, carrying a bag of presents. Catherine took the bag from her and placed it in front of the fireplace.

"Come on," she said, putting her arm around her friend. "I've got my grandmother's Dutch cake, just baked, for breakfast."

"What makes it Dutch?" Judy asked.

"I have no idea," Catherine said, laughing.

Hal arrived promptly at four o'clock while Catherine was busy in the kitchen, preparing dinner. He settled into an easy conversation with her father, who was asking him about his interest in History. Hal went on at length about the Civil Rights Movement and the impact it had on changing things in the workplace for women.

"Representative Howard Smith proposed the amendment that would include sex as a protected class in the Civil Rights Act. He proposed the amendment to kill the legislation, but it passed. Ruth Bader Ginsberg was able to use the language to show that men and women were kept from equal opportunity because of gender."

Catherine could hear most of the conversation from the kitchen and interjected a few comments. As Hal started talking about employment law and sexual harassment, she felt her stomach lurch. Does he have to talk about this right now? she thought, bracing herself against the kitchen counter.

"When my mother was practicing law, what we call

employment law was not what it is today. In fact, it wasn't until the 1970s that we had a name for sexual harassment in the workplace." Judy gave Hal a dark look, and he quickly changed the subject. He started talking about the oral histories he'd written about people who were at the March on Washington.

Catherine sat down on the couch next to her father, a bowl of string beans in her hand.

Douglas said, "I would love to read those. I was there."

"So was my mother. I interviewed her and, later, after her death, I interviewed some of her friends."

"It was an extraordinary day. I'd gone alone, but I didn't feel alone as I marched down the mall. A sea of people, more black than white... a moment of unity amid so many years of hatred and fear." Douglas looked at Hal and then shifted his gaze to Catherine.

"Rev. Finley..."

"Please, call me Douglas..."

"May I schedule a time to come back and interview you? The same journal that published my two oral histories would like me to write a third. Your story about the religious perspective would be an excellent complement to the other two."

"I would be happy to talk with you. Let's schedule something after the New Year."

Catherine noticed her father looking at Hal with great interest, steel-blue eyes taking in the younger man's laugh, his intensity, the graceful but forceful way he used his hands to emphasize or make a point.

Dinner conversation shifted to family traditions. Hal mentioned his Uncle Vince, his mother's law firm partner, who took them to a tree farm each year to cut down a

Christmas tree. "We'd spend an evening trimming it and eating my mother's Christmas cookies," Hal said, eyes wide like a child. "She was a great baker and cook, and she would love this rib roast."

Hal left after dinner, wanting to get back to Philadelphia before another snowstorm started, predicted before midnight.

"Douglas, it was a pleasure meeting you. I'll look forward to talking with you next month. Judy, I hope we'll have the chance to see each other again as well," Hal said as he pulled on his coat.

Catherine put the dessert dishes in the dishwasher and joined Judy and her father in the living room. They sat quietly, watching the yellow and orange flames crackle and hiss. Catherine could tell her father was deep in thought, and she didn't want to interrupt.

"I'm going to bed," Judy said, reaching over and kissing Douglas on the cheek. "It was so good to spend this Christmas with you." Douglas didn't get up but reached up and gave Judy a hug.

Catherine thought she would continue their conversation from the previous evening. Instead, Douglas was focused on the discussion with Hal.

"Catherine, as I talked with that young man today, I felt as though I was transported back in time. I felt as though I was having a conversation with a colleague in the 1960s."

"Well, Hal does bring History alive for his students," Catherine said, enjoying the fire's warmth.

"No. It was something more than that. It was as if we knew each other and had this conversation before."

"I'm glad he came," Catherine said. "It's his first

Christmas without his wife."

"To lose her when he's so young," Douglas said. "Tragic." His gaze was far away.

Part III
Winter 2005

Chapter Twenty-Nine

Hal made the trip to Spring Lake the second Saturday in January. A frigid wind blew off the ocean as he walked to the boardwalk and watched turbulent surf ebbing and flowing. His mind wandered to a time on Cape Cod with his mother.

She was teaching him to swim. He was wading in knee-deep water when an enormous wave engulfed him, and he lost his footing. His mother immediately wrapped her arms around him and held him close. The softness of her breasts against his shaking body comforted him. Her gentle voice, filled with assurance, soothed his panic. She never missed an opportunity to challenge him to move past whatever had frightened him or angered him.

"I'm always here for you, little man," she'd say.

"She is still with me today," he said, the saltwater spray touching his lips.

Carrying the memory, Hal walked back to the house and rang the bell. He'd thought a lot about his conversation with Douglas on Christmas Day. He imagined Catherine's father at the March, alone but taken up in the excitement of the day.

He imagined himself there, marching down the Mall, experiencing what it was like to be the minority for the first time. He'd watched YouTube videos of the speeches, Martin Luther King and John Lewis, and the performances of Joan Baez and Peter, Paul, and Mary. He imagined the crush of the crowd and nationwide awe that the gathering remained peaceful. He had closed his eyes more than once and tried to imagine his mother meeting Douglas at the March. She mocked religion, but would she have seen past his faith to his passion for the change he wanted to make? Underneath her toughness, her cynicism, there was an idealist like Douglas.

Douglas, dressed in khaki pants and a black sweater, opened the door and looked pleased to see him. He took Hal's coat, laying it across the chair in the foyer. They moved from the foyer towards the smell of fresh coffee. Douglas brought the coffee pot to the dining room table where he had laid out cups and a small plate with fresh pastries. Douglas's eyes were bright and alert.

"I'm so glad you could come. I've been rereading my journal and several papers I have kept from the 1960s and 70s," Douglas said, motioning for Hal to take the seat next to him.

"You kept a journal then?" Hal asked, reaching for the coffee pot and filling the two cups.

"Yes. I've always been more comfortable talking on paper first," he said shyly, taking his first sip of coffee.

Douglas took in the young man's, wind-blown jet-black hair.

Hal reached for a raspberry pastry and took a bite before responding.

"I think I'm the same way. When I teach a class, I've written all my ideas down in a published article or in extensive notes. My first exchange is with myself in writing."

Douglas nodded. "We all tell our own stories, don't we, whether we do it through literature or history or theology? I was thinking about this as I reread my journal from the 1960s. I was a young man, full of passion and fervor for the things that needed to be changed in this country. While many focused on legislation that would demand a change in the way people behaved and made decisions about who they would employ, I didn't believe that any of this would matter unless we changed people's hearts. The young black students in the Movement understood this."

Hal listened carefully. He sipped his coffee and opened the small notebook he'd laid on the table. As Douglas talked, he jotted down some notes. His left hand moved across the pages of the small notebook as he pensively ran his right hand through his hair.

"The night before The March on Washington, I was having a drink in the hotel bar. A young woman came in alone. She seemed familiar to me. After she ordered a glass of wine, she smiled at me. I started talking with her and realized I had seen her walking in Valley Green, a park near me in Philadelphia. She told me she was from Philadelphia. Her friend, another attorney, and his wife, joined her in a few minutes. We got into a conversation about the March, and they invited me to join them for dinner. Her friend, the attorney—I can't remember his name—had been one of the Freedom Riders in '61."

Hal didn't want to interrupt, but the young woman reminded him of his mother's story. She had tried some cases with William Thompson. Yes. That was his name. Hal was forming a question when Douglas returned to his thoughts on the theology that shaped his thinking.

"Some of Niebuhr's theology gave me a platform for how I wanted to address the inequities in society. He took the story of the Gospels and provided a structure to address current societal ills," Douglas said, pausing for a moment and sipping his coffee.

"My mother was raised Catholic," Hal said. "She saw government and the church as oppressors, allowing, if not promoting, racism and sexism. She would have found your perspective unrealistic."

Douglas was silent for a moment. He looked at Hal closely, his eyes scanning the younger man's face.

"Is it possible that your mother and I were both correct? Unless we destroy existing structures—the church, commerce, government—and start again, vestiges of racism and sexism, greed, and wrong-headed passion will always be an issue. On the other hand, dismantling those structures would destroy the good they represented and have done in the world over time."

Hal took a few moments before responding.

"My greatest influence is the way my mother lived her life. I could come home from school, bloodied by a fight that I'd started. She would hear my story, comfort me, and defend me, but she always wanted me to try to understand why the other person acted as he did. She didn't seem to need religion to shape her ethics, her morality."

"Empathy," Douglas said, his gaze far away. "Your mother understood the importance of empathy even if in the end, she might reject the behavior or the attitude of the other person. To me, it's the heart of the Gospel. It's the heart of what makes us human."

Douglas took a large bite from one of the small pastries and took another sip of coffee.

Hal shifted the conversation, and said, "My mother told me I was privileged, but I didn't always feel that way. I looked around me and saw children with two parents. I saw fathers who were attorneys, like my mother, making twice as much as she did. She was always alone... strong but always alone."

"What happened to your father?" Douglas asked, leaning in to hear what Hal said.

"He died when I was a baby," Hal said, sipping the tepid coffee, looking away from Douglas. Hal wanted to say more, to tell Douglas all the questions he had about his mother. Why had she never married again? Why was she always alone? He remembered the first time he'd asked her about his father.

Kindergarten... his first week of school. They'd sat in a circle as the teacher asked them, "What did your mother pack you for your snack today? In order," she commanded as they started to talk out of turn. One by one... an apple, peanut butter crackers, a banana, until they got to Samantha, a tiny black girl with a tattered blue dress and dirty white sneakers. "My mommy wasn't home when I left for school." Silence, then, nervous giggles.

The teacher blushed and shifted in the tiny chair.

"What was the last game you played with your father?" she asked, voice uncertain.

Most answered without enthusiasm. Hal defiantly said, "I don't have a father," and bowed his head and folded his hands.

Samantha said, "Catch," and looked over at Hal.

Samantha became his friend, as much as that was allowed in 1969.

That night, when his mother read to him before bed, he wasn't listening. He interrupted, asking about his father.

"Honey, he died when you were a baby," she said.

"Died? Like Gramps?" he asked, rolling on his side and taking his mother's hand.

She nodded. "He had to go away. He couldn't stay with us."

"It's okay, Mama," he said, eyes heavy with sleep. "I don't think Samantha has a daddy or a mommy."

"Tell me about Samantha," his mother said.

He fell asleep, feeling soft fingers stroking his cheek.

Hal listened to Douglas, interrupting less as the conversation continued. He took copious notes and wished he'd asked if he could tape the discussion.

After an hour passed, Hal looked up from his notes and saw fatigue in Douglas's eyes. Was he fatigued with age and illness, or was there a sadness that lingered because the church and society hadn't accomplished what he had hoped?

Hal wished the conversation could go on longer, but he didn't want to tire Douglas.

"Douglas, I appreciate your time. May I send you a

draft of my article to review?"

"Of course," Douglas said. "I'd like to read it."

Hal hesitated, looking down at his notes and then, at Douglas. "Did you ever see the young woman again, the one you met the night before the March?"

"I did," Douglas said, the weariness leaving his wrinkled face as he described her call and their dinner in Chestnut Hill a week later.

"Her name was Grace, a name that suited her. She wasn't in Philadelphia for too much longer before she moved to Boston. We exchanged some letters. Hers were always passionate about cases she was trying, her grief over Dr. King and Bobby Kennedy's deaths. She wrote to me when she was diagnosed with cancer." Douglas had been staring at his hands as he spoke, but as Hal responded, Douglas looked at him.

"Breast cancer," Hal said.

"Yes," Douglas replied. His hands shook as he clasped them tightly, searching Hal's face, seeing Grace's intensity.

"Grace was my mother," Hal said, running his hand through his hair. How is this possible? To meet someone who knew his mother when she was so young, so filled with passionate ideas. He remembered stories she told him about cases she tried, often cases she lost. As he got older, he thought she told him about those cases, so he'd know she was human, that it was okay to fail, but maybe, more important than that, she really loved the people she defended.

The young black woman in Memphis who was raped by white teenagers... She told him about that case when he was studying the Civil Rights Movement in eleventh grade.

She wanted him to know it wasn't just about laws passed... it was about people. James Porter, the father of that young woman, did everything he could to protect his daughter, but she still was raped. Hal's mother spoke about him tenderly.

Hal fought back tears, eyes unfocused as he tried to regain his composure.

"Did she ever tell you about me?" Hal asked.

"No," Douglas said, realizing he may have spoken too quickly. "There was little in her letters about her personal life." Douglas leaned back in his chair, unclasping his shaky hands and placing them on the edge of the table.

"The last letter I received from Grace was in 1974. I don't remember much about the letter, but she seemed happy."

Hal smiled. "She was. She'd received the news in early October that her cancer was gone. I was ten. She took me out of school for a week and we drove to Maine. We took the coast road to Bar Harbor. My mother always had energy for work, for me, but that trip was the first time I saw her enjoy herself, really have fun. We saw a sunrise on Cadillac Mountain. You can imagine how cold it was on an October morning, but the sky was cloudless, and the sunburst on the horizon like a cannonball."

Douglas nodded, remembering the summer morning with Grace on Cadillac Mountain, remembering her words: "You'll always be loved, Douglas, but I doubt if either one of us will ever feel safe."

Hal closed his notebook. "My mother took more time off later that fall, and in December, we did something we'd never done before."

Douglas smiled and leaned in, "What was that?" he asked.

"We celebrated Advent. We had a wreath with candles and a book of readings, but it wasn't just religious."

"How do you mean?" Douglas asked.

"It was political too. She talked about God breaking into history, God fighting oppression. She told me stories from the 1960s when she'd been optimistic about change."

As Hal drove home, he felt an incredible sadness. How different his life would have been if he'd had a father like Douglas... if his mother had shared her life with someone like him.

Living without a father was living with a hole deep inside him. He filled the hole with his hobbies and sports when he was growing up. Then, his studies and his love for Tina. Today, the gaping hole seemed smaller, somehow. Hearing some of his mother's story tugged at his heart. Others were drawn to her passion and energy. Douglas's chance meeting with her at the March on Washington was still vivid after forty years.

Chapter Thirty

Ruth had called this morning with the news. "I rang the bell," she said. "When he didn't respond, I used my key. He was lying on the couch, fully dressed as if he was going to someone else's funeral."

Wind gusts and large snowdrifts slowed the trip. Catherine hunched over the steering wheel, straining to see the lines on the road. Words from Auden's elegy for Yeats ran through her mind:

He disappeared in the dead of winter:
The brooks were frozen, the airports almost deserted,
And snow disfigured the public statues;
The mercury sank in the mouth of the dying day.
What instruments we have agree
The day of his death was a dark cold day.

We had such a good Christmas. He was stronger than he'd been since Mother died, but he did talk about his life as though he were telling someone else's story.

Catherine slowed down as she approached the exit for Route 35. The snow-covered ramp wasn't slippery, she decided, after pumping the brakes several times. When Ruth called with the news, she had the presence of mind to ask Catherine if she wanted her to call the undertaker. "Yes, thanks for doing that. Please tell them not to take the body away before I get there. I'll leave right now," she responded.

The defroster was straining to fight the sleet. Just two more blocks. Catherine pumped the brakes slowly as she navigated an icy patch and pulled up in front of the house. Her hands shook as she took the keys out of her purse. Drifted snow, coated with ice, filled the driveway. The stone stoop shimmered like the surface of a still lake.

The darkness of the stormy day fell away momentarily as Catherine entered the well-lit, orderly living room. A small crèche held center stage on the television. Ruth must have missed it when she helped her father put away the Christmas decorations. Her father lay on the couch, a book open and lying on his chest.

Catherine unbuttoned her cloak slowly, handling each button with unsteady hands. She knelt beside the couch. His frailty was gone. Had the lines in his face been erased by death, or was she just imagining this? She took his cold hand in hers, her other hand touching his warm forehead.

Ruth was right: he did look like he was dressed for someone else's funeral. How many husbands, wives, children and friends of the dying or dead had her father comforted over the years? Soon the house would fill with mourners, there to comfort her.

Rilke's *Love Poems to God* lay open and face down on

her father's chest. Letting go of his hand, Catherine turned the book over:

No one lives his life.

Disguised since childhood,
haphazardly assembled
from voices and fears and little pleasures,

we come of age as masks,
Our true face never speaks.

He probably knew it by heart, she thought.

Our true face never speaks. Our stories become our masks, protecting us from rejection. That moment on Jordan Pond when she was a little girl, she saw his vitality without fear or shame. His memories of Grace allowed him to remember his best self, someone he couldn't be with her mother.

Without a willingness to be vulnerable, others don't know us. He'd been vulnerable with Grace, vulnerable with Catherine over these last few months, hoping she'd see him without his mask and still love him.

She placed the book on the end table and walked into the dining room where a cup of coffee and an empty cereal bowl lay abandoned next to a large envelope with Catherine's name on it.

She read the letter slowly, standing at her father's place, fingertips tentatively touching the table.

Dear Catherine:

You have brought me such peace of mind over these past few months by listening to me talk about Grace. I hope I have not burdened you with more than you can bear. Grace has remained in my heart and in my imagination since the day I met her, which was a huge injustice to your mother. It was impossible for her to forgive me for my infidelity and to accept my decision to go into the ministry.

I have wanted you to know the kind of freedom and passion Grace had. I have seen it in you, even when you were little. I pray that you will know the kind of love and acceptance that I felt when I was with her. I know you don't need a man, but I do think that it is part of the image of God in us to long to see ourselves fully in someone else's eyes.

In my study, there's an iron box. You remember? The one I always said I would grab first if there was a fire? Well, the iron box doesn't contain my will, yours and Caroline's birth certificates, and my passport. Those documents are in the safe deposit box at PNC. The iron box contains my journal and letters from Grace and a beautiful ring she gave me once. I want you to take the box home with you after I die. If you wish to destroy it, you may, of course. If you choose to read its contents, know that you will be reading about a relationship that brought me great joy and, at the same time, great sadness.

I must end this letter because I'm feeling very tired.

I love you, Catherine.

Daddy

Catherine held the letter at arm's length so her tears would not smear the ink on the page. She located the file box next to her father's desk in his study and hesitated before reaching for it. Perhaps this secret should die with him. Did she really need to know about this? She sat down in his desk chair, remembering the many times she sat in his lap as a little girl, holding his pen, asking him questions about the books he was reading.

"So, you're going to be left-handed like your grandmother?" her father asked when she was five. She squeezed the sleek black pen tightly, looking down at the book open on her father's desk.

"Why do you write in your books?" she asked, squinting to see the tiny notes in the margins.

"It helps me remember important ideas," he answered, sliding the pen from her grip and placing it on the desk.

She opened the file box and ran her fingers over the top of the chocolate brown, leather journal. Letters, still in their envelopes, were bound together with a green ribbon. Reaching into the box, she pulled out a smaller box, which contained a gold, masculine ring with a brown stone that Catherine didn't recognize. She placed the ring box on her father's desk before she closed the iron box and carried it out to her car. The sky was dark. The wind cut through her.

Auden's elegy kept running through her mind: "What instruments we have agree/The day of his death was a dark cold day."

Chapter Thirty-One

The temperature remained frigid and gusty winds blew off the ocean the day before the funeral as Catherine made last-minute arrangements with a caterer who would provide lunch at the house.

The priest at Douglas's parish was young and timid, reluctant to officiate at the service. He encouraged Catherine to call the bishop, a friend of Douglas's since the days when they had marched with Martin Luther King, but Catherine declined.

"I told him," Catherine reported to Judy that night, "my father is a simple man. He doesn't need a bishop to usher him into the next life. He's already gotten there on his own." Catherine took a generous sip of the white wine she had been nursing since Judy arrived and moved to the fireplace to put another log on the fading flames.

"I thought you didn't believe in an afterlife?" Judy asked, softly.

"I'm not sure I do," Catherine said, "but my father did.

The Celts believed that when you die, you go through the thin place. The longer it takes to move through the thin place says something about how ready you are for the afterlife. When I got here the day Daddy died, he no longer looked like a frail old man. The lines were gone from his face. He looked like a young boy sleeping. I have no doubt he'd already moved through the thin place."

The phone on the end table rang.

"Judy's here, Ruth," Catherine said, "and I think we'll just turn in early. I'll need you and Al tomorrow. You've been so good to Daddy and me."

"It's been my pleasure looking in on your father," Ruth said. "Our lives are richer because of his ministry and his friendship. Al and I love him and you very much."

"I love you too," Catherine said, her voice catching. "I'll see you in the morning."

Catherine and Judy ordered a pizza and continued drinking wine as they talked about childhood memories, Judy still processing the loss of her own parents over the last two years.

"My parents had a long life," Judy said. "For this reason, people expect us to pick up quickly and get back to life as normal, but I haven't found it that easy. My mother was an important part of my life, in the same way that your father has been part of yours."

"Maybe more people are like my sister Caroline," Catherine said, nibbling the edge of a pizza slice. "Once she got out of the house and had her own life, she seemed indifferent to our parents. Even though our mother did everything for her, Caroline wasn't here much to visit with her."

They finished the pizza and watched the fire.

"Anything you need tomorrow," Judy said, "say the word." The phone rang again as Judy said good night and went to bed.

"Hello. Caroline." As she listened, Catherine fidgeted with the phone cord. "I'm sure that others coming from New York have concerns about the weather. There's an early morning train out of 30th Street Station. I can pick you up at the station here."

Catherine heard a curt "I'll do my best," and Caroline hung up abruptly.

Catherine pulled the afghan over her and curled up on the couch. She took a deep breath and watched the flames flicker.

She and her sister had arrived the night before their mother's funeral. Caroline was dismissive, rude, to their father.

"Why do you have to be so mean to Daddy?" Catherine asked in a whisper as they cleaned up the kitchen after dinner.

Caroline released a sigh. "Do you really think he cares she's dead? I haven't seen you shed a tear."

"He does care. He told me he tried to make peace with her before she died. I don't know what that means to him."

"His fucking Christianity. Be a bastard all your life. Then, latter-day confessions wash it all away. I don't buy it."

"You don't have to buy it, Caroline. It's his faith. You could respect it."

"Not likely. Daddy's little girl can respect it." Caroline spat the words at Catherine. "He's a hypocrite." She threw the dishtowel on the counter and stormed out of the

kitchen.

Caroline was right about one thing. She hadn't shed a tear for her mother. She felt her father's pain, his regret that he hadn't called the ambulance sooner. She stumbled and fell. He thought she was drunk. The admitting doctor had assured her father that a quicker response would have made no difference. The cerebral hemorrhage probably killed her instantly.

Catherine slept until first light and woke up disoriented from busy dreams. Putting on sweats and running shoes, she walked brusquely to the boardwalk and watched the pounding surf.

"I love you, Daddy," she said softly into the wind. "You worked hard this last year to make peace with all that was troubling in your life. No one, not mother, not Grace, and certainly not me, could ask any more of you. Yes, I know you're out of that thin place."

When Catherine returned to the house, she passed on the food Judy offered and drank two cups of coffee before showering and dressing for the funeral. She pulled the simple black dress out of the closet, the one she wore to her mother's funeral. Recalling the bad memories of that day, she returned it to the closet and selected an emerald green dress with a belted waist and a pleated skirt instead.

When the undertaker took Catherine to see her father before anyone else was welcomed into the church, he looked as he did when she found him on the couch, at peace, hands folded on his chest. He wore a red rose in his lapel, and the ring she had found in the iron box was on his ring finger. Her father had never worn a wedding ring. The marriage was over before Catherine was born, and this ring, the ring from Grace, was the one that mattered to him. How heartbreaking to love her so much and be unable to be with her.

Grace. That name she heard as a child trying to sleep but hearing their fighting. Grace... Angry voices, then hushed tones, the days of silence. He said he fell in love. Grace must have loved him. A woman giving a man a ring... how bold... unconventional...

Despite the cold, many came. Elderly people who knew Douglas at Princeton and those who worked with him in the Civil Rights Movement and in his church in Washington. Children from his parish in Spring Lake, now grown, people Catherine had known during her high school years. Caroline arrived when the calling hour was almost over, looking out of place with her chic black suit with white satin cuffs and collar. She slipped in next to Catherine with no apologies for being late.

Catherine reached out to hug Caroline. Caroline's body, stiff and unyielding, sent a chill down Catherine's spine. She kissed her sister's cheek instead.

After the last visitors were received, the undertaker escorted Catherine and Caroline to the casket for a last look before it was closed. Catherine watched her sister closely as she viewed their father's body. Her face, stunning with their mother's high cheekbones and her father's blue eyes, was impossible to read. No emotion. Did it mean no love? What would keep her sister from loving their father the way Catherine loved him? Catherine saw Caroline look at the ring on her father's finger, but she made no comment, murmured no goodbyes.

This lack of emotion continued at the service and at the gravesite. Each mourner placed a red rose on the casket. Caroline lingered, holding tightly to hers before placing it with the other roses.

One last mourner emerged from the group. Catherine recognized his chiseled cheeks, red from the cold. Peter placed the rose with the others and bowed his head. "Rest in peace," he said as he touched the casket.

"Thank you for coming," Catherine said, taking both his hands in hers.

"I should have told you I would be here, but I was afraid you'd tell me not to come," he said.

Old feelings tugged at her heart. "You were an important part of our lives. My father would be pleased that you've come."

Catherine returned to the house and moved through the living room, talking with each guest. An elderly African-American man in a gray suit stood alone by the front door, awkwardly holding a glass of red wine. He had been talking with John McDuff, a friend of her father's who had tried some landmark Civil Rights cases. Catherine remembered him coming through the receiving line at the viewing, and he stood at a distance from the gravesite, head bowed.

Catherine put out her hand. "Sir, I'm not sure we've ever met."

"No, we haven't," he said, shaking her hand warmly. He pulled a linen handkerchief from his pocket and wiped his brow.

"I'm James Porter. I knew your parents before you were born. We marched with Dr. King. Years later, your mother prosecuted the white men who raped my daughter. She took a stand for my family, for black people in Memphis."

Catherine didn't comprehend what this man James Porter was saying, but she nodded as if she did.

"The world's a better place because of your parents, Catherine."

"So, you're from Memphis?" she stammered, feeling stupid.

"Memphis will always be home," he said with a smile, "but now I live in Philadelphia with Loretta. There were many years when I missed her terribly. She left Memphis soon after the trial, found a job in Philadelphia, and married a northerner. She never went back."

"I live outside of Philadelphia, working at Franklin College."

"My daughter's at Temple," he said. "She's a psychology professor. Her name is Davis now. I'm immensely proud of her." He reached into his wallet and pulled out her card and handed it to Catherine.

"Thank you," Catherine said, placing the card on the foyer table as she watched Caroline go upstairs.

Mr. Porter left, and Catherine headed upstairs. She looked in Caroline's old bedroom, but she wasn't there. Moving further down the hall, she saw her sister in their parents' bedroom, sitting on their bed, holding the music box that Catherine had found in her room.

"Caroline, are you okay?" Catherine asked, standing in the doorway.

"Yes, Catherine. I'm sorry I wasn't here to help you with the funeral," she said.

Catherine didn't respond. She wants me to say it's okay, but it's not.

"Is that yours?" Catherine asked.

"Yes," Caroline said, opening the music box.

"I don't recognize the tune," Catherine said.

"It's from Beethoven's Pastoral Symphony," Caroline said, closing the lid.

"We were really little. It was the second time mother tried to kill herself. I was only five, but I pieced it together from things she told me later. She blamed Dad, but the truth is she was drinking a lot. She took valium too, I remember. One day, I came home from kindergarten, and she was lying on the living room floor. At first, I didn't bother her. Flora came a few minutes later and called an ambulance. I had done the wrong thing. If Mommy died, it would have been my fault.

"But she didn't die. When she returned home, she brought me this music box. Flora had told her I saved her life. It wasn't true, but I never let her know anything different."

Poor Caroline. Always craving Mother's approval. Mother did love her, but time and alcohol blunted that love.

At eleven, Caroline told her sister, "Maybe Daddy's right when he says Mother's sick. Alcohol numbs her. Kills pain but kills hugs too. She never hugs us like Nana does."

"She said that a man who had cared for her while she was away gave this to her," Caroline continued. She wanted me to have it. As I got older, she told me stories about the man. He'd made her feel good about herself, told her she could be well. She came home, wanting to be our mother, but she was never able to do it, was she? Right before she died, she told me she'd never forgiven Dad for being unfaithful. She told me to never trust a man."

Caroline didn't move as she talked, continuing as if she'd practiced this speech for this day.

"It's a cliché, Catherine," she said, never changing her gaze or moving, "to say that each child has a different childhood, but it's true of us. We're not even eighteen months apart, but from the time we were babies, Mother and Dad were living different lives.

"I blamed you, Catherine, when we were little. I didn't always know why. I thought Dad loved you more. I didn't think he protected Mother from getting sick, from wanting to kill herself. Dad didn't love her, but I didn't realize until Mother was ill, she didn't love him either. He loved someone else."

"Her name was Grace," Catherine interrupted, sitting down in the caned rocking chair.

"You knew?" Caroline asked, looking hurt.

"Only recently... the last few months I've spent a lot of weekends with Daddy. Sometimes, it seems he was describing a life he hadn't experienced, a fantasy of sorts. At other times, Grace seemed as real as you or me."

"Oh, she was real," Caroline said derisively. "He never stopped loving her."

"Can you forgive him, Caroline?" Catherine leaned forward, hands together as if in prayer.

"I don't think it's about forgiveness. He lived a lie. They both did. I'm glad it's over," Caroline said, her beautiful face expressionless, hands tightly clasped.

Catherine didn't want an argument. Maybe it was over, the family charade anyway.

"Why didn't David come with you today?" Catherine asked.

"I didn't want him to come. The less he knows about

our fucked-up family, the better off I am. Listen, I'm going to change out of this ridiculous black suit and head home."

Catherine eyed the small black overnight bag in the corner. What could she say? She was part of the fucked-up family her sister wanted to leave behind.

"I'm glad you came" was all Catherine could offer. She opened the music box, her mind racing through memories in which her sister had come to her rescue when she was bullied...

the first time she heard Caroline rebuke her father: "Mommy's not sick. She's drunk." Catherine remembered her father's stricken look. The truth paralyzed him.

Why couldn't she be more decisive like Caroline? For Caroline, every step—college, marriage—was a step away from this house and the painful memories of parents who didn't love each other. Caroline cared little about what others thought. If she could be more like that, the drama at the College would be less stressful. Caroline would be clear about what to do about Neil.

Caroline let herself out while Al, Ruth, Hal, Catherine, and Judy sat around the dining room table, Al telling wonderful stories about Douglas. Al's heart attack when Douglas was by his side after the surgery. The children's christenings, first communions, and weddings.

Chapter Thirty-Two

When Catherine returned home after the funeral, she placed the iron box on her writing table in the study and opened it to look at her father's journal. She unpacked the rest of her things and returned several phone calls before she went to the study and removed the journal from the box. Lifting the afghan from the back of the chair, she sat down, pulling it around her. The heat's on but taking its time to warm the house, she thought.

The phone rang. She let it go to voice mail. She nestled further into the chair, running her fingers over the soft leather. She wanted to read the journal, but was this the right time? Maybe she should wait. Wait for what?

Catherine put the afghan aside. Molly jumped down from the window seat in the dining room and followed her into the kitchen. Catherine lifted her and gave her a kiss. "Hungry, girl? I know you are." She scooped cat food into two dishes before she opened the refrigerator and found some cheese.

With a plate of sliced cheese and crackers and a glass of white wine, she returned to the study. Getting comfortable again under the afghan, she opened the journal to the first entry. It was dated September 5, 1963. Before she was born. Caroline was a baby. He was cheating on Mother when she just had a baby. Wow. She took a sip of the cold wine. She hadn't eaten since dinner last night. Somehow, all her timing seemed off.

The phone rang again, and Catherine didn't even look to see who it was. It isn't my father, she thought. How many times will I reach for the phone thinking it might be him? She closed the journal and picked up her father's copy of Rilke's *Love Poems to God*. She read his notes on several pages before she fell asleep. An hour later, the phone rang again, and Catherine got up and went to bed.

Catherine awakened before the alarm clock and went to the kitchen and made coffee. The thermometer outside the kitchen window registered 22 degrees. Snow had been melting slowly over the last few days, but the backyard was still shrouded in a white, icy covering.

Catherine got her coffee and went to the study. Once again, she opened the journal to the first entry.

September 5, 1963

I met Grace the night before the March on Washington. Black hair pulled back in a barrette. Her green eyes sparkled as she chatted with the bartender. The curve of her breasts under a yellow sweater, which reached down to long legs in black pants. When I finally got her attention, I told her I'd seen her walking in Valley Green. A blank look at first. Then, recognition.

Her friends, another attorney and his wife, joined her. He was William Thompson, one of the Freedom Riders in '61. World

War II veteran became a pacifist after Hiroshima and Nagasaki. As we talked about the March, Grace was passionate about the changes that needed to take place in the country. Civil Rights legislation. Protection for voting rights.

The morning of the March, coffee with Grace before we left for the March. I gave her my card and said I hoped our paths would cross again.

I lost Grace and her friends during the March as we moved toward the Mall. A sea of humanity, more black than white; a moment of unity amid years of strife and violence. I was moved to tears by King's speech... "I have a dream that my four little children will one day live in a nation where they will not be judged by the color of their skin but by the content of their character." His dream is the American Dream, reading back to the Declaration of Independence. The powerful rhetoric of the prophet Isaiah, crying out that justice like a mighty stream...

September 7, 1963

Yesterday morning Grace called. She had enjoyed our conversation and wanted to talk with me again. We agreed to meet on Thursday evening at a restaurant on Germantown Avenue, a few blocks from Grace's home.

...the scent of lavender perfume, lips parted slightly in a smile. Her pale hands with light pink nail polish kept pace with her gentle, lilting voice. If I close my eyes, I see the lemon-colored sweater she wore the night I met her. A thin gold chain lay against the silky white skin of her neck. I can still hear her voice.

September 13, 1963

The house was still when I got home. Elizabeth, asleep in the guest room, hadn't talked to me since before the March. Caroline was sleeping, thumb in her mouth. I stroked her forehead and she turned to me, dropping her thumb.

Dinner with Grace. Impressions of the March still vivid in our thoughts. I was mesmerized by King's dream, she with the urgency of John Lewis's message about addressing the economic and social tyranny of white against black.

King wanted to soften Lewis's rhetoric. Not talk about revolution. Lewis is clear why the Civil Rights Bill is not enough.

William introduced Grace to the importance of protest, action. Thurgood Marshall will chip away at injustice, one case at a time. More is needed.

The conversation should have been enough, but I decided it wasn't.

I told her I'd never felt this way... wanting to talk to someone about so many different things. I told her that the night after I met her, I closed my eyes to sleep, and she was there.

Grace looked at me for what seemed like a long time. Finally, she ran her fingers over my open palm and touched her fingers to her open mouth, her tongue touching her middle finger. She ran her fingertips over my hand again before she spoke. She told me she hadn't stopped thinking about me since the day of the March. I was speechless, but I responded more decisively than I ever had in my life. I paid the bill and walked the three short blocks to Grace's apartment.

She led me into the bedroom and undressed me slowly, placing kisses all over my chest and neck before she reached up to kiss me on the mouth. My hands slid under her soft, green sweater and lacy bra. Her nipples were hard, her belly soft and warm.

Catherine placed the journal on the coffee table and closed her eyes. Her father remembering this first sexual encounter, writing it down so it's seared in his memory. Daddy told me that Grace was everything mother wasn't. Why did he stay in this dead marriage if something better was possible? Her parents fought about Grace, so Mother knew. She must have been devastated. Was her mother's drinking the result of her father's betrayal?

September 16, 1963

I couldn't sleep. Four little girls smiling, dressed in white dresses and lace-trimmed gloves and patent leather shoes, dressed for children's church. Cynthia Wesley. Carole Robertson. Addie MacCollins. Denise McNair. Four KKK planted at least fifteen sticks of dynamite connected to a timing device.

Was this a response to the March? The powerful in this country who want to keep black and white apart? Or an angry cry from the powerless, using dynamite to claim the power they think they should have?

> *Margaret, are you grieving*
> *Over Goldengrove unleaving?...*
> *It is the blight man was born for,*
> *It is Margaret you mourn for.*

The CBS News showed the rubble, the church's cornerstone blown out. The stained-glass window of Jesus was still intact, but the face of Jesus gone.

"Suffer the little children to come unto me, for such in the Kingdom of God." Why did they have to die? King envisions a world where these four little black children will hold hands with white children. How many black children must die to make this possible? The face of Jesus gone. Who remains, watching over the other children in Birmingham who must go to sleep at night in fear?

Catherine left the study and went into the living room and took down a photograph of her father from the mantle. He was wearing a white shirt, collar open at the neck. His hair was thick, cheeks full and ruddy. She got her chestnut hair from him, and Caroline got his blue eyes.

Catherine put the photograph back and headed

upstairs to get dressed. She lingered in a hot shower, then put on her make-up mechanically, careful to cover the dark circles under her eyes. I must look better than this tomorrow when I go back to work, she thought, applying some blush and mascara.

Not hungry, she made more coffee, poured a cup, and returned to the study. She opened the journal. Two months had passed between the first four entries and the next entry. Had her father debated whether he should commit these memories to paper? Or had he wanted to relive each meeting with Grace until each was an exquisite moment of being that someone else could also experience?

November 2, 1963

The door was unlocked when I arrived this morning. I knocked... no answer. I breathed in the smell of coffee, but I didn't see Grace. I wandered through the apartment, noticing a set of tiny leather-bound books on the sideboard in the dining room. I stooped to stroke the tiny tabby cat who purred with contentment on the window seat.

Grace was in the backyard, reading. The New York Times lay on a chair next to her, unfolded, in pieces. A book of poems lay open on the table. I held her briefly, soaking up her warmth. She was eager to read a poem to me by e. e. cummings that I didn't know.

I listened as much for the softness and the beauty of her voice as for the words. I latched on to the lines, "'you open always petal by petal myself as Spring/opens (touching, skillfully, mysteriously) her first rose'."

November 22, 1963

I sat in my office today and cried. I was with a client when Ray interrupted our meeting to say that President Kennedy had been assassinated. We listened to the radio. The announcer said, "I have just talked with Father... of the Holy Trinity Catholic Church. He and another priest have administered last rites... The only way to describe things here is grief... grief and shock... The President of the United States is dead."

How was this possible? The young president who gave us so much hope. Gone.

Elizabeth called me to say she wouldn't be home for dinner. Although she had little interest in politics, she was upset about President Kennedy's death and wanted to be with her father and stepmother.

I called Grace and reached her just before she left to join some friends. She invited me to join them. When I reached the crowded bar, the silence was suffocating. A large square television provided coverage of the assassination. Vice President Johnson at a bank of microphones: "We have suffered a loss that cannot be weighed." Jackie's pink suit splattered with her husband's blood. Vice President Johnson taking the oath of office with Jackie by his side.

Disbelief.

There were clips of the President and the First Lady arriving in Dallas, Jackie in the pink suit with the pillbox hat carrying roses. The President, energetic. Smiling.

I didn't stay long. I was exhausted. Grace asked me to walk her home. She stopped outside her front door and took both my hands in hers.

"I need you, Douglas," she said.

I held her for a moment, absorbing her strength as well as her sorrow before I went home to an empty house.

For the first time in weeks, I slept in our bed, hoping Elizabeth would come home and want to talk. I was reading when she got in. She changed in the bathroom and came to bed with a book in her hand. I tried to hold her and asked her how she was. Her eyes were cold. She reminded me of her father the night before our marriage. I turned away from her, letting grief *lull me to sleep.*

Was he trying to make the marriage work? Catherine thought. Had it really been too late?

Did he love Grace, or was it just her spontaneity, her passion, that he never had with her mother? Would he have made a happy marriage with Grace, or did all passion fade?

She turned her attention to the next entry in the journal.

November 23, 1963

Grace and I took a walk in Valley Green. It was unseasonably warm for late November, and I knew that the cool morning air would soothe me. We stopped to look at the waterfall, the sun shimmering on the water. My hand slid across her back and reached for her right hand. I kissed her gently on the lips.

Our thoughts were on the assassination. No words seemed to come to ease our grief, but I was also thinking about the last several months—our lovemaking, our laughter.

I stopped to show a little girl how to skim stones. She gazed up at me, surprised, perhaps, that I would stop for her. She was black with large expressive brown eyes. She looked at her mother to make sure it was alright to respond to my gesture. The mother offered a shy smile, kneeling close to the edge of the water.

Catherine closed the journal. Why is it so hard to find and keep what makes us happy, she thought? Why was it so hard, impossible, for her parents to break the silence and try to heal the pain?

Chapter Thirty-Three

Catherine got to the office before Bette. Stacks of mail, neatly placed on the left-hand side of the desk, were already tagged for each member of the staff. An arrangement of flowers, yellow roses, baby's breath, and tiny orchids covered the coffee table. Catherine put down her briefcase and reached for the card. With deepest sympathy, Lisa Ferguson, it read.

Catherine sat down at her desk and went through the phone messages. Lisa had also called yesterday to ask how Catherine was doing. She noticed two from Jim Murray, Chairman of the Chemistry Department. "Concerns about Mikayla Davenport." Hmm. Don't know who that is.

Catherine checked her email and saw an email from Jim describing the situation.

"Good morning, Catherine," Bette said from the doorway. Still wearing her coat, her cheeks were red from the frigid morning air. "Welcome back."

"It's good to be back. I'm sorry I didn't get here

yesterday, but I felt like I needed one more day."

Bette sat down in the chair next to Catherine's desk. In a motherly tone, she said, "You may find as time goes on that you need a day here and there to continue to process all that you are going through. The loss of two parents in a little over a year..."

"Yes. My friend Judy said something similar. Both her parents died over the past two years, and she still is working through it."

Shifting easily to her professional tone, Bette said, "I tried to keep your schedule clear today, but two things seemed unavoidable. Chelsea Williams stopped by early last week to ask how you were doing. She was so sorry she didn't get to the funeral and wanted to see you to tell you why. When she stopped by again yesterday, I didn't have the heart to put her off. She doesn't seem like herself. I scheduled an appointment for her at 9:00 tomorrow morning."

"That's fine. It'll be good to see her. She's got a lot on her plate right now, so she may not be getting the rest she needs." Catherine knew Bette was too astute to believe this, but she felt she had to say something.

"And then there's the matter of Jim Murray who has a student in his General Chemistry course who isn't doing very well."

"Mikayla," Catherine interjected.

"Yes. He's tried to convince her to withdraw, but she wants to stay with it. He encouraged her to see you this week before Thursday's deadline. I've scheduled her for 1:00." Catherine asked Bette to pull her folder and run her fall grades.

"Bette, thanks for coming to my father's funeral. It

meant so much to have you and others from the College come, despite the bad weather and the cold."

"Catherine, you have already endeared yourself to many here at Franklin. We want to do anything we can to help. I have to say, I've never seen so much genuine emotion at a funeral. From what I heard, your father's done a lot of good in the world." Bette got up quickly before Catherine had a chance to respond. She was already greeting someone in the outer office who had a question about mid-term grades.

Many from the faculty came to Douglas's funeral, and everyone on the staff was there, but there was nothing from Neil... not a call, not a card, nothing. Steve had sent flowers to the house from the Enrollment Management Staff, and Roslyn had sent an enormous arrangement to the funeral home from the Executive Administration.

"Catherine," Hal said, appearing in the open doorway. She gave him a warm hug and motioned for him to have a seat.

"I only have a few minutes," he said, running his fingers through his hair as he sat on the couch and stretched out his legs. "Steve has me running from one meeting to the next today, but I had to stop and tell you I haven't called because I wanted you to have some peace."

"Thanks for that," she said, taking a deep breath. She knew she had to talk with Hal about her father, about Grace.

"See how the next few days go and let me know when you have some time to breathe. I've been thinking about my talk with your father. If it's not too upsetting, I'd like to talk with you about it."

"It won't be upsetting. I'm only sorry you didn't get

more time with Daddy, for your research and for you."

"Me too," Hal said as he got up to leave. "Pace yourself, Catherine. It's really hard coming back after such a loss."

"I know you understand," she said, patting him on the back as he left the office.

At lunchtime, Catherine closed the door, and pulled blueberry yogurt from her briefcase. She found a spoon in her top drawer and wiped it off with a tissue before taking the first spoonful. Looking at her computer, she noted seventy-two unread emails. Not bad, she thought. People really *have* left me alone.

Before she had the chance to take another spoonful, the phone rang. She was going to let it go to voice mail when she saw it was a Connecticut number.

"Catherine Finley," she said after the second ring.

"Catherine, it's Annette Lombard."

"Annette, it's good to hear from you. How are you?"

"The important question is, how are you? I only found out last night from Lisa Ferguson that your father passed away. I'm so sorry I didn't know before now. I called Lisa about a College matter, and she told me the news."

"I'm doing well. I took last week to begin sorting through my father's papers, but mostly just taking some time. You said you called Lisa about a College matter. Did you want to talk with me about it?"

"I did, but perhaps I should call at another time."

"No. I'm here now and am happy to help if I can."

Annette sighed and took a moment to respond.

"I went to Franklin with Michelle Murphy. We were close and have stayed in touch over many years. I'm the reason her daughter Sarah is at Franklin. When I heard that Sarah was moving to Philadelphia to take a job, I talked with her about the graduate program in Psychology."

"Sarah Murphy?" Catherine asked.

"No. No. Her name is Sarah Walsh." Focused on her father's death and funeral, Catherine had let go of much of the anger and fear about what was happening at Franklin. With the mention of Sarah's name, it all came back.

"Sarah Walsh," Catherine repeated.

"Yes. Do you know her?"

"No, but Hal Doyle has mentioned her. You remember Hal from the Capital Campaign."

"Yes. Of course," Annette said, impatiently.

"Sarah told her mother that she was accosted by a drunk professor. I understand that she was able to move into another section, but she's since found out that this has happened before, and no one addressed his behavior."

"Yes. That's my understanding," Catherine said. Clearly, Annette didn't suffer from inertia. She intended to defend her friend's daughter.

"I've called Roslyn Ashcroft about this matter, and she's not returned my calls. That is not acceptable. I called Lisa for her advice. She gave me the name of one of her friends on the Board of Trustees. I intend to call her."

"Annette, I'm so glad you're acting on Sarah's behalf." Catherine felt rage rise in her throat. "I went to Roslyn on another matter of similar consequences in December, and she didn't take my concerns seriously. Perhaps she'll take this concern seriously if she hears it from a trustee."

"Well, I certainly hope so, but she should be listening to you, Catherine. You call me if I can help in any way. I know Lisa feels the same way."

"I will, and with your permission, may I let Hal know

we've had this conversation about Sarah?"

"Absolutely," she said. "We'll talk soon."

Catherine finished the yogurt, feeling some relief that someone else was aware of Sarah's situation. If things escalated again with Neil, she'd call Lisa or Annette and get their advice.

"Catherine," Bette said, knocking softly and opening the door a crack. "Mikayla's here for her appointment."

Catherine opened the door and motioned for Mikayla to come in.

Mikayla held her hand out for Catherine to shake. "It's nice to meet you, Dr. Finley."

"Likewise," Catherine said, indicating that Mikayla should take a seat on the love seat. Catherine sat in the chair next to her.

"I understand from Dr. Murray that you're having some difficulty with General Chemistry."

"Yes," she said, looking at Catherine thoughtfully, appearing relaxed and confident in jeans and a black silk shirt with an orange scarf tied loosely around her neck.

"My mother wants me to be a doctor, so I came in as a Chemistry major, Pre-Med. I did okay in Chemistry in the fall, probably because I had AP Chemistry in high school, but now, I can't seem to keep up."

"If you want to be a doctor, Mikayla, I wouldn't give up on it, but it needs to be your decision. Otherwise, you won't have the motivation to work hard."

"I don't want to let my mother down, but I'm really more interested in History and Public Policy. I'm not sure what I'll do after college if I major in History."

"The possibilities are endless," Catherine said.

"Really? I've never heard anyone say that before."

Catherine suggested she go to the Career Center and explore the way academic majors like History map to various career directions.

"You can major in History and make sure you take all the science requirements needed for medical school," Catherine explained. "Have you thought about retaking the second part of Chemistry at a community college over the summer if you withdraw from it now?"

"Yes. I talked with my mother last night. She's disappointed in me, but she felt better when I told her I wasn't giving up."

"You have time, Mikayla, to explore the major and to explore career directions. In the end, you may major in Chemistry or Biology, but there's time before you have to decide."

"It doesn't always feel that way," she said, looking at Catherine carefully. "It seems like everyone else knows what they're doing."

Catherine smiled. "Sometimes, others seem more confident, but I can assure you they all have doubts and questions too."

Mikayla talked about Hal's course on the Civil Rights Movement. "I wrote an oral history about my grandfather for the class, and Dr. Doyle has helped me with my writing since the class ended in December."

"That course is for History majors, so you've already proved you can do the work if that's the direction you want to go."

Mikayla nodded, smiling broadly.

"You read Dr. Doyle's oral histories in the course," Catherine continued, feeling a tightening in her throat. "He interviewed my father last month, right before he died. He was at the March on Washington. I'm sure Dr. Doyle will want you to read this one when it's ready for publication."

"I'm sorry about your father, Dr. Finley. I would like to read it. My grandfather was at the March on Washington too. It's the central event in what I've written."

"Dr. Doyle's oral history will keep my father's stories alive. You're doing the same for your grandfather."

When Mikayla left, Catherine sat down at her desk, unbuttoning her suit jacket and rubbing the back of her neck. So much potential in a student like Mikayla, but she doesn't see it yet. She needs time to explore and support from all of us while she does.

Catherine's thoughts turn to Chelsea and what happened to her at Middlebury. She didn't find anyone to hear her story and help her deal with what happened with Neil. Neil shattered her undergraduate experience.

Chapter Thirty-Four

Chelsea knocked on Catherine's door a little before nine.

"I'm early," she said, apologetically. "I have a 9:30 class."

"Your timing is perfect. I just finished reading an email from a parent raving about your advising."

"Good," Chelsea said, smiling wanly. She lay her coat and gloves on the love seat and sat down on the other end. Gray sweater and black slacks hung loosely on Chelsea's shrinking frame. Catherine tried to hide her shock, but Chelsea read her expression.

"I know," Chelsea said, nervously tucking her hair behind her right ear. "I'm having trouble eating. Therapy is helping, but I think I have to see a doctor too." Shifting in her seat, Chelsea changed the subject.

"I'm sorry I didn't get to your father's funeral. My band had a gig in New York. It had been planned months in advance. I couldn't change it."

"No apologies needed. I understand you were also teaching some seminars for the MFA program. It's all important work.

"Everything went well despite the cold weather," Catherine said, feeling comfortable as she told Chelsea about the service, about seeing her sister, about her mourning. "I'm going to miss him. He's always been my rock."

"My partner lost his father almost a year ago. He's still grieving, and I'm actually very worried about him."

Catherine took a moment before she said, "I'm sorry so much time has gone by without talking. I want you to know you have my full support. Since you told me about what happened to you, Neil's attacked me twice. I stood up to him and threatened to expose him. In December I spoke with Roslyn, but I got no support."

"I'm sorry," Chelsea said softly.

"I'm so angry, sometimes, I can't see straight," Catherine said, her voice quivering. "Other times, I feel dirty, shamed. I can't explain all the feelings."

"I know," Chelsea said. "I've never felt so helpless, but I refuse to be a victim."

"I'm aware of a student situation, a student who has been accosted by a drunken professor. I received a call from an alumna about her yesterday. This woman is going to bat for the student. Roslyn hasn't returned her calls, but she's calling a Board member about it.

"I'm sharing this with you in confidence because if anything else happens with Neil, I'll go to this alumna and to her contact on the Board if need be. I'll do the same for you, Chelsea."

"Thanks, Catherine."

"We're going to beat this," Catherine said, confidence returning. "Do whatever you need to do to get well, but let's keep talking."

Chelsea looked at her watch, thanked Catherine and promised to stay in touch. She nodded hello to Hal as she left, thanking him for his help in setting up the seminar at the University of Connecticut.

"It went well," Catherine heard Chelsea say to Hal. "When I get my report ready for Bill, I'll send you a copy."

"I got your email," Catherine said, waving Hal in. "I don't have anything until 11:00, so we have lots of time. My 11:00 is the 'Emergency Preparedness Meeting.' I feel more like that chick on the ten o'clock news than a dean."

"She's a meteorologist, Catherine, not a chick."

"Whatever she is, I want to be her. She can be wrong again and again and still have a job." An unpredicted storm had dumped ten inches of snow early Thursday morning, closing the campus. "I'm glad we were able to open late today. We're too close to mid-terms to miss any more time."

Catherine briefed Hal on her phone conversation with Annette Lombard, indicating she was supporting Sarah Walsh. "At this point," Catherine said, "I have to be confident that she and the Board member she's talking with can get some results."

Hal nodded agreement but didn't seem convinced. "I guess we'll have to wait and see," he said glumly.

"On a more positive note, then," Catherine said, not willing to let go of her optimism, "I met with Mikayla Davenport yesterday about her Chemistry course. She's got a lot of options, but she just doesn't know it yet. She loved your course."

Hal described the oral history she wrote about her grandfather's involvement in the Civil Rights Movement.

"I've been working on my interview with your father and hope to have a draft of it ready soon. I'll include it in my course next fall. The immediacy should really bring things to life for students.

"I'm glad I got the chance to meet your father."

Catherine felt sorry for Hal. He was tense, and every word seemed difficult.

"Hal, don't be apologetic about talking about my father. It helps me. I have so much to process, to think about. I know when I get to Spring Lake during Spring Break, I'll want to spend a lot of time with Ruth and Al. Talking helps."

"His death was such a shock," Hal said. "It was a good interview, but there's something else."

"What's that?" Catherine asked. A mischievous smile crossed her face. "Is there really anything you can tell me at this point that would surprise me?"

"I don't know," Hal said, smiling. He leaned back in his chair.

"Something was on my mind since I talked with your father at Christmas." Hal repeated the story Douglas had told them about meeting the young woman the night before the March.

"I remember," Catherine said.

"I know this is hard to believe, but that woman was actually my mother. I asked your father if he'd ever seen her again, and he had. They corresponded for a number of years after she left Philadelphia for Boston."

Hal continued to talk, relaying what Douglas had told him, but Catherine wasn't listening. Hal's mother was

Grace? This can't be possible, she thought.

"I asked your father if she'd ever told him about me, and he said no. He said she never talked about her personal life. Why wouldn't she have told him about me?" Hal stopped for a moment and asked, "Catherine, are you listening to me?"

"I am. I'm sorry. This seems so incredible. I don't know why she didn't tell him about you."

"We promised each other we'd meet again. I had so many questions I wanted to ask him about my mother, but then..." Hal's voice trailed off.

He's so sincere, Catherine thought. We never imagine our parents young, in love. She moved on, met Hal's father. Probably the passion faded, but they remained connected because of their political interests.

"When I met your father at Christmas, I started imagining what it would have been like if he'd known my mother. At first, I thought she would have found him naïve. She had no time for religion, but when I talked with him last month, I realized how much they had in common. They were both so passionate about the things that needed to change in society. As I listened to your father, it made sense. His faith was active, not passive. She would have understood that, at least at some level."

"I'm sorry you didn't have more time with him," Catherine said, reluctant to tell him at this point what she knew about her father's relationship with Grace. "I'd love to read the oral history when you have it ready."

"Okay. I'll give you a copy." Hal got up to leave, and Catherine gave him a hug. "Thanks for all your support with the funeral."

"My pleasure," Hal said, letting go of the embrace.

Catherine sat through the 11:00 meeting thinking about what Hal had told her. His impression was that his mother and her father had made a political connection. Would the truth upset him? The details in the journal of her father's passionate relationship with Grace were so vivid. He wrote it down so it would remain that way, a story that would never fade when memory failed him.

Chapter Thirty-Five

Hal looked up from his computer.

"Catherine, is that you? I'll walk out with you." This had become part of their routine.

She'd stop on her way out, encouraging him to go home. "The work will still be here tomorrow," she would say.

When there was no reply, he got up from his desk and walked out into the dimly lit office.

"Dr. Doyle?" a tall young woman with jet-black hair and large rimmed glasses asked, looking at him and then down at her feet.

"I am," he said. "Were you looking for me?"

"We were," she responded, extending her hand, and indicating another woman behind her. "My name is Bridget, and this is Katie."

Katie looked up for a moment but offered no greeting. She was dwarfed by Bridget. Her jeans hung loosely, and she seemed lost in an oversized navy-blue sweater. Her hands clutched her ski jacket, fingers raw and red without gloves in the cold.

"We're sorry to bother you, but it's important," Bridget asserted. Her lower lip quivered, as if she was close to tears.

"You're not bothering me. Please, come in."

Hal moved to his desk, scanning the desktop quickly. He tried to think if he had met these students before, but nothing came to mind.

"How can I help you?" Hal asked, sitting down across from them. Katie didn't look up. Bridget did the talking. She sat with legs crossed, hands clutching her right knee. She spoke slowly about what had happened on the academic quad in September.

"I had been drinking," she said, "but I wasn't drunk. I remember everything. My head still hurts where he pushed me down on the grass, his right hand pressing my cheek into the ground."

"When it happened to me," Katie said, looking up at Hal, "I hadn't been drinking. I'd come from the library and stopped to talk with one of my roommates who had just come from the pub. She was drunk, so I offered to walk her back to the dorm. He attacked me before I could help her.

"I told my RA, but she said it was pointless to report it. She said it was my word against his. If he raped me, she said, I should go to the Health Center. He didn't rape me because I fought like hell.

"I believed my RA, so I did nothing, but when the nightmares started, I got scared. I went to the Counseling Center and started to talk about what happened."

"Who attacked you?" Hal asked.

"Dr. Rhodes," Bridget said. Katie looked up and nodded.

"I met Katie in a class this semester," Bridget continued, "and we started to hang out. When we got to the material on sexual harassment, we shared our stories."

"Is this the Public Policy course with Professor Engles?" Hal asked, trying to keep his composure.

"Yes," Katie said, looking defiant.

"Last week," Bridget continued, "we were studying late in the Psychology Lounge. I'm a Psych major. We were talking about the class, but we started talking about what happened. It helps, sometimes, to talk about it."

Hal nodded, not wanting to interrupt. My God, he thought. This problem is so pervasive. Why didn't I know?

"We didn't know someone was in the TA study carrel. That's how we met Sarah Walsh. She apologized for listening to our conversation. She said something similar had happened to her, and you had helped her."

"We weren't sure what to do," Katie said. "I went home last Thursday because I was really sick. My mother noticed how much weight I'd lost. I told her what happened. She called her lawyer. She's meeting with President Ashcroft tomorrow afternoon."

Hal's head was spinning. A resident assistant tells a student not to report an attack like this. Who's training these students? And yet, if the word on the street is that it doesn't matter...

"Where will you be tomorrow?" Hal asked, looking from Bridget's confident demeanor to the trembling Katie.

"We both have classes in the morning, but we'll leave after lunch to go to Bridget's house in Connecticut for a long weekend," Katie offered. "We don't, at least *I* don't want to leave Franklin, but our parents want to pull us out of school."

Hal nodded, not sure what to say.

"We're glad we met Sarah. It's good to know we're not alone," Bridget said, uncrossing her legs and seeming to relax a bit.

"You're not alone. I'm glad you found each other, but I'm sorry it's taken this long for you to find Sarah or me." Hal pulled two cards from the cardholder on his desk and began writing his cell number on each card.

"Please call me any time if you need to talk."

"Okay," Bridget said as she got up to leave. Katie nodded her head.

Hal left a phone message for Steve: "Call me first thing tomorrow. It's important." He turned off the lamp and locked the door behind him.

A heavy wind gust blew the outside door out of his hand. It's March, and it's still frigid. Will this winter ever end?

Hal slid into the car and got the heat going. His mind wandered to the endless winter when he was ten. It snowed the day his mother went in for surgery and snowed every day she was in the hospital.

"I like the snow when Mama's here," he told Uncle Vince one night before bed. "Now I'm afraid it will keep me from seeing her."

"Don't worry," Vince said. "The storm is on its way out to sea."

She was home for two weeks after the surgery. There, every day when he came home from school. By the second week, she was up, making him breakfast.

"*You were up late last night,*" *Hal said as his mother placed two pieces of french toast in front of him.*

"*I was,*" *she said, nodding as she sat down across from him. Her color was better, and the dark circles under her eyes were receding. "I was talking with our new research assistant,*" *she said, describing the class action lawsuit brought against Wentworth Industries. "It's complicated because one of the plaintiffs is part owner of the company.*"

"*What do they want?*" *Hal asked, eating slowly, wishing he could stay home from school.*

"*Equal pay for all the women working for the company, the same pay that men get for the same positions. Then, compensation for all the years they worked for less. It's a case that may set a precedent for future litigation.*"

He'd have to look up "precedent" when he had a chance.

As Hal pulled into the driveway, it occurred to him that it snowed until mid-March that year. His mother got stronger as she weighed into that fight, winning the lawsuit for the Wentworth women despite the radiation that made her so sick. The cancer made her stronger.

Chapter Thirty-Six

Catherine got to the office before Bette and started reading her email. She'd put her father's journal aside, letting work command her attention.

"Catherine, you look awfully tired," Bette said, sitting down in the chair across from her.

"I am tired. I've been getting up extra early to read through my father's papers."

"I'm sure the pressures around here are taking their toll too," Bette said softly, breathing deeply as she finished her sentence.

"How do you mean?" Catherine asked.

"Catherine, you have been very discreet about Neil's advances toward you, but he hasn't."

"What?" Catherine said, feeling sweat trickle down her back and her hands turned cold and clammy. He'd kept his distance since the funeral, canceled more than one meeting. She assumed he was avoiding her. Maybe he finally got it!

Bette looked at Catherine closely before speaking, "Neil was at the pub on Wednesday night last week with some of his golf buddies. They were very drunk. Steve was there with a friend, having dinner at the bar and overheard Neil talking about you in the most inappropriate way." Bette's voice was flat. She seemed to be trying to control strong emotion.

"Steve told you this?" Catherine asked, trying to remain calm.

"Instead of having his assistant call me to schedule your monthly meeting with him, Steve called himself. He asked how you were. One thing led to another, and he told me what he heard at the pub."

Catherine was stunned.

"I thought you should hear it from me, not someone else. I'm sorry, sorry this is happening to you."

Bette got up and returned to her desk, leaving Catherine furious. He's bragging about what he's done to me? He can do whatever he wants and get away with it.

Later in the day, Catherine had a brief conversation with Steve. He confirmed what Bette had said.

"Catherine, I'm on my way downhill to drop something off in Hal's office. Let me finish this conversation in person." Catherine heard the click of the phone, and she put the receiver down, releasing it from her shaking hand.

Steve was in her office ten minutes later. She was seated on the love seat with her head in her hands when he knocked gently on the closed door. Her "Come in" was barely a whisper. He sat down in the chair next to her.

His face was clouded with emotions, but she wasn't sure what emotion was the strongest. Anger, sadness, and exasperation were etched on his otherwise tranquil face. His large hands were clasped together. His ringless hands were freckled and strong.

"Last Wednesday night, Neil was at the bar with Philip." Steve began slowly, looking at Catherine with concern. "He and Neil had struck up a friendship when Philip was on the Board of Trustees. They often played golf together. Both have a reputation for drinking, and Wednesday night, Neil was very drunk. He talked about you. His voice was loud. It was awkward, and my friend and I got up to leave but not before we heard Philip say he'd broken up with you."

"How does Neil get away with this behavior?" Her angry eyes scanned Steve's face. "Philip played golf with him? He never told me that." So, when she told Philip what Neil had done to her, he was nonplussed.

"There's something else." Steve hesitated and then went on. "Catherine, I'm sure Philip told you his wife was killed by a drunk driver when she was on her way to Baltimore to meet him."

"Yes, he did." Catherine waited, wondering if she wanted to know what would come next.

"His wife Anne had gone to Baltimore that weekend to confront him. She found out that he was seeing another woman, a woman named Trixie who worked with her and Philip in the export business. Anne was to meet Philip in the bar of the Marriott at Inner Harbor. She waited at the bar for two hours until it occurred to her that she should see if he had already checked in. He had."

"How do you know all this, Steve?" she asked, hysteria in her voice.

"Because Trixie was my wife."

"This can't be," Catherine said, choking on her words.

"When Anne saw them together, she rushed out of the room and started to drive back to Philadelphia. She was distraught. She hit another car head-on. There was no drunk driver."

Somehow, her own pain from Philip's behavior was only a nagging ache compared to the pain his wife must have felt. She had invested her life in Philip and their children only to find out he was a cheating bastard.

Catherine had no words. She sat silently, not wanting to hear any more.

"Catherine, I'm sorry to be the one to tell you this. I'm sorry I didn't tell you sooner. I didn't know you were seeing Philip until the Christmas dinner at Roslyn's house, and then, I guess, I thought it was too late."

"What happened to Trixie?" she asked.

"We separated when she told me about Philip and when I found out about Anne's death. Trixie told me everything. I couldn't stay with her. I was devastated."

"Here at the College..."

"The circumstances of Anne's death were covered up. Her children don't know she was drunk. They know only what Philip told them... that she was killed by a drunk driver.

"Trixie seemed to have no remorse. She said she loved Philip. I hated Philip for his lies, but I saw no reason to cause more pain for Anne's children."

Steve got up to leave, and Catherine stood, shaking as she absorbed what she just heard.

Bette wasn't at her desk, but Catherine saw a note: Dr. Stewart stopped by twice to see you, the note read.

She left the office early that afternoon, feeling

nauseous and anxious. She went to bed and slept for a few hours before waking and rushing to the bathroom.

How could she be so unaware? All the dinners with Philip... the trip to Boston and Maine. She never knew he was Neil's friend. What an actor. He always spoke lovingly of Anne, and he was cheating on her. What a bastard.

Her father did this to her mother. He was cheating on her when she was pregnant with Catherine. Her idea of a home, a safe place, had been shattered. All her mother's rages. Biting, hateful words flung at her father. Was her mother reliving that moment when she found out about Grace, drinking to obliterate the memory?

Chapter Thirty-Seven

Catherine's cell phone buzzed as she stepped out of the shower. It was 6:13 a.m.

Be in my office at 8:00 a.m. ...Emergency meeting ...Roslyn.

Catherine dried her hair quickly and put on make-up without too much attention to what she was doing. One cheek too pink, she thought, rubbing away some color.

As she backed the car out of the garage, her cell phone rang. Hal.

"Aren't you part of this 8:00 meeting?" she asked him.

"Yes," he said. "I was up early and was at Starbuck's when I got Roslyn's text. I tried to reach you yesterday, but Bette said you'd gone home sick. Are you okay?"

"Yes. I'll tell you about it when we have time to talk. Why did you want to see me?" she asked.

"I wanted to tell you about the two students who came to see me yesterday. They are the two unnamed students in the article."

"What article?" she asked. She turned off the engine and sat in the biting cold.

"The article on the front page of the *Philadelphia Inquirer*."

"*What*?" Catherine sputtered.

"The headline read, 'Academic Vice President resigns amid sex scandal,'" Hal said.

"Really?" Catherine said, surprised and somewhat pleased.

"Sarah Walsh has brought charges against the College because of what happened with Jason. Two other students mentioned but not named in the article claim that Neil made inappropriate advances towards them. I'm assuming our meeting this morning is Roslyn's attempt at damage control."

"Protecting the College," Catherine said, almost without thinking. "Hal, I'm going right to Roslyn's office. See you there."

When Catherine arrived at Franklin Hall, Michelle quietly ushered the cabinet into the large Board room adjacent to Roslyn's suite of offices. Kristin Rosin, Vice President for Development, was already seated at the table. Bill Stevens was huddled at one end of the room, talking with Steve and Hal.

As soon as Roslyn entered the Board room, everyone took a seat, like actors taking their cue, like children in a family knowing their place. Steve sat to the right of Roslyn, and the Vice President for Finance, Ginny DiNato, sat to her left. Now that Neil was gone, power would shift to Steve or to Ginny. Time would tell.

"I don't know if any of you saw the *Philadelphia Inquirer* this morning, but the press has picked up an unfortunate development here at the College," Roslyn said, prepared, or so it seemed, to keep things under control. "The paper reports that Neil has resigned, but this is not true. What *is* true is that a graduate student is threatening a lawsuit because of a run-in with a faculty member."

There's that word again... a run-in... as if it was a minor dispute, disagreement. Catherine was having trouble staying focused. It's all spin. We'll never know the truth.

"The student claims she took the complaint to Neil, and he did nothing about it. Her complaint, then, went to Hal, where she found some sympathy." Roslyn looked at Hal, eyes cold.

Everyone turned to look at Hal. Hal looked at Roslyn, waiting for the right moment to speak.

"Based on what Neil told me," Hal began, "and what I know from the campus grapevine, this is not the first time that Jason has accosted a student while drunk." Catherine knew Hal was choosing his words carefully. She had never heard him so rigid, so devoid of emotion.

"No allegations against Jason have ever gone to court," Roslyn said, scanning every face at the table. "Let's keep it that way. The allegations that have surfaced about Neil from these two students can be quickly discredited."

Where was she going with this? Catherine thought.

"Both students are friends of this Sarah Walsh," Roslyn said, spitting the name as if it was vinegar. "It's simply their word against his."

"Friends of Sarah Walsh?" Hal asked. "That isn't my understanding." He scanned the room, noticing looks of surprise. Fear. Was he going to contradict the President?

"Are you going to say more?" Roslyn asked, her look of certainty fading quickly.

"No, Roslyn. What the students shared with me was shared in confidence, but I will say this. Unlike Sarah, who is a graduate student, these students are undergraduates. One is a first-year student and not yet eighteen."

"Can an arrangement be made," Kristin Rosin asked, looking at Roslyn, "so there's no more bad press?"

"It may not be that simple," Bill Stevens said. Roslyn glared at Bill. He paused before he spoke again. "As President of the Faculty Senate, I'm aware of charges against Neil from a faculty member."

"Just one faculty member?" Roslyn asked, glaring at Catherine. Catherine didn't take her eyes off Bill's face as everyone waited for his response.

"Roslyn, with all due respect," Bill began, holding Roslyn's gaze, "if it's one or a dozen, it's all the same to me. I brought this particular situation to your attention two months ago, and it was your responsibility to address it with Neil."

He's making her mighty uncomfortable, Catherine thought, watching as Roslyn picked up her reading glasses, folding them and unfolding them before she put them back on her binder. Her composed face tensed as she absorbed Bill's accusation.

Catherine asked Roslyn to speak to Neil before Christmas. Did she speak to him then? Catherine's mind was racing with questions.

"Let me be perfectly clear, Bill," Roslyn said. "If this becomes a scandal, you'll be equally liable. You knew about the allegations and did nothing."

Silence. Bill must know, Catherine thought, that what

Roslyn was saying wasn't true. Bill had done what was required of him. He'd talked to Roslyn as Neil's supervisor.

"I suggest we keep our attention on the two students," Roslyn said, shifting uncomfortably in her seat. "Both had been drinking. I have someone looking into additional information about them."

"Only one of the students was drinking," Hal interjected quietly.

"Their stories are very similar," Roslyn continued, glaring at Hal. "Each claims that Neil accosted them on the academic quad, following them back from the pub. One alleged incident occurred in September, the other in October. Neither filed a police report."

"For now, the only statement from this office is that Neil's on administrative leave for one month while an investigation is underway. Bill will be Interim Vice President during this time."

"What do you want us to tell staff and faculty when they ask about the situation?" Hal asked, looking first at Steve and then at Roslyn.

"I'll be issuing a statement on behalf of the President," Steve said. "That will have to be sufficient for the campus community." Hal nodded his understanding to Steve.

Roslyn stood and walked out of the conference room. Her heels clicked against the hardwood floor. She brushed past Michelle who stood regally in the outer office and closed her office door behind her. No one spoke. One by one, they filed out of the conference room.

No orthopedic shoes today, Catherine noted.

Catherine went to her car. She put her seat belt on and sat for a few moments in the cold. It's out of my hands now, she thought. No matter how much damage control she does, the word is out there now. If the charges against Neil stand and I'm subpoenaed, I'll tell the truth. For now, I'm just going to get through the day.

Catherine drove downhill and parked in the lot adjacent to the gym. She walked the short distance to her office in Tyler Hall, slowly navigating the icy sidewalks and emailed Facilities, asking them to get someone out salting the walkways.

Within the hour, Steve's email to the campus community was posted:

> Dr. Neil Rhodes is on administrative leave, pending an investigation of allegations against him.
> Dr. William Stevens, President of the Faculty Senate, will be Interim Vice President for Academic Affairs until this situation is resolved.

Tyler Hall was quiet. If staff were gossiping, Catherine thought, they aren't talking to me.

Bette knocked gently on Catherine's open door. Without waiting for a response, she walked in and sat in the chair next to Catherine's desk. "We've had two calls, one from the *Philadelphia Inquirer* and one from the *Newark Star Ledger*."

Catherine laughed as she took the messages from Bette. "The *Star Ledger*? It must be an awfully slow news day."

"I've taken the messages, but I haven't promised them a call back." Bette smoothed out her chartreuse skirt and placed her left hand on Catherine's desk. She looked at Catherine thoughtfully and asked, "Are you holding up all right?"

"I am. Thanks for your concern." Catherine sighed

deeply and looked, for a moment, at the snowy playing fields. "I've been thinking since I got the news this morning that the situation with Neil is now out of my hands. If the charges against him stick, I'm sure I'll be subpoenaed."

"I hope it doesn't come to that," Bette said. "The scandal could cripple the College." Bette got up and returned to the ringing phone on her desk.

Even the best of them wants a cover-up. Scandal is worse than the truth.

Catherine emailed Hal. "I'm leaving to have lunch at home. Do you want to join me?"

Hal's email—a simple "Yes"—came immediately.

"You look exhausted," Catherine said as she took Hal's coat and draped it over the couch.

"The calls have been nonstop," he said, following Catherine into the kitchen. "Since I was named in the article, everyone wants to speak with me. I'm not going back this afternoon."

"Good idea," she said, pouring iced tea. She placed cheese and crackers in the center of the table.

"Let's eat something. Surprisingly, all this drama has made me hungry," she said, taking a seat at the head of the table.

Hal sat down and reached for a piece of cheese. He smiled at Catherine and said, "I'm glad to see you're in good spirits."

"I feel relief," she said, taking a sip of the tea. "It's out of my hands, but Roslyn's role in this still nags at me. It's ironic, though, that her firm grip makes me believe that we may get to the truth.

"The only person who spoke to me this morning was Bette. She hopes the allegations don't stick. She says the College can't withstand a scandal."

"People are afraid... afraid they'll lose their jobs," Hal said, moving the salad around on his plate.

"That doesn't follow. Maybe they're just afraid of the truth," Catherine said.

"How do you mean?" Hal asked.

"If the truth comes out, Neil may lose his job, and he may go to prison if the sexual assault charges stick. If the district attorney is aggressive, he may go after Roslyn, but she can put a new spin on the story and make it work for her. The Board can step in and make it right. I don't think the rest of us have to be negatively impacted. Too much energy is wasted on protecting people like Neil and keeping secrets."

Hal nibbled on a cracker before saying, "In one of my last conversations with Tina about work, she said I hated being a dean. I think she was right. I don't have the energy for these politics like my mother did."

"Maybe," Catherine shot back without too much thought, "your mother believed she could make a difference, and she did. We can make a difference and give these students our support. They need to be heard."

They ate in silence for a while. Catherine's cell phone rang. She looked at it but didn't pick up.

"Hal, the faculty member Bill referred to today is Chelsea Williams. Neil propositioned her, and she came to talk with me about it. I told her to be on record with her Chair but also to consider going to Bill as President of the Faculty Senate. I'm surprised she went to him. She was so distraught that I thought she'd just shut down. I'm learning from my own experience that emotions are all over the map when something like this happens."

"That was Chelsea who just called?" Hal asked, gesturing toward her cell phone.

"Yes," Catherine said. "I'll call her back later."

"Do you want to tell me about the two students?" Catherine asked. Hal recounted what the students told him.

"Katie's therapist cautioned her about reporting the incident, suggesting she might not be believed and would have to relive what happened."

"What changed their minds about coming forward?" Catherine asked, no longer hungry.

"Both Bridget and Katie signed up for Doris Engles's course, 'Gender Law and Policy.'"

"Really?' Catherine said.

"They shared their stories with each other. Then, one night when they were studying in the Psychology lab, Sarah Walsh overheard them talking. After she heard what happened to them, she suggested that they talk with me."

As Hal relayed the students' story, Catherine thought about Hal's mother. Her work over thirty years ago had made it possible for Katie and Bridget to tell their stories and be heard.

"I wish I had been able to intervene earlier," Hal said, "but Katie's mother already had a lawyer involved, which is what's making Roslyn squirm."

"I think it's good that you're involved, Hal. This may be the first time the College has stood up for a student in this situation," Catherine said. Hal didn't respond. She knew he needed time to process what had happened.

Hal thanked Catherine for lunch and headed home.

Catherine reached Chelsea and had a brief conversation.

"Chelsea, I think this is better for both of us if the charges against Neil stick."

"I'm not so sure," Chelsea said. Catherine could hear the fear in her voice. "I'm not sure I can handle reliving the humiliation. I'm remembering more about what happened in college."

"I've had trouble processing what Neil has done to me. Sometimes, I pretend it never happened, but I can't bury this," Catherine said, pacing in the kitchen and stopping to sip her tea. "He needs to be stopped and my story can be part of the case against him that derails him."

"I know," Chelsea said. "I know you're right."

"Call when you feel like talking," Catherine said.

Catherine sat down in the living room. Bridget and Katie. These allegations replicate what happened to Chelsea at Middlebury. No one standing up for them until Sarah Walsh hears their stories. A therapist saying it will be brutal if they must relive the attacks, and they may not be believed. Is that worse than carrying this secret, never resolving it?

Catherine took a deep breath, trying to let go of the anxiety that had settled in her chest.

Part IV
Spring 2005

Chapter Thirty-Eight

Catherine left the house untouched when her father died. With the scandal about Neil hovering over the College, she decided to spend the whole week of Spring Break in Spring Lake. As soon as she got to the house, Catherine walked the two blocks to the beach and watched the surf roll in. She looked out at the ocean, now populated by three surfers with colorful boards and black wet suits waiting for a wave.

Her father worked so hard to make peace with his life at the end, but why wait until then? Were memories of Grace so powerful that they strangled any possibility of reconciliation with her mother? Her parents' marriage was like warfare. Seldom a ceasefire or restful retreat. Would anyone choose to live like that?

Abandoning a snack in the kitchen after school because of the fury, she would ride her bike on the boardwalk, seagulls like dive bombers dropping seashells in her path.

Cold, moist air created by the salty spray numbed her cheeks and soothed her anxiety about what might happen between her parents.

"I'll never get married," she told her Nana when she was seven. Daddy seemed only to have peace when he was away at a march or reading his books late at night.

"Why does he put up with her?" she asked at eight. "She's mean."

"He made a promise, not just to your mother but to Caroline and to you." Nana always had an answer.

"Well, he can break the promise to her and keep the promise to us," Catherine snapped. "We're not mean."

Nana pulled her into a hug and told her a story about her grandfather. "We had such adventures, hiking in every state on the East Coast. He worked hard, but the weekends belonged to us. What a storyteller. Every adventure, he'd make up tales about the people who'd hiked there in the past."

She never knew her grandfather, but she saw the love and gentleness between her father and her grandmother. Why didn't he know how to get this from her mother? He just retreated like a scared animal.

Had she done the same thing with Peter? Retreated when she found him in bed with Meghan? When she saw Peter at her father's funeral, she reimagined him without the worries about his drinking. If she hadn't been so quick to judge, could they have made it work?

Catherine walked back to the house and sat down in her grandmother's chair in the corner of the living room. Mother hated it: the faded blue and white handmade slipcover clashed with the other furniture. Catherine's father insisted that it stay.

She checked the thermostat and turned up the heat. She opened the drapes in the study. Late afternoon sun warmed the room. She retrieved the iron box and the bag of groceries from the front seat of the car. Placing the journal and the small stack of letters on her father's desk, she reached for the keys she had found in the box, all different sizes, some rusty, some thin, others long, heavy, gold.

The desk was mahogany with enormous drawers on either side. A center drawer, flat and long, required a small key, but nothing she had seemed to fit. Finally, one of the larger keys, one with a purple ribbon, opened the lock on the top left-hand side. The drawer was deep. Peering into it was like standing at the opening of a dark, empty cave. Catherine felt like she was violating her father's privacy, but then, again, he left the journal and letters for her to read. He had left the keys in the file box.

Gingerly, she reached into the desk like a child, almost afraid that something would grab her hand or push it away. She felt around the edges. Was it empty? No. Her fingers slid under an envelope, a large white envelope. She lifted it from the drawer and opened it carefully.

Inside were two pictures. One was a copy of her parents' wedding picture, her father in a gray tuxedo looking shy and terribly thin, and her mother in white satin with a lace-covered veil that filled all the empty space behind the couple. She had seen this picture many times. Until her mother's death, the picture held center stage with other pictures in the living room. She studied it, trying to imagine how they felt on that day.

Did mother have girlfriends like Aunt Rosemary who

gave her advice about the wedding night? What to expect if she'd never had sex? Did she love Daddy then? Was she excited to be this beautiful, young bride starting her new life?

Underneath the picture was a smaller picture of a woman in an emerald dress. Her jet-black hair fell softly over her shoulders. Her smile was filled with energy. Flirtatious, Catherine imagined, for the man behind the camera. There was something about the smile, the eyes, which were familiar. She studied the slender figure—full breasts fitting snugly in the dress, accentuating a tiny waist. A beautiful cameo, also familiar, hung around her neck. This must be Grace, Catherine thought. She's beautiful, and if she was as brilliant and witty as Daddy said, no wonder he couldn't resist her.

Catherine returned the wedding picture to the desk drawer where she found it and placed the second picture on the desk, leaning against the banker's lamp. She looked at the photograph as she read the journal.

December 23, 1963

Elizabeth took Caroline to visit a friend in Carlisle today, so I spent the whole day with Grace. We walked in Valley Green. Every now and then, I would stop, caressing Grace's gloved hand, running my fingers over her soft cheeks. I kissed her eyelids.

As we returned to Grace's apartment, I imagined doing this every day.

We lit the four Advent candles and read a passage from Isaiah.

We made love. Our lovemaking had an intensity, a finality that I didn't understand. Was I losing Grace? Had passion already faded?

I told Grace I wanted to be with her, but I needed to find the right time to tell Elizabeth. Grace told me she could wait until I found the right time. She said she loved me. Her words washed away my anxiety.

Elizabeth's car was in the garage, and she was waiting for me. She followed me into the kitchen. I poured a glass of milk and sat down at the dining room table. The refrigerator hummed. She stood over me, beside me, as I sat, sipping the cold milk. I couldn't breathe. She moved close to me, and I could feel her warm breath on my neck. Clutching at my shirt, she inhaled the air around me. I took a few deep breaths and pulled away from her. She stepped back from the table.

I told Elizabeth I loved Grace and wanted to start over again with her. Did my love for Grace gave me this courage, or had I finally found it myself?

Elizabeth glared at me. Hand raised, poised to hit me, she quickly regained control. A suffocating silence fell over the room. Is this how I'm going to feel for the rest of my life... like a cornered animal, unable to protect myself? Like a man, shut down by life? My heart was frozen, as cold as the milk I drank as she stared at me in silence.

Elizabeth told me she was pregnant. She reminded me about the last time we had sex, two months ago after Ray and Rosemary's Halloween party. She told me she'd kill herself and my baby if I left her.

Anger gone, her pale face showed no emotion. She ran her hand over her trim waist, covered by a beige-belted dress. Elizabeth stormed out of the room without another word.

Catherine looked up at the photograph. "He gave you up for me," she said. "Mother referred to me as his child." The distance between her parents, her mother's indifference to her. It made sense now, she thought. Mother knew Daddy didn't love her, and she didn't want me.

December 29, 1963

I can't leave Elizabeth when she's pregnant. She's too fragile.

Grace is in Boston for New Year's, meeting her law school friend's father who is the senior partner in a law firm.... a possible job after months of interviewing and no prospects.

January 5, 1964

I got into the office early and called Grace. A voice filled with sleep answered the phone. I told her I needed to see her.

When I arrived, she was in the living room, reading. I told her Elizabeth was pregnant. "I didn't know you still had sex with her," Grace said, her voice flat, disengaged. I told her it was only one night in October when we both had too much to drink.

Grace got up slowly and walked into the living room. I watched her move, black and white lines moving gently against a familiar background, a place I might be seeing for the last time. She sat down on the couch, stroking the tiny tabby. Then, she scooped her up and held her close to her chest. I could hear the cat purring, but I couldn't hear my own breathing. Silent tears rolled down Grace's cheeks.

I told Grace I can't leave Elizabeth now. She's threatened to kill herself and the child.

Grace looked at me in disbelief... disbelief about what I said? I didn't know, and I lacked the courage to ask.

Silently, Grace let the cat go and moved toward me. She touched my cheek and asked me to leave. I kissed her on the forehead and left for Valley Green. I walked for hours. The morning was chilly. My hands were raw. When I walked here with Grace, the warmth of her hand in mine and the lilt of her gentle voice had cut through a chilly wind.

We stepped on patches of ice, steppingstones to avoid the mud. I found an old cloth to clean her beautiful sable-colored boots when we returned home. Today, I slipped and trampled in the mud. I didn't care what was beneath my feet.

Catherine reread the last two entries. My mother was pregnant with me. She thought about killing herself and me before I was born. Did she really mean it, or was it just her way to keep my father? Keep him in their miserable marriage?

Catherine picked up the picture of the woman in the green dress, running her finger over the woman's face. You loved my father, she said to the picture. He let you go because of me. Catherine struggled with her grief in this moment. What a deeply unfair burden he'd left her.

Catherine woke up before dawn, a heavy rain and wind blowing against the windows. She pulled a robe over her silk nightshirt and went to the kitchen to make coffee. She smiled as she saw the gourmet cookies, unopened, behind the coffee beans from Starbucks. Daddy loved his treats, she thought.

When the coffee was ready, Catherine poured a cup and carried it to her father's desk and continued reading from the journal.

March 9, 1964

Our client base is growing. Ray tries to pull me out of my funk with his bawdy sense of humor. Sometimes, he succeeds. I feel useful when I'm working with our clients. Most love the products they sell, but they don't know how to manage money. Parish ministry will be a bit like this, helping people conquer the day-to-day struggles that keep them from having an abundant life.

Elizabeth is beginning to show. We never spoke about Grace again. I wake up early on Saturdays and think about her. How does she fill the time that used to be ours?

May 1, 1964

Caroline's first birthday... I plan to get home early to help Elizabeth with dinner. Her father and Suzanne will come to celebrate. We've made no friends with other couples who have children.

Grace has taken a job with a law firm in Boston. I can stop imagining that I'll run into her in Valley Green. I've lost her.

Catherine leafed through several entries... some thoughts on the Civil Rights Act, signed into law on July 2, 1964, and then an entry about her birth.

July 15, 1964

Catherine Elizabeth Finley. Born at 7:30 p.m. Named for my mother. Mother was thrilled when I called to tell her the news. 6 pounds, 13 ounces. Elizabeth's labor was easier than it had been with Caroline. Catherine's tiny fingers reached up to me when I held her for the first time.

Nothing about Grace. Was he unable to express his feelings about losing her? Had he let her go?

December 10, 1964

King received the Nobel Prize today and said he was receiving the award as 'a trustee for the twenty-two million Negroes in the United States of America who are engaged in creative battle to end the night of racial injustice.' This will make Grace happy.

March 7, 1965

There is nothing "more powerful than the rhythm of marching feet." – MLK

The girls were down for a nap. Elizabeth was out to lunch with her stepmother. Ray called to tell me to turn on the television. Marchers in Selma were crossing the Emmus Pettus Bridge, facing a sea of helmeted, uniformed Alabama State Troopers. John Lewis led the march. Tear gas was released as they moved toward the troopers. Marchers were attacked with billy clubs. The local organizer, Amelia Boynton, was knocked down, Lewis was clubbed in the head. The world was watching. Would there be action now, change?

I heard Catherine cry, so I turned the television off and went to the nursery to hold her. I want a better world for you. I bounced her up and down until she stopped crying.

March 10, 1965

The second march was today. They crossed the bridge but retreated as troopers stepped aside. King feared they wouldn't make it to Montgomery without violence.

March 13, 1965

I told Ray I wanted to take some time off and go to Selma for the march scheduled for next week. When I told Elizabeth, she said nothing.

Her mother's silences screamed at her now. Why didn't her father understand the damage he was doing by ignoring the distance between them?

March 24, 1965

The march was peaceful. 54 miles from Selma to Birmingham. Protected by National Guard, some with Confederate flags sewn on their uniforms.

I spotted my friend James Porter as we crossed the bridge. We walked together the first day. They were fighting for the vote in Memphis. His little girl, Loretta, is in college. Spelman.

Black people on the side of the road looked hopeful and frightened. Local officials called us "outside agitators" and "white Negroes."

We stayed at St. Jude's that night. I walked through the camp while others ate, looking for Grace. She spotted me first and embraced me. She invited me to join her with several of the organizers. They asked how we had met, and we told them at the March. We all had stories about that day.

I slept that night with Grace's voice, her laughter in my head. She seemed to carry no anger toward me. We walked together on the last day. She asked about my girls, and I shared lots of stories. I carried their pictures in a book in my rucksack. She described the senior partners at her firm who didn't like having a woman on board.

Dr. King's speech... the need to access the ballot box. For the Great Society to succeed, the Negro Revolution must succeed. Revolution. The word King didn't want Lewis to use in '63. Grace whispered to me, "See. Lewis was right."

August 14, 1965

I put up a swing in the backyard. Catherine crawls to me and stands up against my legs, holding on for dear life.

"Swing me," she says. She giggles and squeals. I take her outside and hold her squirming body... warm, soft, and chubby, before I place her in the baby swing.

Exchanging a three-piece suit and a gold pocket watch for comfortable clothes, I'm on the road a lot. Memphis, Selma, Washington, following the Movement, hoping it will make a difference by being there. I seldom see Elizabeth. When I get home, I fall into bed, exhausted. Side by side, we never touch.

Her father was selfish, Catherine thought as she

paused and looked at the picture of Grace. He cheats on Mother but stays in the marriage because she threatened him, but to become part of a Movement her Mother didn't understand and then expect what?

So, this was the estrangement he described when Peter asked. Estranged and doing nothing to bridge the divide between them?

Her father tried to make peace with her mother before she died. Maybe Caroline was right. Mother didn't have his faith, so why would he expect her to understand forgiveness after so many years living without it?

September 21, 1965

I'm still working for Ray one day a week, mostly to help his new partner get acclimated. Seminary classes are my full-time job now. Elizabeth has taken on some volunteer work at the university, so I have Catherine with me two days a week while Caroline is at pre-school. Catherine is a beautiful baby... chestnut curls and big expressive hazel eyes. She has an old Raggedy Ann doll she carries everywhere. She is already talking, much earlier than Caroline did. After I give her lunch, we settle down in my study. She plays quietly most of the afternoon, but sometimes she crawls over to my desk and reaches up, asking to be held. I hold her, reading out loud so she can be part of what I'm doing. Maybe it's silly, but I imagine that she's really listening, taking it all in.

"I was listening, Daddy," Catherine said out loud. "You gave me my love for words."

Catherine closed the journal. Brief entries from 1966 and 1967, mostly about seminary and his girls. Nothing about Grace. One entry for 1968, the last one in the journal.

She picked up the bundle of letters, untied the ribbon, and fingered each envelope. Each letter was addressed to her father at Uncle Ray's office, each beige Crane & Co. envelope had a green lip, edges ragged. Sheets of beige stationery in each envelope were covered with small, impeccable handwriting. Had Grace labored over every letter, or were the letters as spontaneous as the woman her father described?

Catherine pulled out a letter, dated June 10, 1968. Was this the first contact since they'd seen each other in Selma? In the letter, Grace says she was in Memphis the week Dr. King was killed, defending a twenty-four-year-old black woman who had been raped by teenage white boys. She didn't know about King's assassination until she got back to Boston that evening.

She wrote, "Where is your God in all this, Douglas? Are we still waiting for him to show his face? When will he hold us in the 'great hands of his heart'? Do you still believe he's here for us?"

Her father's faith had touched Grace, still after so many years. This must be the letter he answered by asking her to meet him.

Catherine opened the journal and read the final entry.

July 1, 1968

We talked for hours, made love. It was as if no time had passed. We canoed on Long Pond. Hiked around Jordan Pond. She was more driven than ever, talking about cases with William Thompson and the ACLU. She was softer, somehow. Interested in my girls and how they were managing with Elizabeth's drinking.

I asked her to marry me. She said no. I tried to convince her, but she persisted. The lawyer in her told me I'd never get custody of the girls with my infidelity and my father-in-law's money. I wanted to try.

She said no. She loves me, but she said no.

Catherine thought about all the women she'd admired. Grace was like them. She wouldn't have said, "Stupid, stupid girl. No sense of reality." She would have loved her questions the way Daddy did.

He was ready to leave Mother and start over with Grace. His most decisive act, and she said no. Grace probably knew no court would consider Mother unfit, but why wasn't she willing to let him try?

Catherine pulled a letter from an envelope postmarked 1974, but there was no date on the letter.

Dear Douglas:

I hope you are well. I got some bad news this week. I have breast cancer. It looks like I'll need surgery, and then the doctor will decide if I need radiation or chemotherapy. I'm frightened. I've never been sick.

Unlike you, I don't think about heaven and hell when I think about dying. Remember when we talked about my father's death? He was so worried about going to heaven. The Church had him terrified about that. I think about what I'm leaving behind, the people I'll miss, the work I won't finish.

Do you ever think about the March on Washington, and all the things we did only a decade ago to make a better world? Remember our spirited disagreement about King's vision versus John Lewis's demand for action? It speaks volumes about who we were, how different our stories were.

Did any of my victories in court matter? Was marching in Washington and Selma a waste of time?

Protesting the war? I have three friends with husbands who have returned from Vietnam, one without legs, one more arrogant than when he left, one addicted to drugs. Did anything we accomplished really make a difference? Did Dr. King and Bobby Kennedy die for nothing?

I wish you could answer my questions. I don't think I'll ever stop asking you all my questions.

Grace

Grace. The turbulence of the 1960s. Assassinations. Marches for economic justice. Voters' rights. So little about his marriage. Was he trying to tell a story about Grace and how their passion was rooted in the turmoil and hope for change in the 1960s? Would Grace's own story complement the one he told?

Catherine put the letter on the desk and walked to the kitchen and filled the tea kettle. The wind chimes sounded on the porch as the ocean breeze cut through the still night.

Laughter... her grandmother's laughter mingled with her father's reassuring voice. They sit at the kitchen table, sharing a story and a cup of tea before he headed out to the hospital to visit sick parishioners.

Teaspoon against cup and saucer... more laughter.

What was Mother doing when Nana and her father were enjoying each other's company? Did she feel left out, a stranger in her own home?

Catherine filled the teapot and returned to the study. She thumbed through several other letters.

September 30, 1974

Dear Douglas:

I was in Philadelphia last week meeting with colleagues. I took a walk in Valley Green. Do you remember the little black girl we saw in the park the day after President Kennedy was assassinated? You stopped to show her how to skim stones.

I felt like I was in a time warp. A man and a woman, older, maybe 50, stopped by the stream. Her auburn hair framed her round face. She looked so happy, watching her friend, husband, I didn't know their relationship, engage with a little girl. I lost myself for a minute, imagining it was you and me. We'd stayed together, had a child, and still looked at each other the way we did when our love was new.

I imagine a son with your intelligence and heart but with my wicked wit. He'd make us thankful every day that we gave him life. He'd make us proud of who he'd become, of the choices he would make. I see him playing with the little girl in the park, unaware of her color.

> *Love,*
> *Grace*

These letters must have tormented her father, Catherine thought. She was imagining having a child with him, a son. Uncle Ray had told him he'd never find in Grace a woman who'd want to have children. Did Uncle Ray even know her?

Catherine put down the journal and reached for the windbreaker on the back of her chair. It was dark. No moon illuminated her path as she reached the beach. The salt spray invigorated her. Trudging through the hard sand, she walked close to the waves lapping along the ocean's edge and thought about Grace's last letter. She'd read it over and over, practically memorized it.

December 7, 1974

> *Dear Douglas:*
>
> *I hope you're doing well this Advent. The whole idea of waiting with great expectation for God to break into history appeals to me.*
>
> *I'm still waiting, I guess. I remember the sunrise we saw on Cadillac Mountain... a tiny sun in the vast, cloudy sky. Perhaps that was God breaking into history. Like a baby's first cry or his first smile... that's enough for me.*
>
> *I've decided it's time for me to stop writing to you. It's my way of letting you go. Not that you aren't already gone, but I've carried you in my heart for so long. My heart needs to give someone else my undivided attention.*
>
> *Grace*

"I carry you in my heart," Catherine said aloud. "I think that's a line from a poem... a baby's first cry or his first smile... Hal. But she never told him about Hal?"

Catherine turned around and headed into the wind coming off the ocean. Braving the cold, she took off her shoes and walked in the chilly water. An older couple walking, hand in hand, passed her and nodded hello.

When Catherine got back to the house, she sat down in her grandmother's chair and thought about all she had read in the journal. She walked to her father's desk and looked once again at the woman in the green dress.

"There was someone else," she said out loud. "You had a child, his child... a son. Because you didn't tell him the truth before, when you were pregnant, you decided you couldn't do it when he was willing to leave Mother and marry you. You had to hold onto the life you had, the life you had made with your child, with Hal."

Catherine placed the picture inside the journal, tied the letters together with the green satin ribbon, and placed them all in the iron box. The car was already packed, so she placed the iron box on the front seat after she had checked the doors to make sure the house was locked securely. It might be a month or six weeks before she'd be back.

Catherine got home to two hungry cats. She fed Molly and Maggie and crawled into bed. She awakened the next morning from a dream. She and Caroline were making a drip castle with a little boy with dark hair and blue eyes. He smiled like Daddy.

Chapter Thirty-Nine

Catherine walked down the hall to Hal's office, carrying her father's journal and Grace's letters tied together with the green ribbon. Hal waved her in as he finished a phone call. Standing in front of the two pictures on his bookcase, Catherine pulled Grace's picture from the journal and stood it against the picture of the woman in the emerald bikini, holding baby Hal. Catherine turned as Hal got up and stood beside her.

"Where'd you get the picture of my mother?" Hal asked, smiling at Catherine.

"It was in my father's desk drawer, with a picture of my parents on their wedding day."

"What?" Hal asked, baffled.

"When you met with my father in January, he told you he knew your mother," Catherine said. "But there's more, more than just a couple meetings and letters exchanged."

She sat down in the chair next to Hal's desk and laid the journal in front of him.

"My father was in love with your mother. It's all here in his journal." She placed the tiny stack of letters on top of the journal. "These letters were written to my father from your mother, the last one dated 1974, just like my father told you."

Hal untied the ribbon and opened the letter on top of the stack. "This is her handwriting."

"I've read all of it since we talked before Spring Break," Catherine said. "I wasn't sure before I read it all."

"Sure about what?" Hal asked.

"A few months before my father died, he told me about Grace, a woman he'd fallen in love with soon after my sister Caroline was born. I'd heard the name before as a child when my parents were fighting."

"Catherine, I don't understand," Hal said.

"When I talked with my sister the day of my father's funeral, she confirmed what I now think I understand. Daddy never stopped loving Grace. They were together enough even before I was born to have conceived a child. Your father only died metaphorically when you were a baby, Hal. He was lost to your mother because my mother threatened to kill herself and me if my father left her."

"But why wouldn't she have told me?" Hal asked. "Why would she lie to me?" Unmasked, Catherine saw his vulnerability. Anger at the mother he adored. He ran his finger over the tiny printing, stopping on the cursive "G" of her signature.

"I don't know," Catherine said, searching Hal's face, seeing her father in the tilt of his head and his steel-blue eyes, seeing Grace in his thick black hair and sensuous lips. "But it was a different time, then... the shame of having a child when you weren't married.

"I've just started to process the sense of loss my father must have felt. In the last few months of his life, I think he was trying to make peace with all of this by telling me about Grace. I'll never know, though, if he realized the day you talked with him in January that you are his son."

They sat in silence for a few minutes. Catherine continued to study Hal's face while he leafed through the letters. He looked like a little boy who just discovered that Superman has no special powers. His mother had an important story she'd never shared with him.

"I want to leave the journal and the letters with you," Catherine said, wishing she could say something to ease the pain. "Read them. Then, let's talk again."

Hal nodded his head in agreement, his fingers lightly caressing the worn stationery.

Chapter Forty

Hal opened the guest room door slowly, catching a glimpse of old Winnie the Pooh sitting on the bed. A gift from Uncle Vince when Hal was a baby. Vince's mother had made Pooh from a McCall's pattern. Yellow-orange terry cloth. Black felt eyes, brows, nose, and mouth. His mouth drooped onto his chin and his left eyebrow hung over his eye. His red cotton shirt, faded to pink, was torn but still intact.

Hal sat back against a pillow and put his arm around his old friend. He smiled, remembering Uncle Vince using Pooh to tell him stories before bed.

"Once upon a time, Hal, I was just a pile of cloth. Yellow-orange terry cloth. Red cotton. A swatch of black felt. A wizard named Lucille worked her magic, and I appeared."

"Was she really a wizard?" Hal asked at three.

"Yes. Yes, she was," Vince said, making Pooh's head

nod at Hal. *"She had a white cape and a white pointed hat. She was a good wizard, creating Winnie the Pooh and Tigger too for little boys like you and me."*

"Was I made the same way?" Hal asked, eyes wide with delight.

"Sort of," Vince said, scrunching up his nose and looking pensive.

"A wizard named Grace," Vince began.

"Mama," Hal squealed.

"Mama," Vince repeated. *"She took a little flesh,"* pinching Hal's tummy. *"She took a little bone,"* squeezing Hal's kneecap, *"and breathed life into you."*

Hal smiled, remembering it was Uncle Vince who had the talk with him about how babies were made when he was twelve.

She gave him a father in Vince, he thought, squeezing the old bear, but she never told him the truth about his real father.

Hal placed the journal and the letters on the tiny roll-top desk his grandfather had brought from Philadelphia when he was three. He loved its tiny drawers and cubbyholes, places to hide chewing gum and chocolate bars his mother didn't permit.

"This was your mother's desk," Gramps said proudly as he carried it up the steps and asked Grace where to place it. *"Your mother loved to roll the top up and down like this, vroom, vroom, just to irritate her mother."*

"Don't give him any ideas, Dad," Grace said, laughing.

The walnut surface was worn from use. Hal's mother scolded him just a little for placing his Skylab and astronaut stickers on its surface.

Tina loved the desk and its tiny bench with pedestal feet, the only piece of furniture they took from the house in Boston where Hal grew up. This room would become the nursery when they had their first child. All the furniture, except the desk, would go, to be replaced by the baby's crib. Hal always imagined telling his son or daughter, "This was your grandmother's desk."

Hal stayed in his office that evening after Catherine had given him Douglas's journal and his mother's letters. With light from his desk lamp, he read each journal entry carefully. 1963, before he was born. The historic events... the March on Washington. The death of the four black girls in Birmingham. President Kennedy's assassination. Each shaped Douglas as a young man, memories and experiences Douglas had shared with his mother.

Hal blanched when he read the description of Douglas's first sexual experience with his mother. His mother's boldness. Douglas describing himself as more decisive than he had ever been. His mother said she loved Douglas that day, the day he promised he'd ask his wife for a divorce. She told Douglas she could wait until he found the right time.

Douglas captures his mother's shock the day he told her his wife, Catherine's mother, was pregnant. She didn't get angry. She cried silently, looking at Douglas in disbelief. Douglas stays in his marriage to save his daughter's life. Why didn't his mother get angry that day?

His mother got angry a lot. At the washing machine when it made a terrible noise and walked across the basement floor. At toys she put together backward and then called Uncle Vince to dismantle and reconstruct.

She had no time for her sniveling colleagues who wouldn't defend a client who needed help.

"There's justice, and then, there's Grace's justice," Uncle Vince explained one Saturday afternoon when Hal was a teenager. "Some find her intolerant. Maybe, but she's focused on the goal, getting justice for the client."

Grace left that morning for New York, slamming the door behind her. She had lost a case, a suit against a prominent Boston banker who had sexually assaulted a twenty-seven-year-old employee. The young woman took her life, and Grace was headed to her funeral.

"She feels responsible," Vince told Hal. "She didn't get justice for her client. This makes her angry."

"But justice doesn't bring her client back. It doesn't make the pain stop," Hal said. "Doesn't she understand she can't fix it? Being angry doesn't help."

"No. Believing she can fix it, though, keeps her in the fight," Vince said, leaning close and giving Hal's shoulder a squeeze.

Maybe she knew Douglas well enough to see that anger wouldn't move him to stay with her. Douglas describes a gentleness in his mother that others don't see. Maybe she only recognized that gentleness in herself when she was with Douglas, but Hal, the son Douglas didn't know he had, saw it as well.

Catherine had described Douglas as a prisoner to her mother's rage, caught in marriage like a trapped animal. His mother wouldn't want to further entrap Douglas because she was pregnant.

Hal read the entries about Selma again. Raw anger shot through him. His mother had asked about Douglas's girls then, but she never mentioned him. Why wasn't he on her mind? Why wasn't she thinking about what it would be like for him when he had to say, "I don't have a father."

Hal walked to the bookcase and ran his finger over the picture of his mother holding him, resisting the urge to smash it, to smash the trust he'd always had in her. He returned to his desk with the picture in his hand, laying it face down.

Anger coiled in Hal's stomach, ready to burst and spread, but it wasn't just anger for himself. It was for Douglas. Douglas needed his mother, just like Hal always needed her. He needed her strength and certainty that neither of them possessed.

That night, he fingered the green ribbon as he thought about what he'd read in the letters. He reread the letter from September 30, 1974, lingering on the last paragraph.

I imagine a son with your intelligence and heart but with my wicked wit. He'd make us thankful every day that we gave him life. He'd make us proud of who he'd become, of the choices he would make. I see him playing with the little girl in the park, unaware of her color.

Was Douglas supposed to get it that she was talking about his son, not some figment of her imagination? Did he respond to that letter? Hal pounded his fist on the tiny desk, wanting to break it. Wanting his mother there with an answer that would make sense.

The tiny bench fell backward as Hal got up. He reached down and put it back on its feet. He picked up the last letter from December 1974 when she said it was time to let Douglas go. He read it again. She gave up on Douglas.

She had taken Hal to Maine that fall to relive the time she had spent with Douglas, that happy time in '68 that ended with her saying no to his marriage proposal. Would 1974 have been different if he had responded, asked her again?

Hal walked to the window and pushed the curtains aside. The sun faded into a pink sky, the light painting the houses across the street in an eerie glow.

She didn't want to break up Douglas's marriage, but hadn't she already done that? Catherine said her mother knew about Grace. The damage had been done.

The cancer came back when Hal was away at college, this time in her bones. Three years she fought it with chemo and radiation. He came home over every break, hoping the treatments were working.

She could have given him a father, then. Told him who Douglas was, so he could know him. Ask for his love and support when he lost his mother, be present on his wedding day and share his happiness with Tina.

She could have given him a father, a father who could have taught him about faith, about that God of his who broke into History, a God who cared about the oppressed.

If his mother had been with Douglas, would she have surrendered some of her cynicism and been less disappointed in the world she had hoped to change?

Leaving the curtains open, Hal sat down on the bed and pulled old Pooh close. Light fading, the darkness was comforting somehow. He'd read it all again tomorrow. He wasn't ready to talk with Catherine.

Chapter Forty-One
August 2005

Throwing keys and a few dollars in her beach bag, Catherine pulled the bag over her shoulder and closed the front door behind her. Hal would be here later this morning. She'd invited him to stay for the weekend. Over the summer, she'd redecorated her sister's room, making it more inviting for a man. The light-colored quilt, pillow shams, and dust ruffle were replaced with a medley of browns. A simple beige afghan she'd made once and put away in a drawer was folded over the back of the caned rocking chair.

It'll be good to spend some time with Hal away from the College, Catherine thought, as she walked towards the beach. Five months since the announcement of sexual harassment charges against Neil and his departure from the College. Five good months getting to know Hal better, hearing about growing up with a single parent, finding out about Grace.

Daddy was single too, wasn't he? Mother was married to vodka and valium. What was the world like for her mother? All a haze? Or did she have lucid moments when she experienced some happiness?

Hal had read her father's journal several times before asking to talk. They sat in his office one evening until close to midnight, two hoagies from Wawa, unwrapped and untouched in front of them.

"I have more questions than answers," Catherine had said, sipping iced tea. "I wonder if he knew you were his son that day in January. I still wonder if he thought of the connection when he met you at Christmas... when he said he felt his conversation with you was like conversations he had in the 1960s. I wasn't listening. I wasn't paying careful attention, or I might have understood."

Hal leaned back in his chair and shook his head. "I see his face and try to remember his expression when he said he knew my mother. I felt something when I met him at Christmas, but I didn't know what it was.

"She never mentioned me," Hal began. He gripped his pen, looking close to tears.

"She mentions you. She's reminding my father about the year he taught her about Advent."

"Yes, of course," Hal said, anger flashing across his face as he got up and walked to the bookcase. He picked up the picture of his mother, holding him.

"Yes, I'm the baby... baby's first cry was enough for her, but it's never been enough for me. I wanted a father."

Catherine thought about her own anger toward her mother, but this was different. Hal loved his mother. How can he reconcile that love with this awful lie?

He placed the picture on the shelf and moved back to

sit at his desk. He scanned Catherine's face before he said, "Until I met Tina and fell in love with her, I worried that I was too attached to my mother. I always wanted to be like her, strong, certain, but I wasn't.

"When I read your father's journal, I realized I'm like him. Full of ideas but no certainty. All my life I relied on my mother for that certainty. Then, I saw it in Tina. Nothing fazed her, not even the cancer that took her."

Catherine reached over and laid her hand on his.

"I've missed my father every day since his death, but I can't even begin to imagine the loss you're feeling right now. My father was indecisive in many ways, but he was sure about two things."

Hal looked at her blankly, waiting for her to continue.

"He loved his children, and he loved Grace. He gave her up to save my life. If he'd known in 1968 when he asked her to marry him... If he'd known she'd had a son, his son, he would have moved heaven and earth to be with her and with you."

"I don't know," Hal said, shaking his head.

Catherine had left Hal in his office that night, admitting to herself that she didn't know either.

We can never know, she thought, as she placed her chair close to the water's edge. She opened her father's book of Rilke's *Love Poems to God* and scanned a couple of poems until she settled on the end of the poem her father was reading the day he died:

> Somewhere there must be storehouses
> where all these lives are laid away
> like suits of armor or old carriages
> or clothes hanging limply on the walls.
>
> Maybe all paths lead there,
> to the repository of unlived things.

She closed the book and her attention wandered to some ships on the horizon.

The news about Neil's acquittal had broken on NPR Thursday night. Catherine left the office early, wanting to be home alone when she heard the news. A friend from the *Philadelphia Inquirer* texted her at 4:20 p.m.: "The acquittal will be on the front-page tomorrow."

The grand jury decided there wasn't enough evidence to convict him.

She waited until she was on her way to Spring Lake to stop and get a paper. No *Inquirer*, so she bought a *Star Ledger*. The story was on page two.

Roslyn held a press conference Thursday evening in the Board Room in Franklin Hall.

"While we are pleased that Dr. Rhodes has been cleared of all charges, we are sorry to report he has submitted his letter of resignation, effective immediately. Dr. Stevens will continue as Acting Vice President while a national search is conducted for Dr. Rhodes' successor."

"Sorry, my ass," Catherine said out loud as she got back on the road. "You're damn lucky they didn't bring you down as well. Maybe the Trustees will, though, after they give this some thought." Catherine felt the sweat that started at the back of her neck. She could still feel his hands... feel the humiliation of talking about it before the grand jury.

Catherine pulled her chair back from the water's edge and placed it on the dry sand. Slipping keys in the pocket of her sweatshirt, she walked brusquely through the warm, August ocean. Pieces of jellyfish littered the water's edge.

As she headed back to her spot, she saw Hal standing on the boardwalk, Starbuck's coffee in one hand. She waved several times before she caught his attention.

He spread a towel next to her chair and hugged her close before he let go and sat down. Khaki shorts and a brown polo made him look unusually boyish.

"You look pretty rested for a man who went to work yesterday," she said, looking at him carefully through sunglasses.

"The silence was eerie on campus yesterday," he said. "I had two phone messages when I got in, one from the *Inquirer* and one from the *Chronicle of Higher Education*. I talked with Steve about what to say. I wasn't even sure he'd want me to respond, but he did. We prepared a statement."

Hal took a sip from the coffee before continuing. "I was so angry when I heard the decision. I took a long walk in Valley Green. I wanted to talk with my mother about the case. I wanted her advice on how to get past it. She would have listened, Catherine, really listened. She wouldn't have an answer, but she'd keep going, keep fighting. That's what I need to do."

Catherine took off her sunglasses and smiled at Hal. She'd thought about resigning when the scandal broke in the spring and, again, several times over the summer. Anger came in waves, and she didn't imagine the anger would ever go away completely. For now, though, Neil was gone. And she was going to stay at the College and see where things go.

They sat together quietly, scanning the horizon. The cloudless sky meshed with the tranquil surf. Catherine experienced the contentment she'd always had with her father. The moment of happiness, she thought. Perhaps I haven't experienced it yet.

Acknowledgements

Writers need solitude to write, but we also need community to have the courage and resilience to keep writing. I am grateful to the writing colleagues and friends who have been that community for me.

Alison Hicks, Director of Greater Philadelphia Wordshop Studio, has been an encouragement and sounding board as I worked on this novel as a participant in Wordshop (2010-2015, 2020-2021). A special thanks to Kerri Schuster, who read an early draft of the novel. My editor and coach, Anne Dubuisson, has pushed me to write a better novel and encouraged me throughout the process.

To Norma, who has believed in me since I was a little girl and was delighted when she read an early draft of the novel, I will always be grateful for your presence in my life. I am sorry you had to leave us before the novel was published.

Imagination transforms the cotton wool of everyday life into exquisite moments of being. My heartfelt thanks to the many colleagues who inspired me to create the fictive world of Franklin College.

About Atmosphere Press

Atmosphere Press is an independent, full-service publisher for excellent books in all genres and for all audiences. Learn more about what we do at atmospherepress.com.

We encourage you to check out some of Atmosphere's latest releases, which are available at Amazon.com and via order from your local bookstore:

Comfrey, Wyoming: Birds of a Feather, a novel by Daphne Birkmyer
Relatively Painless, short stories by Dylan Brody
Nate's New Age, a novel by Michael Hanson
The Size of the Moon, a novel by E.J. Michaels
The Red Castle, a novel by Noah Verhoeff
American Genes, a novel by Kirby Nielsen
Newer Testaments, a novel by Philip Brunetti
All Things in Time, a novel by Sue Buyer
The Tattered Black Book, a novel by Lexy Duck
Hobson's Mischief, a novel by Caitlin Decatur
The Black-Marketer's Daughter, a novel by Suman Mallick
The Farthing Quest, a novel by Casey Bruce
This Side of Babylon, a novel by James Stoia
Within the Gray, a novel by Jenna Ashlyn
Where No Man Pursueth, a novel by Micheal E. Jimerson
Here's Waldo, a novel by Nick Olson
Tales of Little Egypt, a historical novel by James Gilbert
For a Better Life, a novel by Julia Reid Galosy
The Hidden Life, a novel by Robert Castle

About the Author

Nancy Allen has worked as a college administrator and adjunct professor of English at several colleges and universities in the Philadelphia area and at the University of Pittsburgh. She is currently at work on a prequel to *Grace*. She lives in Wyndmoor, Pennsylvania.

Find out more at www.nancyjallenauthor.com.

CPSIA information can be obtained
at www.ICGtesting.com
Printed in the USA
BVHW082004270321
603543BV00002B/8